WHITE KNIGHT

John H. Cunningham

Other books byJohn H. Cunningham

Red Right Return

Green to Go

Crystal Blue

Second Chance Gold

Maroon Rising

Free Fall to Black

Silver Goodbye

WHITE KNIGHT

A BUCK REILLY ★ ★ ADVENTURE ★

John H. Cunningham

WHITE KNIGHT

Published by Greene Street, LLC

Print ISBN: 978-0-9987965-5-0 Electronic ISBN: 978-0-9987965-4-3

www.jhcunningham.com

This book is for

Robert and Sharon Cunningham, my aunt and uncle who introduced me to the Florida Keys, saltwater fishing, helped me get certified as a scuba diver, and gave me my first Travis McGee novel.

BRITISH
VIRGIN ISLANDS

NECKER IS.

GUANA IS.   GREAT
           CAMANOE

Jost Van
Dyke   Coral Gardner
                    Bay   Tortola   SCRUB IS.

Sandy   Little
Cay   Bay

Great
Thatch Is.   BEEF IS.   Virgin Gorda

HANS LOLLIK IS.
                                          St. John   GINGER IS.

Magens Bay   SALT IS.   COOPER IS.
St. Thomas   Red Hook   PETER IS.

          Cruz Bay

WATER IS.   NORMAN IS.
          Frenchman's Reef

UNITED STATES
VIRGIN ISLANDS

The Buccaneer   BUCK IS.

St. Croix

SECTION 1

WOMAN UP, WOMAN DOWN

1

THE LOOK IN HER EYES SAID IT ALL.

That and the fact that she wouldn't engage mine. Whoever said you can't go backward was right. Even with a kid involved—*especially* with a kid involved.

A plane with a foreign flag on its tail descended toward Cyril E. King Airport on St. Thomas, where Scarlet and I stood outside the departures entrance. The airport was devoid of passengers, but planes continued to arrive. Black helicopters circled and hovered around the perimeter. Several black and silver limos were parked near the entrance to the airport.

"What the hell's going on around here?" I said.

"See, you don't even watch the news," Scarlet said.

"The news is always bad."

"But you don't know what's going on."

"I know what's going on around me. Right now that's bad news, too."

Scarlet grimaced and glanced at the cars, then up at a hovering chopper. "You're not curious about all this?" She pointed to a throng of security guards dressed in suits.

"Didn't I just ask what was going on? Bet you it's—"

Scarlet held up her palm. "I'm sorry this didn't work, Buck. You wanted to try, and we did."

I glanced back to the taxi still parked at the curb behind us. Charlie was nose down in his phone like he'd been the entire forty-eight hours since he and Scarlet arrived.

"Did we?" I said. "We were supposed to sail around the Virgin Islands to get reacquainted, so I could get to know my son, and we didn't get further than St. John before you wanted out. Why? What did I do?"

"Are you staying?"

"I chartered the boat for ten days. I've got eight days left. Yeah, I'm staying."

"Okay. I'm sorry, Buck." Scarlet reached for the taxi's door handle. "This was just too much too fast."

"He had his nose in that phone the whole time. Why do you let him do that?"

She rolled her eyes. "It's their generation. All kids are the same."

"Lost Generation. This trip could've changed all that—been an adventure he'd never forget."

"Buck Reilly adventures are always memorable." She glanced at her—our—son seated inside the taxi. "Maybe when he's older he'll be more interested."

"And you?"

"I've had enough adventures. I was hoping you had, too."

I looked into her eye for a long moment. "Do you know me, Scarlet?"

She pulled the door open. "Let's go, Charlie. We'll miss our flight—the last one out before the airport is closed." She glanced at me. "Thanks to the incoming VIPs."

VIPs?

Charlie—Charles Buck Roberson—climbed out without ever taking his eyes off the glass screen six inches from his face. Scarlet stepped over and gave me a one-armed hug and then walked past me towing her suitcase. Charlie followed as if an invisible umbilical cord kept him at a set distance from his mother ship. He never looked up.

"Charlie!" I said.

The boy, now nearly eleven, five feet tall with sandy blond hair and thin limbs, froze. Startled, he glanced back at me. I bent down and hugged him tight.

"I enjoyed being with you. Sorry it didn't last longer."

"Thanks, Buck. The boat was cool."

With that the boy refocused on his phone and sauntered after his mother.

I stood as still as an Easter Island statue and watched them disappear inside the open-air terminal. If the Beast had still been here—my 1946 Grumman Goose—I'd probably have gone home to Key West, but Ray Floyd, my friend and business partner, had dropped me off and taken the plane for a series of charters, so I was stuck.

As Scarlet and Charlie vanished in the background, a swarm of men in dark suits coalesced in my immediate foreground. One with dark glasses, slicked back dark hair, and an earbud stepped up to me.

"Time to move on, sir. This area is now closed to the public." The man had a midwestern accent.

My mind snapped out of the funk as I looked at him and his four colleagues. They were all dressed the same and had the same skin-colored devices in their ears. Men in black suits weren't a common sight in the Virgin Islands.

Security of some sort.

Somebody famous landing? Or super-rich?

What the hell is going on here?

2

THE MUTTON SNAPPER SHOOK WILDY on the end of my spear, which had gone clean through its gill plate. Blue water rushed around me as I pulled the fish close to stuff it into my yellow mesh bag. The black tip shark I'd seen hovering at the perimeter of the visibility's haze turned toward me as the wounded fish launched urgent sonar signals through the water.

With my breath nearly spent I kicked hard toward the surface, twenty feet above me, where the sun dappled across the light waves and my dinghy bobbed in white rings caused by a passing boat's wake. The pull of buoyancy popped me out of the water—

PPPOOSSSSHHH!

I blew my remaining air from the snorkel to clear it of water and sucked in a fresh breath, scanning in a circle for the shark. No sign—but a three-foot barracuda darted toward my yellow dive bag, its mouth wide and full of large white teeth. I jerked the bag out of the water and threw it aboard the dinghy and then kicked hard with my fins toward the silver predator locked in on the scent of blood—so locked in he'd have been just as happy to take a chunk out of my calf.

The bubbles and wash of my fins altered the barracuda's approach—then I spotted the shark behind it.

I kicked hard and lunged toward the dinghy. After catching hold of the starboard side—there was a strong tug on my fin—I kicked harder, which lifted me high enough to scramble aboard. I glanced down at my left leg and saw no blood. My fin, however, had a three-inch chunk missing from its left corner.

"Bastard."

I crawled down into the dinghy, lay flat and stared up into the Tar Heel-blue sky. Without turning, I reached over to the small ice chest, lifted the lid, and retrieved a cold Virgin Islands Pale Ale. I spun off the cap and took a long slug. The beer was cold and tasted like liquid gold. The sun was on its downward arc but I still squinted face up into it.

Nothing about this trip had gone as planned, but getting maimed by a shark or a barracuda would be the last straw. Thankfully, I'd escaped with my snapper in tow and had a fresh dinner guaranteed. Scarlet and Charlie's departure had left a sour taste that no amount of Caribbean beer would wash away. Turned out they'd departed just as foreign dignitaries had begun to arrive—I'd learned there was a Group of Eight summit being held on St. Thomas—which explained all the security at the airport.

I shook water from my right ear, and when it was clear I heard a steady buzz coming from the west. I was in the Sir Francis Drake Channel, between waters of the U.S. and British Virgin Islands. The sound registered as a low-flying helicopter. When I spotted it in the distance, something else appeared—

WHOOSH—KABOOOM!

A thin white streak had materialized from nowhere and hit the helicopter, which erupted into a ball of fire and dropped like a rock from its altitude of a few hundred feet.

My eyes were locked onto the helicopter as it splashed into the channel.

I scanned the waters—no boat was in sight.

A quick glance to the west, where the white streak had come from—was it a rocket? Still nothing visible.

I sprang to my feet, nearly flopping over the side of the rocking dinghy—my beer went flying—and dived toward the twenty horsepower engine, which started on the first pull. The anchor rope burned my hands as I fought to retrieve it—*must be stuck on a coral head*. I shoved the throttle into reverse and backed away from where I'd been anchored. Behind me, the helicopter was sinking—I jammed the throttle forward but the anchor held firm.

"Come on!"

I yanked the diving knife from its scabbard on my calf and sawed at the nylon rope until it broke free. I jumped onto the small bench seat, grabbed the wheel with my left hand and the throttle with my right, and shoved it all the way forward. The bow of the dinghy lifted high for a moment and we skipped over a few waves before getting on plane. I aimed straight for the smoldering chopper a quarter mile away, still scanning the horizon for the source of that deadly white streak.

Was it really a rocket?

There was still nothing visible in any direction. It only took a few minutes to close the distance, during which time the smoke ceased to billow from the chopper, probably because it was now mostly submerged. There were no people swimming around the sinking craft, so unless they were trapped inside, all occupants must have been dead. I drove the dinghy to what had been the starboard aft side of the chopper, its long tail now bobbing out of the water like a weather vane pointed toward the horizon.

Without hesitation I dived into the clear water. The chopper had four doors, two on each side, the rear starboard door now on the waterline. I sucked in a breath and ducked down under the waves.

The windscreen on the front of the helicopter was a charred hole. Two figures—men in the front seats—were underwater, their faces and bodies scorched black. I rose to the surface on the left side.

The rear passenger compartment was nearly underwater but still had a big air bubble in the back holding it afloat as the nose pointed into the depths. I bobbed in the wake and grabbed hold of the left rear door handle. If I opened the door, the air bubble would escape—water would pour in and potentially sink the craft.

A woman was strapped in behind the pilot, facedown in the water. Past her was another woman, face covered in blood, crammed into the rear corner of the passenger compartment. She wasn't wearing a seat belt so floated free instead of being held below the surface.

I swam hard around the back of the foundering chopper. My dinghy was floating away, and I grabbed the severed anchor rope and wrapped it around the exposed landing skid. The helicopter's tail spun in a circular motion as the craft struggled, held afloat only by the small bubble in the cabin. I swam hard to the right rear door, being pushed around by the surf. I reached for the handle—missed!

I swam closer, and as the helicopter bobbed up on a wave, I grabbed hold of the handle and saw that inside the window, the woman's head was still facing up. Blood covered her face but she was moving—she was alive! Water sloshed inside and I realized the bubble had shrunk significantly since I'd arrived. No way it could hold the chopper afloat much longer.

After inhaling a deep breath, I tugged at the handle—it was jammed.

Shit!

The woman's eyes opened, and a death-curdling shriek sounded from inside the passenger compartment.

I lifted my feet to each side of the handle and pulled with all my strength. The door creaked open an inch but stopped. A quick inspection found that the door's hinges had crumpled on impact. No way it was opening.

The woman's eyes were locked onto mine. The fear there burned into my soul.

"Hang on!" I said.

I swam around the back of the chopper—the angle of the tail was now dropping away from me. The left handle was pointed toward the sky—I couldn't reach it. I climbed to the front, now exposed, and scurried up the side of the helicopter. The air bubble inside was gone!

My cracking open the right door had let water in and forced the air out.

The frame on this door was fine. When I pulled the handle, the door lifted straight up. The woman clawed over the body beside her, gulped air, and jumped straight out of the craft, past me and into the water.

With the seal of the rear doors broken, the helicopter began to sink quickly.

The dinghy!

It was tied to the landing skid—now underwater—and the line pulled taut. The nose of the dinghy had been dragged under. Could it support the sinking helicopter?

The woman floated face up in the channel.

"Can you swim?"

Her eyes stared straight into the sky, unblinking.

Damn! She was in shock.

I dived off the nearly submerged chopper, grabbed her arm and then her hair, and pulled her toward the dinghy. The engine's propeller was now pointed toward the sky and the nose had been pulled farther under because the anchor rope was tied to the skid. I reached for my dive knife and found that it was missing from the scabbard on my calf.

I let go of the woman and launched myself onto the nose of the dinghy. Everything had fallen into the bow, as it was standing nearly straight up in the water at this point.

I shoved the cooler and the yellow dive bag aside—there!

I grabbed the knife and twisted left, slashing the blade across the piano-tight anchor line. It sliced through the nylon rope like it was sun-melted butter.

The dinghy shot up in the air like a balloon released from the bottom of a swimming pool. The boat landed square and bounced, launching me back into the water next to the woman. I grabbed her and dragged her to the dinghy and helped her over the low-slung port side.

Breathing as if I'd just sprinted a 10k, I hung on to the side of the dinghy for a solid minute, trying to slow my racing heart. The helicopter was gone, sunk to the depths of the channel with nothing left to mark its location. One more deep breath and I used what strength I still had to pull myself onto the side of the dinghy. The woman was crumpled, facedown, hopefully not dead.

Had it been shot down? The windscreen was obliterated, the pilot and co-pilot charred, so it damn sure seemed that way.

I took one last glimpse around and saw nothing but an oil slick.

3

WHEN I ROLLED THE WOMAN OVER, I SAW SHE'D TURNED BLUE.

Crap!

I knelt next to her as the dinghy bobbed unsteadily, bent her head back, and checked inside her mouth for obstructions—none. I commenced CPR.

Breathe, breathe, push, push.

Repeat.

After what seemed less than a minute, she convulsed, so I quickly rolled her onto her side as she vomited seawater into the dinghy. When she was done, she coughed and glanced up at me with an expression somewhere between total confusion and sheer terror. The blood that had covered her face was now washed clean, but there was plenty still caked to the side of her scalp, and more was starting to trickle.

"You're okay," I said. "Just stay calm and I'll get you back to my boat."

"What happened? Where am I?" Her voice was meek, and she spoke with what sounded like a French accent.

"It's okay, you're safe now."

"From what? How did I get here? Where are we?"

She got up on an elbow and looked over the side of the dinghy. Confusion twisted her features. The blood on the side of her head was still pumping.

"You have a gash on the side of your head—" I ripped my dive shirt off and held it to her temple. "Hold this in place with as much pressure as you can while I drive."

Her eyes fluttered.

"But, where—who are you?"

"It's okay, I'm a friend. Let's get you onto my boat—a bigger boat. It's about a half mile away, so hang on."

I started the dinghy and corrected our direction toward Tortola, which was a silhouette of gray above the azure sea to the west. I gently pushed the throttle forward until we skipped comfortably across the water. My gaze alternated from the course ahead to her face as she stared up into the sky, her hand pressing my shirt against her skull. Back over my shoulder, the water and the sky were clear. No sign of the helicopter, no other boats, no sign of anyone who might have shot it down.

What the hell happened? I had no radio on the dinghy, so I couldn't call for help or alert the authorities. No GPS to mark the location either. The ride turned choppy, and I had to keep the speed down so as to not inadvertently eject the woman—what was her name? I had yet to ask.

As we progressed farther into the Sir Francis Drake channel, there were more boats, but none had the flashing lights of police or Navy crews dispatched to search for the crashed helicopter. I glanced back at the woman. Her eyes were closed. Her hair was brown underneath the blood. Aquiline nose, taut muscles. Looked to be in her late thirties. She was dressed in quality resort wear, long slacks and tropical-weight blouse with a bold pattern—probably designer. She had no wedding ring, but the skin around her ring finger was white, so I guessed she was recently divorced or separated. She also had on a Cartier infinity bracelet. I'd bought one for Heather when we'd been married—they weren't cheap.

I hadn't heard from Heather, my ex-wife, since seeing her in Jamaica, where she'd been shacked up with Jack Dodson, my ex-business partner. Ugh.

I'd never given anything that nice to Scarlet Roberson, aside from a son—whom she'd kept from me for ten years. Was it just this morning I'd said good-bye to them?

We bounced on a wave from the ferry's wake as it traveled from St. Thomas to St. John to Tortola, and the woman jolted upright with her eyes wide. She glanced around, clearly terrified, until her gaze stopped on me and she calmed. I pointed ahead to the fifty-four foot Moorings catamaran that was anchored another quarter mile away. She showed no emotion but simply lay back down with her head on the rubber bow of the dinghy.

Vomit swirled around my feet in the inch of water on the bottom of the dinghy. Poor woman was lying in it, but at least she was alive. I again scanned the perimeter and found nothing out of the ordinary. Boats, ferries, divers, fishermen, brown scrub islands set against a baby blue sky and surrounded by aquamarine water.

The Virgin Islands hadn't been kind to me over the years. I married the wrong person on Peter Island, was arrested for a murder I didn't commit on Tortola, had been threatened at gunpoint on St. John, had been kidnapped on St. Thomas, and had been shot by a Russian billionaire on waters not far from here.

What the hell had I been thinking bringing Scarlet and Charlie here?

The BVI offered some of the best short-run bareboat sailing in the world—that had been my rationale. Several high quality islands, anchorages, beaches, bars, snorkeling and diving spots, and close proximity to Florida, the state where we all lived, albeit several hours apart. And it was beautiful.

It seemed like a good idea at the time.

I backed off the throttle a hair as we approached the catamaran. The woman's eyes opened again. She glanced up at me and followed my gaze toward the boat. Her expression showed no relief. Who could blame her? Her helicopter had crashed, killing all onboard, and I was a total stranger. There'd been three bodies in the chopper. Were they friends? Co-workers? The catamaran was as I'd left her a couple hours ago.

The yellow mesh bag was partially submerged in the water and vomit on the deck of the dinghy. So much for a mutton snapper dinner.

I reduced throttle to a crawl and circled back to the aft end of the cat.

"I'll pull up behind—this is my rental—and tie us off. Then we can get onboard and call for help. Okay?"

Her eyes were wide and she didn't respond. Probably still in shock, soaking wet and cold.

"Hang on."

With the dinghy sideways behind the back of the cat, I grabbed hold of the line I'd left hanging off a cleat, untied it, and stood up. "I need to get past you to tie this off on the bow here."

She crawled back toward the bench seat and made way for me. Once I'd retied the line to the ring on the dinghy's bow, I turned off the ignition to the motor.

"Ready to climb aboard?" I said.

She still didn't respond but watched as I pulled the line to bring us close to the swimming platform on the back of the catamaran and then stepped aboard. I turned around, bent down, and offered my hand. She didn't budge.

"It's okay. We'll call for help as soon as we get onboard."

"I don't remember anything."

"You had a bad knock on your head, but the bleeding's pretty much stopped. There's a shower where you can wash the blood off your clothes, if you'd like."

Her eyes narrowed. "Who are you?"

Jeez, I hadn't even introduced myself yet. "Sorry, I'm Buck Reilly. I'm vacationing here—on this boat. I was out snorkeling when I saw your helicopter, ah, crash into the water."

Her forehead wrinkled with surprise. "My helicopter?"

Oh shit.

"Let's just get you safely aboard." I smiled and kept my distance. Didn't want to crowd her. If she had amnesia, this could be complicated. I needed to get a look at the cut on her scalp to make sure it wasn't too deep.

She got slowly to her feet and wavered as the dinghy rocked in the current. She started to fall and held her hand up, and I caught her by the wrist.

"It's okay, I've got you," I said.

She didn't seem afraid as I pulled her onboard. Now, as she stood next to me, I realized she was quite tall, maybe five feet ten inches, and for some reason I felt like I'd seen her before.

4

"WHERE AM I?"

"We're in the British Virgin Islands, near the island of Tortola. Again, my name's Buck Reilly and this is my rental boat."

"Are you alone?" she said.

"Ah, well, I wasn't until this morning, but I am now."

"What happened?"

The woman was involved in a helicopter crash and had amnesia and she wanted to know what happened to me. She seemed calm and sat on one of the settees in the salon.

"My guests decided to leave, so I took them to the airport in St. Thomas and went snorkeling, which is when I—"

"I was on St. Thomas," she said.

"Great! You're remembering now."

"At least I think I was. That sounds familiar."

"What's your name?"

A glazed expression overcame her face. She didn't answer.

"You mind if I check that cut on your scalp?"

She reached up to touch her head, and when she lowered her hand it was bloody. She instantly turned pale and tumbled over to her left. I caught her before she fell onto the deck and laid her on her side on the settee. Her breathing was normal. I leaned over her head and parted her blood-caked brunette hair to find a three-inch gash. It was deep, and blood continued to seep from the wound.

Damn.

I grabbed a wad of paper towels and sat next to her, gently pressing the towels against her head. I didn't know how much blood she'd lost, so I sat for fifteen minutes applying pressure to her head while she slept, her head in my lap. I wanted more than anything to call for help, but the radio was up on the bridge and I didn't want to leave her alone. The smell of vomit on her clothing and my feet was a sour stench in my nostrils. The yacht was lying into the wind, so the salon was shielded—which in this case allowed the stink to linger.

Finally, she stirred. I let go of the paper towels and was pleased to see that the pressure had stemmed the flow of blood. I stood slowly so as to not alert her. Her eyes flickered before she sat up, and when she did, the corners of her mouth were turned down into a frown.

"*Quell est cette odeur?*"

French. I knew I'd heard an accent.

"Can we speak English? You swallowed a lot of salt water and then threw up in the dinghy."

"Who *are* you?"

This was starting to seriously worry me. "I'm Buck Reilly. I was snorkeling a mile from here and saw your helicopter crash into the water—"

"My helicopter?"

Oh, man, here we go again.

"There's a shower in the guest cabin and I have some women's clothes onboard. Why don't you get cleaned up and I'll call the police to report the crash."

"No!" Her eyes had narrowed in what looked like anger combined with something else. Fear? "No police."

"But—"

"No, please, not the police. I, I, I'm not sure why ... but no police."

Good grief.

"Okay, no police yet."

"No, not *yet*, not at all. I can't explain. I ... just know."

We sat staring at each other. She was a half-drowned ragamuffin, and I was shirtless and getting a chill in the afternoon shade.

"But I will shower," she said. "I smell disgusting."

She followed me into the interior salon, which was replete with a dining table, full galley, refrigerator, and stocked bar and wine rack.

"Water, please?"

I opened the refrigerator and pulled out two bottles of Evian, removed their caps and handed her one. We both drank deeply. I spied her from the corner of my eye. Standing very straight, she had excellent posture and presence. She radiated elegance and confidence.

"Can you tell me your name?" I said.

She stopped drinking. Her eyes fluttered again and she leaned against the kitchen table. "I don't know ..."

I hesitated and hoped that a warm shower and dry clothes would be what the doctor would have ordered if she'd let me call one. She followed me to the aft port stateroom, which had been unoccupied during my brief cruise with Scarlet and Charlie. The boat had four staterooms, each with its own en suite bath. The bed was made, and a thick white terrycloth robe hung behind the door.

"You can shower in here. Be careful with that cut on your scalp. We don't want that to start bleeding again. When you're finished there's a robe here. I'll hang some dry clothes outside your door."

She stared at me like a lost sheep. "How did I cut my head?"

"In the, ah, well, when your, ah ... Let's talk about it after we both get cleaned up and dry, okay?"

"Is this your shower?"

"No, mine's on the starboard—the other side—in the back. I'm going there now. I'll see you in the salon when you're ready."

She nodded slowly. Her eyes were a deep brown and fixed onto mine. "*Merci, monsieur.*"

"Reilly, Buck Reilly. My pleasure." I reached for the door, and she grabbed my bare shoulder. Her hand was clammy.

"No police, Buck Reilly, promise me."

I half turned in the narrow exit space and glanced at her over my shoulder. Three people had died on that helicopter—*someone* needed to know. I didn't know what I'd gotten into the middle of, but I needed her to stabilize, and the mention of police wasn't helping.

"Understood. No police. I'll see you in a little while."

I left her cabin and pulled the door closed behind me. I heard the click of the lock falling into place. Before going to my cabin to shower, I went to the starboard front cabin and opened the closet where Scarlet had kept her clothes. Her departure had been so abrupt she'd left a lot behind.

I stood there for a moment staring at the wardrobe. I hadn't been looking for an insta-family—I'd only wanted to get to know my son and get reacquainted with Scarlet. After two days of being in close quarters, with Charlie focused exclusively on his phone, the space between Scarlet and me had become close, so close you could cut the tension with a breadstick. I'd been enjoying our time together, but even at fifty-four feet, the catamaran had felt claustrophobic to her.

I chose a black maxi dress, a pair of slacks, and a long-sleeve top to provide the mystery woman with choices of fit and style. As promised, I hung them on the hook outside the door of the cabin where she was showering, and then I hurried to my own cabin. It was hard not to call the police, but I decided to honor her request.

For now.

The shower made me feel as if I were being born again. Covered in salt, vomit, and blood, I'd been wretched, but the scalding fresh water cleared it all away. Once dry, I put on some khaki shorts and a blue Last Resort Charter and Salvage T-shirt, unlocked my door, and walked into the salon. The clothes outside her door were gone.

The sky outside had turned a burnt orange, which reflected onto the sea. Darkness would soon consume the Caribbean, but millions of stars would then light the heavens in brilliant pinpoints. I flipped on lights, inside and out, even underneath the boat. Dying of thirst, I took a Virgin Islands Pale Ale from the still-packed refrigerator and drank half of it in one swig. When I turned around, she was standing behind me, wearing the black maxi dress, with her brunette hair clean and hanging over her shoulders.

It was as if I were seeing her for the first time. Tall, athletic yet sinewy, with smooth, lightly tanned skin—she cleaned up well. In fact, she was beautiful.

What the hell had I gotten myself into now?

5

SHE STOOD STARING AT ME SO LONG I WAS AFRAID SHE DIDN'T remember who I was. Again.

"Do you have another beer, Buck?"

I smiled. Hopefully, that was a good sign.

"You probably shouldn't drink—"

"My head is killing me."

From a drawer in the kitchen I pulled out a bottle of Advil. She swallowed four, washing them down with another bottle of Evian. It was bright in the salon, and rather than lowering the lights, I suggested we sit outside on the back of the boat.

Outside, I shifted two chairs to the aft cockpit just above the swimming platform. As I'd hoped, the sky twinkled with stars. A half moon had just risen on the horizon, and it reflected across the water. Tortola was a series of lights that dotted the contours of the island topography behind us, but we were an oasis of light afloat a sea of blackness.

The woman was quiet. When I was in the shower, I'd tried to think of names to refer to her by, but nothing stuck. She'd remembered my name, so perhaps she now remembered more.

"Are you in pain anywhere else?"

"My neck is sore, and my hands, too."

"The impact of hitting the water would do that. And you weren't wearing your seat belt, so you must have hit your head when you crashed."

"The helicopter," she said.

"You remember?"

"I remember you told me about it."

Damn.

I killed the beer and wanted another but didn't want to break the moment. The woman sat tall, perching her arms on the armrests like a sphinx. Her long brown hair wafted in the light breeze. I suddenly had a fantasy that we were here together, on a Caribbean bareboating cruise. Scarlet and I hadn't sat outside like this even once.

"I do remember a flash, and what felt like a sudden concussion that knocked me out," she said. "Based on what you saw, this must have been on the helicopter."

"Were you on an island tour? A tourist? Do you know what island—"

"I'm sorry, Buck, but I can't recall anything more than broken details, flashes of images."

I bit my lip. Questions built up inside me like a balloon being overfilled with helium. I might explode if I couldn't let a few out, and the longer it went before I contacted the police, the more upset they'd be when I did. Based on my past experiences, the police already didn't like me in the British Virgin Islands.

A bright shooting star carved a long arc across the heavens.

"See that?" I said.

The woman crossed her arms. She started to shiver and her teeth rattled. It was nearly eighty degrees outside.

"Are you okay? Did you remember something?"

She didn't respond.

I jumped up and opened a storage bin in the cockpit. It was filled with thick beach towels. I took two and wrapped them around her shoulders as she stared straight out over the water. I pulled my chair closer to her. The silver moon reflected in her eyes, making them bright like a cat's.

"I saw a streak come up from below us," she said with a shiver. "Then the flash, and next thing I knew I was nearly underwater. That's when I saw you." She turned to face me. She stared unblinking into my face, studying my features. Was she trying to remember if she knew me? She drew in a deep breath and blew it out hard. "I don't understand."

"Do you have any idea why you were on the helicopter?"

She shook her head slowly. "No, but I have a feeling that I was running away from something."

Running from what? Was that why she didn't want the police? Was she fleeing a crime? Did the police shoot her down? Couldn't be— they would have come searching, for sure. Who would shoot her— them—down and not come to check?

"Why would you be running?"

She was quiet. Her eyes had a thousand-yard stare, as if she were deep inside her head, hopefully in recollection. I decided to change tack.

"There were three other people on the helicopter. Two in front were men, probably pilots, and there was one woman in the back with you. Any idea who she or the others were?"

She shook her head again and glanced toward me. "They were dead?"

"Yes. The windshield was gone, and the men in front had been burned badly. The woman next to you might have been injured— maybe her neck broke in the crash—but she was strapped in tight and locked into her seat, which was submersed."

The woman sat forward as she inhaled a sharp breath and brought both hands up to cover her face. "*Mon Dieu*, how terrible."

"I'm sorry. I was just trying to help you recall."

She suddenly stood, the towels on her shoulders falling to the deck. "I'm afraid, Buck." She looked all around in the darkness, took a step backward and stumbled—I caught her as she fell backward. She caught her balance and stood up straight. "Please take me to land, to Tortola. I feel that's where I was going. I'm afraid. I don't want to be out here on the ocean."

"Okay, okay, relax. There's nothing to be afraid of here."

"I don't know you. I don't even know myself, but I do recognize fear, and I need to go!"

I felt like saying, *You were shot down and you did say you were running away.* Fear seemed like a logical and healthy response to me. "Can I call the police?"

"No! Please. I'm sorry. Not until I remember what happened." She looked up into my eyes. "Can we sail to Tortola, now?"

"Even better, we can use the engine."

I wasn't a fan of boating at night, but the course in and out of Soper's Hole on the west end of Tortola is well traveled and marked. Plus it's where I picked the boat up a few days before, and they told me I could use a slip there anytime during my cruise. And unlike me, this woman wasn't on a pleasure cruise—she was a missing person who'd been shot down and left for dead, and all she remembered was being on the run.

Within twenty minutes I'd secured all the open hatches, used the winch to lift the dinghy out of the water, hosed out the inside so it wouldn't stink to high heaven by morning, plotted my course, and got situated at the helm. These cats were designed to be sailed single-handedly and were equipped with the best push-button options available. From my seat I started the engines and pulled anchor at the same time. The GPS was illuminated and the radar showed clear sailing. I pushed the throttle forward and engaged the twin Yanmar V-drive engines. I slowly turned the wheel until the boat was pointed due east, which would take us through the passage between northern St. John and Great Thatch Island, then up around Little Thatch and into the harbor at Soper's Hole on Frenchman's Cay. The small irony that I was carrying an unknown Frenchwoman toward Frenchman's Cay hit me.

The light on my radio pulled at me like a carton of discount cigarettes at a two-pack a day smoker. I turned on the FM radio. Nothing wrong with cruising to local island music.

And news.

The woman appeared over my right shoulder and squeezed past me to sit on the bench seat on the bridge. There was a slight chill in the air, and she scooted closer until our legs touched. Flirting? I didn't think so.

The local news came and went and I listened to every word. Not one mention of a missing helicopter. I glanced at her, but she watched the water ahead as we navigated through the large dark islands peppered with lights to the south on St. John. Great Thatch, however, was just a large dark mass to our north.

I felt her shudder.

"I'm sorry, Buck, but I'm cold."

"Go ahead down to the salon. It's warmer there."

She scooted closer and put her head on my shoulder. "I don't want to be alone."

We sailed on, and truth be told, I appreciated her body heat. I didn't ask any more questions, focused on the task of driving the fifty-four foot cat through dark Caribbean waters with a mysterious woman on the run from God knows what or who. The smart thing would be to get her off my boat and out of my life as soon as possible. But she was terrified and had nearly been killed—I couldn't just walk away.

And since when did I ever do the smart thing?

6

JUST AS I'D BEEN PROMISED, AN OPEN SLIP AWAITED ME at the marina in Soper's Hole. A half dozen catamarans, all like identical sextuplets, were lined up next to each other. Only one had a light on inside. The harbor was quiet, surrounded by steep hills on three sides that created a great sense of place. There was a physical intimacy to the anchorage, which would hopefully set the woman's mind at ease. If a good night's sleep didn't help her recover her memory, I'd have no choice but to deliver her to the local hospital and alert the police about the crashed helicopter.

Once tied up in the slip, I joined my guest inside the salon. The bottle of Advil was back out, and she'd opened a bottle of French Margaux I'd bought for a special dinner with Scarlet that never materialized.

"I'm French," she said. "I drink wine for a concussion."

"Do you remember that you're French, or is that a guess?"

"Seriously?"

"You could be Canadian, or from the French West Indies."

"Either way, I drink wine to calm my nerves and settle my head-ache."

"Americans do that, too."

She pulled another wine glass out of the cupboard and filled it for me.

"*Ta santé*," she said.

"Cheers."

We touched glasses and I swirled the ruby-colored wine in my glass. The taste was as good as I'd expected it to be. The mystery woman had chosen the most expensive bottle I'd purchased for the trip.

"I can cook us dinner," I said.

"No, thank you. I'm going to bed. Images are swirling in my head, and I feel if I can get a good night's rest that maybe my memory will return tomorrow."

We stood assessing each other. She no doubt wondered whether she could trust me. My wheels spun over her earlier recollection of running from something. Would that be from someone trying to hurt her or in response to something nefarious she'd done? Given the fate of the helicopter, the former scenario seemed more likely—unless she'd really pissed someone off badly.

I once again escorted her to the aft port stateroom and showed her the light switches, the location of a small refrigerator stocked with water, a closet with extra blankets and pillows, and finally the intercom system and which button to push to reach me. She absorbed it all, or at least didn't ask questions, and was patient through the tour.

"I'm sorry, Buck Reilly."

I noticed a tear leak from her eye before she quickly wiped it away. Poor thing, she'd been through hell. Then another tear.

I stepped closer and held my arms wide. She stepped inside them and I bent toward her and gave her the best brotherly hug I could.

"Tomorrow will be a new day. We'll figure it—you—out then, too."

When we parted, the corners of her lips were bent slightly upward.

"*Merci*, Buck. Again, I'm sorry to be a burden."

"Not a problem. My plans had already been wiped clean. You're a fascinating mystery and I'm happy to help. But we do need to make some progress in the morning."

"*D'accord.* I understand."

When I closed the door behind me, I again heard the lock quickly pushed into place.

I made a sandwich in the galley, drank more of the Margaux—at $200 a bottle, I wasn't going to let it go to waste—and pulled up the Internet. Virgin Island News Online was the best source of local news

I'd found here. Scanning the home page and the news section, I found no mention of a missing helicopter. Scarlet's rebuke this morning—today actually—that I didn't know what was going on had motivated me to review the events section, where I'd learned about the Group of Eight meeting being held on St. Thomas. The United States, the United Kingdom, Germany, Japan, Italy, Canada, France and Russia—all were in attendance at the annual meeting to seek consensus on global issues like economics, global security, energy, and terrorism. It had just started today. That's why all the big jets with flags on their tails were flying in, along with the helicopters and the security teams. And Russia's being here was a big deal, according to the article I saw, since it was the first meeting they'd been invited to in over a decade.

No wonder Scarlet talked to me like I was a buffoon. I was, and some may say I still am, but the truth was as I'd told her. Ever since I'd been crucified in the press after my company e-Antiquity went bankrupt and my partner Jack Dodson absconded with our corporate bank accounts, I could no longer watch the news without having the equivalent of a PTSD panic attack. If that meant I was out of the loop on some major events, like a G8 summit happening in the Virgin Islands during the middle of my bareboating trip, then so be it.

If the mystery woman was indeed French, or Canadian, for that matter, could she be connected to one of those delegations? Or could she be here to disrupt the meetings somehow? An act of terrorism, perhaps? Good grief.

After I polished off the remaining Margaux, the fatigue of the day hit me like a sucker punch. I turned out the lights in the galley, locked the door out to the rear cockpit, and entered my cabin. I closed the door quietly, paused and latched the lock.

The headboard on the bed in the master suite had a secret compartment where I kept my valuables. Piracy was rare but did occur throughout the islands, and bareboat charters were frequent targets. One of the benefits of having Ray Floyd fly me down here in the Beast was that I was able to bring a 9mm Sig Sauer along that Ray had lent me. I didn't like guns, but I wasn't going to risk any harm to Scarlet and Charlie. With them gone, that was no longer a concern, so I kept it in the hidden compartment on the top of the bed, which I slapped now and it popped open. I placed my wallet inside and closed it.

The gentle rocking of the boat had me sound asleep. When I opened my eyes, my ancient Rolex Submariner indicated it was 6:10 a.m. I knew from planning the trip that sunrise had occurred just twenty minutes earlier. I lay in bed for a few moments listening to the creaks and groans of the floating home and replayed the events of yesterday from my snorkeling trip onward. No point in dwelling on Scarlet. Today was about finding answers and redirecting my wounded dependent to the authorities. I was convinced she must have a connection to the G8 summit, one way or another, and whichever way the chips fell there, it was way beyond anything I needed to be in the middle of.

My groaning stomach interrupted my thoughts. The sandwich last night hardly did the trick after the full day I'd had. Breakfast and coffee was of immediate concern. When Scarlet, Charlie and I set sail from here a few days ago, I remembered being impressed with the bakery at the ship's store at the marina.

Wearing a fresh T-shirt and shorts, I left the close comfort of my cabin and found the galley as I'd left it. A quick glance down the port hallway told me the woman's door was still closed. I was tempted to see if it was still locked—only to confirm she was still there, not to gain entry. But if she was gone, then the problem of the day would be solved. I'd call the authorities, let them know what had happened, and face the consequences for not doing so sooner.

After lingering briefly to try to detect sound from inside the cabin, I continued with my plan to get breakfast. Even though I'd heard nothing, I'd still get enough for the two of us. The door to the back cockpit was locked from inside. Still here.

A small single-sail ketch caught my eye as it passed in front of my catamaran. The white sail had a black skull and crossbones with dueling swords underneath painted on it. A lone man stared at me from the tiller. He had a long white beard, braided down to his chest, piercing blue eyes, a wide straw hat, and was dressed in a white long sleeved shirt, and white pants. He was maybe seventy years old, but those eyes were sharp, and he stared at me like an osprey considering a baitfish. He continued silently past like a living *memento mori*, which caused my skin to go momentarily clammy. I felt like I'd met him before but couldn't place where.

On the dock, there was the familiar morning activity of the charter company provisioning another pair of catamarans that must be launching today. The smell of coffee wafted from the open door of the ship's store, and inside were a pair of locals chatting over steaming cups. They stopped to watch me as I studied the baked goods under glass.

"Help you, sir?" a dark-skinned woman in a clean yellow polo shirt said. The Moorings logo was on the breast of her shirt.

"Good morning. Can I get two butter croissants and two chocolate croissants, please? Also a double espresso and a large cappuccino."

"Coming right up, sir."

While she set about assembling the order, I glanced around the store. The two men I'd interrupted when I entered were now oblivious to me and continued their chatter.

"Don't care about their story. They got no right coming here and being all pushy," one of the men said.

That caught my attention. From between sunscreen bottles one aisle over, I stopped to listen to them. Both were in their late sixties or early seventies, and each wore blue shirts with the Moorings logo on their sleeves. They were porters. I'd met men in the same attire attending to final details of our departure before we had set sail.

"I hear that. Foreigners, too. No need for that."

"Sir?" The woman said. "Your order's ready."

I walked out from the aisle of supplies, and when I was halfway to the counter, an uneasy feeling crept into my gut. I couldn't help myself.

"Excuse me, gentlemen. Did I hear you talking about some un-friendly foreigners being pushy around the dock today?"

They looked at me a moment and then back at each other before one spoke up.

"They's still out there, son. Going boat to boat asking questions. You on a boat, you'll meet 'em soon enough."

For some reason this news caused my stomach to drop. I threw a $20 at the cashier, grabbed my bag of croissants and two coffees, and double-strided toward the door. Before exiting, I glanced down the dock and saw nothing. Up the dock, however, I saw three men wearing dark clothing and serious expressions speaking to a man dressed casually—another charter customer, I guessed.

They were two boats away from my catamaran.

Uh-oh.

7

CONCERN INCREASED MY PACE. I DROPPED THE CAPPUCCINO in the trash can and walked as normally as I could back to my boat without looking over at the men. I didn't see but could feel their eyes on me and I knew they'd be knocking on my door in minutes.

Once onboard, I locked the door, dropped the groceries, and turned and found the woman seated at the galley counter. She was again wearing the black maxi dress. The smell of fresh brewed coffee and the smile on her face were nice to find, but when she saw my serious expression, she stood up. "What's wrong?"

"There are three men on the dock going boat to boat asking questions."

"Three men?"

"Foreigners in dark clothing—not exactly seafaring types. You had said you'd run away—"

"I have to hide—where can I—you have to hide me!" She stood and shuffled around in a circle, staring in every direction.

My gut said to help her, and while my gut had rarely let me down, this time I wasn't sure. But there was no choice.

"Back to your cabin," I said. "There's a space where you can hide."

I led her into her bathroom. There was a clip on the wall to the left that, once pulled, released a panel on the floor. Under the panel was an empty storage bin.

"Get in here," I said. "It'll be dark—"

Just then came the sound of a solid knock on the outside door from the cockpit into the galley.

"They're here!" Her whisper was tortured.

She crawled down into the compartment and lay sideways so I could close the lid. Her expression of terror pulled at my heart. The next round of knocks on the door was more urgent than the last. I closed and latched the lid quickly. I sucked in a deep breath, brushed my hands down the front of my T-shirt, and walked into the galley.

I stepped purposefully to the door and saw a man through the glass. I unlocked it and pulled it open. It was one of the men from the dock.

"Did I grant you permission to come aboard?" I said.

"I'm sorry, sir, but—" His accent was thick, and his skin color and facial features led me to believe he was Sicilian or Northern African.

"Maritime law's clear on not boarding someone's boat without—"

"Mr. Reilly?" Another voiced interrupted from the dock.

Past the man I'd been lecturing were two other men standing behind my boat on the dock. How did he know my name?

"We need to speak with you, sir," the man on the dock said.

I motioned the man who'd come aboard toward the dock, closed the door, and followed after him.

The man who knew my name was a few years older, maybe forty, had a stout build, a trim moustache, close-cropped dark hair, olive skin, and black eyes. He stood in front of the other man, a younger, thicker version of him and a near twin of the man who still stood on my boat.

"Permission to come aboard, Mr. Reilly?" the older one said.

"Who are you and how do you know my name?"

"I'm sorry to disturb you, and I'll be glad to answer your questions, but can we speak in private, please?" His polite words did not match the intensity in his eyes.

"Not until I know what this is about—"

"It's an emergency, sir. There's no time to spare, I assure you, or we would not be so rude."

I glanced around the dock and saw the two porters from the coffee shop standing outside and watching us. I waved to them—I'd rather someone knew what was happening—but they just stared back at me.

"You can come here to the cockpit and tell me what the emergency is—and how you know my name."

The older man stepped aboard, sure-footed even though he never took his eyes off me. The other two men glanced around my boat from where they stood, even craning their necks to peer inside the windows.

"What the hell's going on?" I said.

The older man stepped close to me, and even though I had a good seven inches and thirty pounds on him, he leaned in as if he would cut me in half if I made one false move.

"Did you see a helicopter when you were sailing in the Sir Francis Drake Channel yesterday?"

"Excuse me? How do you know who I am or where I was—"

"The local government is cooperating with us, Mr. Reilly. We have all of the identification codes for all chartered and other boats registered in these waters. We've tracked all vessels for the past twenty-four hours and saw that yours was anchored for much of the afternoon and evening near the channel." His eyes never left mine, and his gaze was so intense I hadn't noticed until now that his two colleagues had vanished.

"Whoa, whoa, whoa, hey? Who are you and—wait, where are they going? Do you have a search warrant?"

"Time is of the essence, Mr. Reilly. Now tell me, did you see a helicopter?"

I crossed my arms, uncrossed them, and took in a slow breath. *Pull it together, Buck.* "I was spearfishing for several hours—"

"How many fish did you get?"

"Snorkeling and spearfishing—"

"What about the helicopter?"

I needed to shift to offense and fast.

"Did I see a helicopter? Really? With the G8 summit going on, there's been helicopters everywhere!"

"Not over the channel yesterday. I have every flight plan, and none crossed over there." His eyes narrowed and he leaned closer. "Our research on you reveals that you run charters—"

"And salvage."

"But your past is somewhat questionable. You're an ex-con, Mr. Reilly. That makes you a person of interest. You went bankrupt and your business partner went to jail. You were accused of murder right here in the British Virgin Islands."

I swallowed, hard.

"What the hell are you talking about?"

The man seemed highly impatient and glanced from side to side. Nobody was in earshot. His men were climbing all over the bow and helm of the yacht, like parasites seeking entry.

The man leaned closer. "Let me be specific. We believe a helicopter carrying a VIP crashed over the Sir Francis Drake Channel within a mile of where your boat was anchored. Did you see anything like that, Mr. Reilly?"

"Listen, I told you I was underwater most of that time, and if I'd seen anything, I would have called the Navy, or police, or someone that could have helped."

The man studied my face closely, waiting to see if I twitched the wrong way.

"What happened?" I swallowed. "Who is the VIP?"

"You don't watch the news?"

"Not when I'm on vacation."

He narrowed his eyes. "Are you alone here?"

"No—well—I am at the moment."

"Explain."

I cleared my throat and tried to avert the anxiety-induced closing of my esophagus. "My son and his mother were with me, but they left early this morning for the Dolphin Discovery Center here on Tortola."

"That's very early for a tourist excursion, isn't it?"

"Not if you want to be first in line. It's a popular place and we're planning to set sail later this morning." I took in a slow breath. I had to turn this around pronto. "So who's the VIP you mentioned?"

"Madame Giselle Huibert, the first lady of France, and her security detail."

His words sucked the wind out of me so fast my vision experienced a whiteout. After what felt like an eternity but was only a couple of seconds, I inhaled and realized the man had opened the door to the interior cockpit and stepped inside.

"Do you mind if I look around, Mr. Reilly?"

What the hell could I say now? I had to cooperate, and—Jesus—if they managed to find the woman—the first fucking lady of France—locked in a storage compartment in the bathroom?! They might shoot me on the spot.

"Feel free."

Did he notice my voice crack? I sounded like a frog, even to me.

The man—he'd never stated his name or shown me credentials—went to the starboard side of the boat first. I watched, unsure if I should follow or give him free rein. The other two men appeared behind me and entered through the open door.

"Jacques?" one said.

"In here. Check the other side." The voice came from my cabin.

I leaned against the galley table and tried to appear casual. My espresso was there. I sipped it but could only taste the acid reflux that had surged up in my throat.

Giselle said she'd run away. From what? Or who?

These guys gave me serious creeps. I couldn't imagine a life surrounded by them, or anything else about public office.

The guy who'd been questioning me—Jacques—appeared outside my cabin. "You are alone in that bedroom? What about your wife?"

"She's not my wife. She's the boy's mother. I'm his father. It's complicated."

He grunted and mumbled something about Americans in another language. He walked into the forward cabin. Thank God Scarlet's clothes were still there, and the mystery woman's—Giselle Huibert's—were in the dryer. The sound of a door opening from the port side caught my attention. The other two men were in the other cabins.

The man in the port forward cabin walked down the hall, glanced toward me, and followed after his associate into the aft cabin. I could hear the men talking. Jacques came up behind me and I nearly jumped out of my flip-flops when he spoke.

"The woman's clothing in the front bedroom belongs to whom?"

"Her name is Scarlet Roberson. Her name is on the boat rental contract, too, if you care to look."

"Jacques?" The voice came from the aft port cabin.

The man in charge followed the voice. My feet were glued to the ground as if I'd stepped in wet concrete. An urge to run sparked in my brain, but communications to my limbs had been disrupted.

A moment later Jacques emerged carrying some women's clothing—the second outfit I'd offered to Giselle last night. "Why are these back here if Ms. Roberson is using the front bedroom?"

I feigned a smile. "Women, you know? She said something about the light being better back there when she was getting dressed last night."

The other two men came out of the cabin. Jacques looked around, his gaze stopping on the bag of croissants, my espresso, and then the coffee maker full of fresh steaming coffee on the counter. He turned toward the door.

"If you think of anything, or remember seeing any boats or helicopters from yesterday, call me immediately." He handed me a card. It had only a number, no name, no title or organization.

"Absolutely. If I think of anything I'll call the police—"

"Not the police. Call me. I lead the private security team for Mrs. Huibert."

Private security? Don't the French have their own version of the Secret Service?

The three men filed out of the salon without looking back. My bladder nearly let go when Jacques stopped and looked back inside the door, but then he turned and climbed off the boat. I stepped outside and watched as they walked down the dock. There was a black Cadillac Escalade with tinted windows, running, with another man behind the wheel. My three visitors climbed inside and the vehicle's tires chirped as they sped away.

8

INSIDE THE BOAT I DIDN'T KNOW WHETHER TO BE FURIOUS or just terrified. I was leaning toward the latter, so it would depend on how the woman—Giselle—responded to the truth.

In the bathroom, I thought for a second about how to play the news. I knelt and knocked on the lid. "It's me, Buck. The men are gone, I'm opening the compartment."

With a click of the button the lid popped up an inch. I grabbed the edge and lifted it. The woman's eyes fluttered in the light. She'd been cooped up for fifteen or twenty minutes.

"You okay?" I said.

Her body trembled and I realized she was crying. I took her arm and gently pulled her to a seated position. Tears streaked her cheeks, and she wouldn't look up to meet my eyes.

"Don't worry, they're gone." I paused. "Could you hear anything?"

She shook her head slowly from side to side. "Only when a man, or men, entered the bathroom. They walked on top of me and the floor creaked. I was certain they would examine the hatch to find out why." When she glanced up, her brown corneas were surrounded by red and her face glistened with tears.

"Let me help you out of there."

The news of her identity burned through my mental circuits. Squatting in a catamaran bathroom storage bin was less than fitting for most people, much less the wife of a major world leader. The Royal Palais in Paris flashed in my mind.

Good Lord.

"Who were they? What did they want?" she said.

I took her hands in mine and stepped backward to help her stand and step out of the storage space.

"They were asking if I'd seen a helicopter yesterday. They knew who I was and that my boat had been anchored in the Sir Francis Drake Channel."

She took a tissue from the box on the counter and wiped her eyes, and when she looked up her resolve had returned. "How did they know that? What did you tell them?"

"I lied."

Her jaw quivered but she fought the tears away. "Thank you."

"The local governments are cooperating with them to search for the helicopter. They tracked all of the GPS signals from every boat in the vicinity and are locating them one by one." I let the gravity of the information register. "You should stay in the cabin in case they left anyone behind to watch the marina."

She left the bathroom and sat on the bed. "Who were they?"

I stood my ground in the door of the cabin. "We haven't had the chance to talk this morning." I paused. "Have you remembered any more since last night?"

Her face fell. "Some, yes."

"Your identity?"

She lifted her gaze and held mine with fresh fire in her eyes. "Yes."

I bowed. "A pleasure to meet you, Ms. First Lady."

"Stop it," she said. "My marriage is over."

"But you're here with your husband—"

"And I left him on St. Thomas. I was on my way to Tortola to fly back to France."

A long silence played out.

"When did you remember all this?"

She stood and paced the small cabin. "In the middle of the night, after my headache finally subsided. I would have woken you, but I decided to wait until morning."

"And the helicopter?"

"I don't know what happened. I mean, a rocket did hit us—exploded and all went black—but I don't know why."

"Are you leaving your husband for another man?" I thought of the other passenger in the back of the helicopter. "Or woman?"

Her laugh was bitter and harsh. "Hardly. Something happened at the hotel on St. Thomas, but I can't remember what. And he'd beg to keep me—his approval rating back home is abysmal. Riots, strikes, demonstrations. As the youngest first lady ever, the people are fond of me, though. Him not so much. If something happened to me, he'd be even less popular."

"Then why did you run?"

She rubbed her palms over her face and then delicately touched the side of her head where the deep gash was. "I don't remember yet, but I'm certain it had something to do with what happened at the hotel. When I think of it, terror takes hold of me, and I, I …" She shuddered and grimaced, fighting back tears.

I stepped toward her and she fell into my arms. Her body shook with silent sobs and she felt feverish, a heat caused by fear and tension.

"I'm sorry to have gotten you involved in this, Buck."

"I got myself into it, Giselle. May I call you that?"

"I'm not a fucking queen. Just the wife of an overly ambitious politician. And what do you mean you got yourself involved?"

I took a step back. Her eyebrows lifted when she noticed my smile.

"I came to your helicopter and pulled you out. You didn't ask me to. I wasn't going to let you drown."

"My white knight." Her voice had a tinge of sarcasm.

"I would have pulled anyone out. It just happened to be you. And until now I had no idea who you were." I hadn't cared then, and frankly I didn't care now.

"Why didn't you turn me over to—who were the men who came here? Police?"

I hesitated. I didn't want to scare her any further, but I didn't know what to do with her either. You can't hide a first lady for long, and those men meant business. Unofficial business, I believed. "Can we eat something first? I'm starving. I bought us some croissants."

"I made coffee."

"Wait here and I'll bring some in."

In the galley I poured coffee and put it in the microwave and then cut the croissants in half and put them in the toaster oven. I was just buying time. Those men, Jacques and his henchman, were the last people I'd call. The whole blank card, telling me to call them instead of the police, was very weird.

Now what? If she wanted to go to the airport, I'd take her there. If she wanted to stay in hiding, that was a different story. Why was she afraid? What could have happened at the hotel?

The microwave beeped and the toaster dinged. I used a tray and brought the load, along with sugar, cream, butter, and jam, into the aft cabin. Giselle was lying face up on the bunk with her eyes wide open. I hesitated and then put the tray on the small night table.

"What do you want to do, Giselle?"

"Tell me about the men who came."

I sat in the side chair. "There were three of them. One was clearly in charge."

"French?"

"Possibly, but darker-skinned. I thought maybe Algerian."

"There are many Algerians in France. But in France there are no African-French, and no Algerian-French like in America. You are either French or something else. Did they show you any credentials?"

"No. But they gave me a business card." I dug into the hip pocket of my shorts. "There's no name, but one of the other men called him Jacques."

"Like John in English."

She looked at the white card that had only a phone number. "It's not even a French phone number. Certainly not the Groupe de Sécurité de la Présidence de la République—our equivalent to the Secret Service in America, my detail." Her hand covered her mouth. The man and woman on the helicopter, along with the pilot. Dead.

"They didn't give me that Secret Service kind of vibe, that's for sure."

She sat up, swung her legs toward the table and stared at the croissant.

"Where can I take you, Giselle?"

"Ready to get rid of me?"

"It's not that, but right now there are people searching for you. You can't just disappear. You're a public figure—"

"Why not? I'll start a new life here, under a mango tree."

That made me laugh. She glanced up, startled, and seeing my face she began to laugh, too. In a moment, we were laughing so hard we couldn't talk.

"You … can sell … coconuts … on the beach," I said.

We laughed harder.

"Or … mangoes." Tears were again streaming down her cheeks as she laughed. The lunacy of the situation had us both punchy, but laughter helped to break the grip of fear.

It was my turn to rub the tears from my cheeks. What a mess this was. I took the other croissant, spread strawberry jam on it, and took a bite. The crunch of the toasted bread caused Giselle to laugh again, which got me laughing. I nearly choked and finally spit the bread onto my palm, which sent her into hysterics.

Once we settled down, I was afraid to say anything. She rolled onto her side and took the remote control for the small television mounted on the wall and turned it on. Her lips parted and she wetted them as she stared at the television. I licked my own lips. If laughter led to affection, I was feeling very, *very* fond of her right now.

Giselle's face suddenly turned to stone.

I followed her eyes to the small TV and immediately recognized the man on the screen.

François Huibert, the president of France.

Her husband.

SECTION 2

POLITICS IS A DIRTY BUSINESS

9

THE SCENE ON THE TV WAS OF THE FRENCH PRESIDENT AT THE AIRPORT in St. Thomas. He wore a black suit, surrounded by other men in suits. The camera panned to a U.S. Coast Guard helicopter landing on the tarmac in front of them. After a moment, the rotor slowed and the side door slid open.

Cut to President Huibert's face. Stoic, eyes puffy, pallor gray, fearing the worst. A banner floated across the top of the screen: "First Lady of France's Helicopter Is Found. Multiple Bodies on Board." Pan back to the helicopter, where the Coast Guardsmen were removing body bags as a black van pulled up to the large orange chopper, blocking the camera.

Giselle's jaw was clenched tight. No more tears.

I turned up the sound. The reporter whispered as if he were commentating a golf match. "No confirmation yet as to whether Giselle Huibert, the first lady of France, was aboard the helicopter, but multiple bodies have been recovered."

The screen shifted to Giselle's official picture.

"I hate that photo," she said.

I'd seen it before. Dressed to the nines, resplendent in makeup, jewelry, a red jacket, short black skirt, black stockings, and high heels. I knew she'd been familiar, but sitting here now in casual clothes with no makeup, she bore little resemblance to the fancy woman in that picture.

"Looks pretty good to me," I said.

Her head snapped over to face me. Whoops.

The commentator continued as the on-screen image shifted back to the Coast Guard helicopter. "The helicopter was tracked using its last known GPS imprint and side scan sonar aboard the Coast Guard ship. Sunk in nearly one hundred feet of water, the recovery of the helicopter was handled by divers from the Coast Guard."

I hit the mute button.

Giselle climbed off the bed and put her face close to the screen. She watched with narrow eyes.

"What are you doing?"

"Seeing who else is there. Watching François' reaction."

"He looks pretty upset from here."

She grunted. "Politicians are the best actors."

"Reality stars," I said under my breath.

The position of the van blocked the cameras from filming the off-loading of bodies from the helicopter. The black van drove off slowly. The camera panned to president Huibert as he entered a black limousine with the French flag on its door.

I turned the sound back on. "... on its way to the morgue, where the identification of the bodies will occur. No information has been made available on why the helicopter crashed, but experts from the NTSB will be reviewing the flight data recorder since the helicopter left from the U.S. territory and was found in U.S. waters."

The camera followed the slow-moving black limousine. It reminded me of the recent funeral for president George H. W. Bush. Had the Coast Guard detected that the helicopter crashed due to being hit by a rocket? Would they state that or would it be classified information? Had a terrorist group claimed responsibility for the helicopter's being shot down—who else would have done it? Still no insight on any of that, but if there was even a hint of foul play, the networks would have the story named, branded, and set to dramatic music.

Giselle pressed the power button on the TV and the screen went black.

"It'll take a couple hours before all positive identifications are made and next of kin is advised," I said.

"I need air. I have to leave the boat," she said.

"You can do what you want. We can go inside the ship's store right now and call the police. I happen to know them well on this island—"

"No—not yet. I need to remember what the hell happened first. If my helicopter was shot down, it was for a reason. If I expose myself now, without the memory of why I fled, then whoever shot it down will find and kill me before I remember."

"Well, then you can't go out there on the dock. Not after those men were here and your picture is being broadcast all over the world. The people here are proud. They'll take your potential death hard, so if you were to survive, they'd be elated. When the coroner reports that neither the men nor the woman—"

"Jennifer Gascoin." She winced. "My personal assistant."

"When people find out your body wasn't recovered, they'll start a mad search of the waters and islands. There'll be no place to hide." I didn't acknowledge her assistant's name, nor did I think she'd want to revisit details of Ms. Gascoin's having drowned.

"Can we sail to another island?" she said.

"To what end?"

"I need to remember what happened! After that I will leave you alone, I promise."

There was no reasoning with this woman. Headstrong, persistent, and unbreakable. I smiled.

"We can sail out of here and be at another island in a few hours. The wind is light, but we can use the engine if need be."

"Good. Let's go."

On my way out of her door, I stopped. "I told those private security men that my son and his mother were at the Dolphin Discovery here on Tortola and that we'd be setting sail when they returned."

"So?"

"If they're watching the marina and see me leave without them, they'll be suspicious." More suspicious than they already were, that is. I hadn't told Giselle that they knew all about me, including my past legal issues here in the BVI, but now wasn't the time.

"It's a risk we'll have to take. They already know where you are, Buck, so we're—what's the phrase?—sitting *canard* here."

"*Canard?* Ducks, right?" I paused. "I agree we should relocate, but you need to stay in your cabin, please. I can handle the boat myself. Once we're at sea, I'll come get you."

All I got was a pinch-faced nod.

My Costa del Mar sunglasses hung from a hook, and I put them on as I exited the salon. I jumped onto the dock and glanced around. I continued up the dock to the small parking area where my unwelcome visitors had departed from. No black Cadillac Escalade was parked there, and I didn't see anyone sitting in a car, so I walked back to the boat.

One of the two porters I'd overheard in the ship's store this morning was standing outside smoking a cigarette. I gave him a nod.

"How you like the boat so far?" he said.

"Very nice," I said. "Handles well, comfortable inside. Getting ready to sail now."

"No wind today," he said. "Which way you headed?"

It was a good question. I had friends on Jost Van Dyke who would help us, but I wasn't sharing that information with anyone here. "Was thinking about sailing to Sandy Spit for a picnic."

He shook his head, took a drag of his smoke, and exhaled a plume. "No wind that way and there's a strong current running. You'll be able to power through it, but you'll burn a lot of fuel and take half the day to get there. And the Spit was wiped clean by the hurricanes. Not much there to see but piles of coral."

"Maybe we'll head to Peter Island then."

He nodded. "Better wind."

"Mind helping me cast off?"

He took another drag and flicked his cigarette into the bushes. I stepped back onboard and he approached my port aft line.

"Bet there's a lot of Coast Guard traffic down there," I said.

"They found what they was looking for."

"Any word on why that helicopter crashed?"

"Nothing on the tele yet. Damn shame. G8 coming here was a boon for business, now this. One step forward, ten back." He tossed the line onto the stern of the cat. "Start it up and I'll get the bow line and throw the fenders over the side."

"Much obliged."

The twin engines fired up, and the porter did as he said. When he was finished he gave me a thumbs-up. I waved back and engaged the transmission. If anyone came back asking questions, they'd get a solid piece of misinformation from a credible source.

Before I pressed the throttle forward, I took intentional action to break my contract with the charter company. Upon giving Scarlet and me a tour of the yacht and walking us through all the operational procedures, they'd given us a tutorial on the electronics: sonar, radar, GPS, radio, emergency channels, and so on. The transponder was next to the GPS, and it was strictly prohibited for charter customers to turn it off. Moorings wanted to know where their boats were at all times in case we had a problem or in case we got lost or ventured beyond the predetermined sailing radius. They were more worried about their million dollar yachts than about bonehead sailors, not that they'd said that, but it made sense. The transponder signal was how the private security team had found me. I wanted to make sure they couldn't do it again. I held the power button down until the screen on the transponder went dark and then, for safe measure, disconnected the power line.

The porter was still on the dock, both hands on his hips, waiting to see me pull out of the slip. I gave him a final wave.

We were officially off the grid.

I smiled. Scarlet's words at the airport came back to me. Buck Reilly adventures were always memorable.

Indeed.

10

THE SKY WAS A BRILLIANT BLUE, AND THE HILLS SURROUNDING the harbor were golden brown, spotted with white, yellow, and blue homes topped with orange terra-cotta roofs. Boats moved in all directions around the waterfront, and we sailed due west, straight out toward open water. Normally when sailing to Jost Van Dyke, I'd steer northwest right out of Soper's Hole, but if anyone, including the porter, had eyes on us, I wanted it to look like we were heading southeast toward Peter Island.

The last thing I wanted to do, however, was reenter the Sir Francis Drake Channel right now, and even though the conditions didn't sound advantageous to the north, I'd give passage to Jost a shot.

Using the binoculars I'd brought from the Beast, I scanned the waters behind us. Yes, there were plenty of boats, but none seemed to be on our line or following my course. No boats were close by on the port or starboard sides, and it was clear sailing ahead, so I engaged autopilot and abandoned the bridge to give Giselle the all clear.

Before I could step down into the cockpit, though, I found her—reclined in a deck chair, wearing Scarlet's green bikini. My eyes bugged wide. Giselle filled it out in a way Scarlet couldn't.

"Are you supposed to be out here?" I said.

"Aren't you supposed to be driving the boat?"

"I was coming to give you the all clear sign, but I see you already gave it to yourself."

Her smile was radiant. "I'm wearing a disguise."

"Lovely."

"I know you think I'm being terribly selfish, and you're right. Many of the French people will be concerned about my going missing. But soon the television will report that I was not one of the bodies recovered, and I want to enjoy this brief respite from the public eye. So yes, I'm going to be selfish. Besides, no one looking for me would ever expect me to be sunbathing on a yacht with a dashing American captain."

I couldn't help but roll my eyes, which got me a very cute giggle.

"I hope your girlfriend won't mind that I borrowed her bikini."

"She's not my girlfriend. She ditched me. Plus, by the look of it, you'll have stretched that top out too much for her anyway, so it's yours now."

She sat up and reached behind her back. "I can take it off if you're worried—"

"No! That's okay. Enjoy yourself. And if you're wondering, I'm about to head north toward Jost Van Dyke. It's a small sparsely populated island in the northern BVI, and I have a friend there who can help us."

"*Magnifique.* Thank you for indulging me, Buck. I promise I'm not really a horrible person, but convalescing here may help my memory to return. Then you'll be free to get on with your life."

I again bowed at the waist. "At your service, Madame First Lady."

Whap!

A plastic tube of sunscreen smacked the fiberglass next to me, and I scampered back to the bridge. The smile on my face felt good. When Scarlet and Charlie left, I was determined to dive and sail these waters all on my own, to get the most out of this impromptu vacation—the first one I'd taken since moving to Key West several years ago. I could never have anticipated what would happen, and while it was interesting for the moment, sooner or later reality would hit.

I just hope it didn't hit with an armed gunship.

The passage north was slow going, as the porter on the dock suggested it would be. The current was moving strongly toward us and there was little wind. The engines were too low in horsepower to push the big cat against the current. Being exposed on open waters like this was risky, given that the search was likely to escalate as soon as they announced Giselle was not one of the confirmed dead. I checked the weather report on the iPad mounted at the bridge. Winds would be better tomorrow and the current was supposed to ease up. Even though it wasn't a long sail to Jost Van Dyke, I decided to make skip-steps in navigation, which would allow me to assess the search situation on each leg.

Well north of Tortola's west end, I tacked the catamaran to the east by simply pressing a couple of buttons. Now we were sailing with the current, and it accelerated our speed. I didn't bother telling Giselle, as she had enough to think about, and as she'd said, maybe the downtime would help her relax enough to remember why she'd fled her husband.

The passage was beautiful. A huge leatherback turtle popped its head up as we sailed past, its shell at least six feet across. Rare for these waters, mariners considered sightings of leatherbacks good luck. Moments later a pod of bottlenose porpoises appeared off the bow and I counted at least a dozen of the beauties swimming ahead of the ship, jumping and playing in the spray of the port bow. High overhead, a frigate bird floated directly over top of us for at least fifteen minutes. Frigates, too, were considered good omens.

Alone at the helm, I took in the nature but was concerned that the passage of time would only make matters worse. I let out a long breath and hoped the various signs here on the water really were harbingers of good things to come.

In another hour we sailed straight into Cane Garden Bay on the north shore of Tortola. There were options to get food or shelter there, provided they'd been renovated since the rash of hurricanes that had devastated the Virgin Islands over a year and a half ago. Wreckage had still been evident on St. Thomas, where less than half the hotels had reopened since the hurricanes hit. Surely at least one beach bar would have reopened here, and from there we could coconut-telegraph our way to finding a small inn, where we could be on solid ground for a night and I could hopefully hand Giselle off to someone in a better position to help her.

After putting us back on autopilot, I went to inform Giselle of the change in plan.

On the aft deck I found her now lying on her stomach, topless and asleep. I stood staring at her for a long moment. Certainly beautiful, and married to one of the most powerful men in the world—at least in the top eight of industrialized nations, if you bought into the whole Group of Eight concept. But here she was on my chartered boat, on the lam, and lounging like a woman freshly liberated from her husband.

"Giselle?"

No response.

Louder this time. "Giselle?" Still nothing.

With the sun behind me, my shadow fell over her as I touched her shoulder. "Giselle—"

WHAP!

WHOOF—

She had exploded from her nap with a right jab that caught me in the gut and knocked the wind out of me—all while keeping her left arm over her boobs.

"Buck?! I'm so sorry! I was asleep—you surprised me."

I held a hand up as I remained slumped forward and tried to catch my breath. She sat up and tied the strap around her back. "Are you okay?"

"Fine, just surprised. Nice jab."

"One of my hobbies during the past few years has been martial arts. You never know what can happen. I'm *so* sorry!"

"Just wanted to alert you of a change of plan. The conditions aren't good for getting to Jost this afternoon, so we're headed to Cane Garden Bay instead."

Thankfully, she pulled a robe on as I was fighting with my eyes not to glance down and admire her physique. She was remarkable for forty years old.

"Makes sense to stay on Tortola," she said. "But I do want to get off this boat."

"Understood. I have a plan for that."

"Can your plan start with food? I'm famished."

"Yes. I'll be dropping anchor in maybe fifteen minutes, so go ahead and find another outfit in the closet. Understated and low key—unless you're ready to call for help?"

She shook her head. "Still no recollection of what happened. So I will make myself as frumpy as possible, which, given the wardrobe I've seen so far, shouldn't be difficult."

I wanted to defend Scarlet's attire, but Giselle was accustomed to being dressed in originals by French designers. Off-the-rack clothing borrowed from a Florida mom would no doubt shock her fashion sense, but she didn't have to call it frumpy.

"No offense," she said.

As usual, my expression must have given me away. "None taken."

Back on the bridge, I steered the boat to a familiar spot in the middle of the beach. Several open mooring balls awaited. With the mainsail dropped and the engines engaged, I was able to steer directly for my target. The familiar lines of Myett's Restaurant, a favorite watering hole from a few years ago, were no longer there. However, a larger structure had been built where the main restaurant had been, and it glistened in the afternoon sun. The sign there said Pusser's, too, which was a new affiliation. Yellow umbrellas dotted the beach next to empty lounge chairs.

I reduced power on the engines. It would have been nice to have some help, but I hurried from the bridge, grabbed the boat hook, dived to my knees, hooked the orange ball, and took the line from the center of the trampoline and passed it over the ball.

The effort went well, but my shirt was damp with sweat.

The sound of clapping sounded from the helm. "Well-done, Buck. But I would have been happy to help."

"If there's a next time, I'll take you up on that. Let's get in the dinghy, grab some lunch, check the news, and figure out what's going on."

11

M YETT'S MAY HAVE BEEN REBUILT FROM THE GROUND UP, but the hospitality remained the same.

Across from me sat the first lady of France, wearing a large straw hat, dark glasses, and a colorful wrap over her green bikini and laughing at my attempts to keep the situation tolerably light. I didn't need to pinch myself to know she wasn't here for me but due to circumstances outside her control. We were quite the pair.

"I've found that people can adjust to new circumstances, new realities beyond our control," I said. "We adjust, and the new situation becomes the new norm. Lord knows I learned that from experience."

"Sounds scientific. And what happened to you for such a conclusion?"

"I was adopted—by an undersecretary of state. Became an archaeologist, was famous before I turned thirty, built a net worth north of fifty million dollars, and married the top supermodel in the world—"

"Ooh la la." Giselle smiled.

"Only to see it all slide through my hands like sand. Due to circumstances largely beyond my control."

Her smile faded and she leaned forward. "Have you adjusted?"

"In many ways, yes, but in others I'm still working on it."

Her smile returned.

Our late lunch consisted of a fine chicken roti over yellow rice and a bottle of French rosé—Giselle had insisted—and we were having coffee while we awaited the results of the manager's efforts to find us a room at one of the small inns nearby. They had availability at Myett's, but I wanted to be at a smaller hotel, somewhere up on the hillside where we would be less visible. Our lunch conversation had been light, and I shared some of my past high points from e-Antiquity to keep her mind off her own plight.

"Quite the successful entrepreneur, *Monsieur* Reilly."

"Yeah, well, that's history now, but I'd rather not ruin my meal by talking about what followed."

"Very mysterious." Giselle's smile revealed straight white teeth behind expressive, full lips. She leaned closer. "I can't remember the last time I dined at a restaurant without bodyguards or being recognized. I could get used to this."

The television inside the bar was tuned to a soccer match. The network interrupted the game to provide breaking news. When the French flag appeared, I tapped her shin with my bare foot and nodded toward the screen.

Too far away to hear what was being said, we picked up our coffees and headed to the bar.

The commentator's face was very serious. "We have just now received official news from Charlotte Amalie about France's first lady, Giselle Huibert."

Giselle took my right bicep between her hands and held on snugly.

"The French president, Mr. Huibert's statement is being presented now. We are switching over to a live feed—"

Giselle's grip became tighter on my arm.

The image on the screen changed to François Huibert standing at a podium in an open-air courtyard. Other officials were gathered around him, but all eyes were glued to the president of France.

"I would like to thank the American Coast Guard for finding my wife's missing helicopter and for recovering the bodies from off the ocean floor." He paused to wipe a tear from his eyes with a white handkerchief.

Giselle's breathing next to me had gotten raspy, her grip still tight.

"It is with deep regret and sadness that I must inform you that one of the bodies found in the wreckage was my beloved Giselle. The others were the pilot and the head of her security—"

Giselle's grip clamped down hard for a second—then her arm swung up and she swatted the hat off her head. "What?!" she said.

She took a step back. I grabbed the hat off the ground and tried to put it back, but she blocked my arm.

"What the hell?"

She sat suddenly on a chair. I got the hat back on her head. Her eyes were narrowed and she was shaking as she stared at the television.

I pushed a cloth napkin into the water of our ice chest and dabbed her cheek. She brushed my hand away and jumped back up to stare at the screen. I glanced around the nearly empty bar restaurant to see if anyone was watching us.

"A state funeral will follow the return of her body, which has been cremated per her wishes ..."

The camera panned the other officials who stood with the president. All were ashen gray, several openly crying, except one—

I heard a sudden intake of breath.

"Him!" Giselle stabbed her index finger toward the screen.

The camera was back on the president, but Giselle's breathing had become ragged. She kicked a chair over, and I took her arm and tried to steer her outside. Our waiter came rushing over.

"What's wrong, sir?"

"Too much sun. She's dehydrated." I tipped the straw hat down to cover her face.

I was able to steer Giselle outside. Some women may have responded by collapsing and crying, but Giselle trembled with fury.

"There's a hammock over here, sir!"

I stood, my arm around her waist, holding her close, and followed the young man to the side of the bar, where a green mesh hammock hung under a tree near the beach. He helped me lay her in the hammock, placing her feet gently inside.

"Bring ice water, please," I said.

I still had the wet napkin in my left hand and tenderly rubbed her forehead and cheeks. Her eyes fluttered and her breathing accelerated again.

"Giselle." I glanced around and realized I'd better not use her name. "It's okay, just rest."

The waiter appeared and handed me the water.

"She's fine. Thanks for your help. I'll sit with her. Don't worry."

He walked a few feet away and stopped and peered back. I waved.

"That bastard! I'm not dead—cremated? I have no living will with those instructions!"

"It's okay, calm down. Drink some of this."

She took a sip of water, but then she fell back in the hammock with her eyes fixed straight up on the tree branches. Intuitively, I knew something had clicked in her head—I just hoped it wouldn't make matters worse. And I needed to find out before she blew up or freaked out and exposed her identity.

I glanced up to see the manager, who'd gone to his office to call hotels for us, now walking this way with the waiter.

"Be careful what you say. The manager's coming," I said and quickly added, "I'm so sorry. Maybe someone lied to François. Maybe he doesn't know."

Her eyes quivered for a second, and then she looked into my eyes with total clarity in hers.

"I know what happened. I remember."

That's when the manager arrived.

12

"MR. REILLY, IS EVERYTHING ALL RIGHT?" the manager said. He was young, early thirties, in good shape, and wearing a nice gold batik shirt with broad brown leaves and a parrot on the back.

"Yes, thank you. The water is helping. We've been sailing all day—I warned her to stay hydrated. She'll be fine."

He stood next to her, but I'd positioned her hat so her face wasn't visible.

"Good news," the manager said. "I was able to find you a room at the Tamarind Club, about five miles from here. It is secluded, as you requested, with a small but good restaurant."

"Wonderful, thank you so much." I dug into my pocket and gave him a $20 tip. "We'll head over there as soon as, ah, Scarlet feels better."

"As you wish, sir. Just tell them that Dominic from Myett's sent you. Can I arrange a car for you?"

"That won't be necessary, but thank you again."

The manager nodded confidently and walked purposefully back inside the restaurant. I pulled my cell phone from my back pocket and scrolled through names until I found Valentine Hodge, my friend and driver here on Tortola. The fewer strangers we encountered the better.

"Buck Reilly? Dear God, man, I hope you're not back in jail!"

"Thanks, Valentine. Nice to hear your voice, too. Glad you recognized my number." I explained that we were at Myett's and asked if he could give me and my lady friend a lift to the Tamarind Club.

"They probably have room at Myett's. It's a lot nicer—"

"They do, but we're looking for more privacy. Are you nearby?"

"Everything on Tortola's nearby, Buck. Just playing dominoes down in Roadtown. I'll come now."

"Sorry to interrupt your game."

"I'm winning, so this gives me an excuse to walk away."

We hung up, and when I turned, Giselle's eyes were fixed on me.

"I remember everything now. Why I ran. It was ghastly—"

The waiter approached with our check for lunch.

"Sshh, hang on," I said.

I glanced at the bill and gave him cash plus a hefty tip. He sauntered off smiling.

Giselle shook her head. "I can't believe it—"

I leaned down close to her. "Hold, on, Giselle. First off, I'm going to start calling you Scarlet, since her name is on the boat rental with mine. Second, a friend will be here any second to pick us up and take us to a hotel—"

Her eyes grew wider.

"We'll get two rooms, but more importantly, let's wait until we're there, safe and in a private setting, before you tell me what happened. Okay?"

Her eyes softened. She put her hand on mine and nodded once.

Just then I heard the familiar sound of shrieking brakes. If I wasn't mistaken, that would be Valentine's car. I reached down and took Giselle's hands and helped her up. She stood unsteadily at first but then adjusted her hat and sunglasses and offered me a weak smile.

"I'm ready."

I led her through the restaurant and found Valentine standing outside his ancient blue Ford Crown Victoria. The car was a bit more faded and scratched up since I'd last seen it, and on closer inspection, so was Valentine. His broad smile, however, could melt ice.

"Buck Reilly, I'll be damned."

"Still haven't got those brakes fixed, huh?"

He ignored me and gave a coquettish smile to Giselle. "And you are?"

It dawned on me a half second too late—

"My name's Scarlet," she said.

"Let's hit the road, okay?" I said.

Giselle passed by Valentine and removed her hat to get inside the car. I caught Valentine's eyebrows arch sharply, and he turned quickly toward me. I ignored him and steered her toward the car's open back door. After I closed the door, I felt his hand on my back.

"Scarlet, huh? Sure changed since I last saw her."

"I'll explain later. For now, we need some quiet—and no questions."

He studied my tight lips and squinted eyes. "I can be quiet, not a problem. No sirree, my lips are sealed."

Tortola, like most of the Caribbean islands, is a series of sharp hills, with most of its businesses and restaurants down along the shore, the beach, and in the major harbor of Roadtown. That's why I wanted to be up in the hills. I'd driven by the Tamarind Club before—it wasn't much, but it was small and secluded, which is what we needed most.

Valentine's old car swayed and rocked as if it were a baby's bouncy chair with a rambunctious child inside. He kept glancing back at me in the rearview mirror, but I wouldn't engage. None of us said a word on the ten-minute drive to Tamarind. He pulled up out front and the shriek of his brakes made me wince.

He jumped out and popped Giselle's door open. "Ms. Scarlet, it was a pleasure to meet you."

"*Enchanté*," she said. "Nice to meet you, too."

When I got out the other side, I found Valentine staring at me over the roof of the car with eyes the size of hard-boiled eggs. She walked around the trunk, and when she passed me, she mouthed, "Sorry."

"Thank you, Valentine—"

"Buck, you got a second?" he said.

Damn it.

"Just wait by the door, honey. I'll be right there."

She nodded and walked toward the front door, fifty feet away. I gritted my teeth. One of the things I loved about Valentine, as a local who'd been born here and who now had to be over eighty years old, was that he didn't miss anything and always spoke his mind. That had worked in my favor in the past, but this time—

"Hell's going on here, Buck?" His voice was a whisper, the usual broad smile gone. "TV said she was dead—her own husband—she is married, right? She is who I think—hell, her picture's been on the TV for days!"

I held a finger to my lips. "I know, this is crazy—"

"Crazy? This is way past crazy."

"Listen, I don't know all the details yet, but she's on the run for her life. What they haven't said on the news was that her helicopter was shot down."

"What? But the Coast Guard found it."

"I was there. Saw it happen. I pulled her out and she was unconscious. Everyone else on board was dead. I had no idea who she was."

"How the hell you didn't know—"

"I don't watch the news, okay?" Our faces were pressed so close together that from behind either of us it would look like we were making out. "Something happened that caused her to flee on that helicopter. She was headed to the airport here, with plans to fly back to France."

"Flee from what?"

"I don't know yet. She just remembered that when we were at Myett's, after she saw the news conference on television. We haven't had a minute alone for her to tell me yet."

He stepped forward. "Let's go find out."

"No, Valentine. Let me deal with this for now. She's terrified but trusts me. We will need your help, though. Depending on what happened, I'm hoping I can talk her into either calling the French security agency or the police here."

"Detective Bramble? After what he tried to do to you?"

"Otherwise I'll get her to the airport, where she can get help. But I need to talk to her first and find out what the hell happened."

"Why'd her husband—the *president*—say they'd found her body? Does he want her dead?"

"Again, I don't know."

He took a deep breath, rubbed a heavily wrinkled hand across the gray curly stubble on his head, and exhaled loudly. "I seen you do some crazy shit, Buck Reilly, but this takes the cake."

"I'm just trying to help the lady, that's all."

"First lady, you mean." He snickered. "Don't fool yourself, boy. There's a karma between you two. I could feel it."

"Don't be silly, Valentine. Thanks for picking us up, but more importantly, thanks for keeping this to yourself. Can you plan to get us in the morning around nine? Hopefully we'll have a plan by then."

"I'll be here. Count on that."

"Oh—and could you take a ride over to Soper's Hole and keep an eye out for any foreigners who look sketchy—kind of Middle Eastern or Northern African looking, probably Algerian? See if anybody's asking about me or my rental catamaran or even Giselle Huibert. Roadtown, too, around the marinas."

"Good God almighty. Beautiful Giselle Huibert, back from the dead."

No smile bent my lips. "It's my job to keep it that way."

13

"DID HE RECOGNIZE ME?" GISELLE SAID.
"We can trust Valentine, don't worry. But yes, he did. You need to keep your hat and sunglasses on. Pictures of you have been on television nonstop since the story broke about your helicopter crashing."

"You mean getting shot down." Her voice had an edge I'd not seen from her before. Good. Fear and fury are good traits to help you survive when the cards are stacked against you. Something I'd felt more than my share of times.

"That hasn't been reported yet," I said.

"Why not? Didn't you say the front windshield was blown out? And that the pilot and Robert, my personal bodyguard, had been burned badly in the explosion?"

"Yes, but they wouldn't have had time yet to do any tests to determine that it wasn't an internal explosion from the helicopter. Maybe when they do they'll change their story. It's possible a terrorist organization was behind it and they'll take credit—"

Giselle crossed her arms quickly and her features again took on a pointed look. "It was not a terrorist action. My husband—"

The front door to the Tamarind Club opened next to us, interrupting her. A small man in his early forties wearing dark pants, a white Polo shirt and horn-rim glasses stepped outside. "Excuse me, but are you Mr. Reilly?"

I stepped in front of Giselle, who turned away from the man.

"Yes, I am. Are you the proprietor?"

"I am. Dominic from Myett's called me on your behalf." His voice had a singsong Caribbean lilt, common in the British Virgin Islands. "I have a nice king room available for one night. Will that be satisfactory?"

Oh jeez.

I didn't want to draw too much attention by asking for two rooms. It's easier to blend if you don't make requests that cause people to wonder. Don't be an anomaly.

"That could work, but we'd prefer a suite if you have one. Maybe one with a sitting room and kitchenette?"

He clasped his hands, stepped to the side, and gazed directly at Giselle, hesitating a second before he turned back to me. "Ah, yes, I do have one suite facing down the hill. It has a wonderful view of Roadtown below but no kitchenette, I'm afraid. Our restaurant opens at seven in the morning and goes all day until 10 p.m., though. And we do offer room service."

We had no choice. It would have to work.

I pivoted toward Giselle. "Why don't you go around the side and enjoy the view while I check us in." I winked. "Honey."

Gisele walked away without a word. I followed the proprietor inside. He kept glancing out the windows as he walked. Giselle could be seen walking parallel to us.

I cleared my throat. "How old is the hotel?"

He stopped walking for a moment, and I'd been following him so closely, with both of us staring out the window at Giselle, that I bumped into him.

"Sorry," I said.

When he turned around, his mouth was open and I thought I saw his eyes flicker behind his glasses.

"Did you ask a question?" he said.

"How old is the hotel?" From the corner of my eye I saw Giselle disappear behind the building.

"The oldest part of this structure dates back to the mid-1800s, but it didn't become a hotel until the 1970s." He squinted and pursed his lips. "I'm sorry, but is your lady friend a model? I'm sure I've seen her before somewhere."

"No, but I'll tell her you thought so. It'll make her day."

He hesitated again and then continued to the small reception desk in the back of the room. I glanced around and saw that the restaurant was next to reception, and there was a patio out back where Giselle stood overlooking the town and the Caribbean Sea below. I filled out the paperwork using my Key West address and allowed him to make a copy of my passport. In exchange I was given a key to Room 12.

"The suite is on the back of the hotel near where, ah, your lady friend is enjoying the view. There's a stair there to the second floor." He put on a practiced smile. "Will you be dining with us tonight, sir?"

"I'm not sure yet. We need a nap and then we'll decide."

"No reservation needed. Just come down if you'd like, or we can bring food up to you. Thanks for choosing the Tamarind Club. I hope you enjoy your suite."

Indeed.

I walked through the dining room, past a small bar, and out the open double doors to the stone patio, where Giselle still stood facing away from the building.

"Nice view?" I said.

"I haven't noticed." I saw that her cheeks glistened with tears. "Did you get a suite?"

"I'm sorry, but I thought asking for two rooms would arouse his curiosity. He already thought you were a model, was certain he recognized you. We're in Room 12 upstairs."

Once inside the room I was relieved to find a floral-covered loveseat in the front room. Giselle continued into the bedroom and glanced around, and her shoulders sagged. She continued into the bathroom and closed the door. Poor thing.

It dawned on me that we'd shown up empty-handed and the hotel manager didn't ask if we had any luggage. Maybe Dominic from Myett's mentioned we were on a boat? The lack of luggage, even just an overnight bag, was another anomaly, and if he hadn't already noticed, it might occur to him later.

The room had green carpet that smelled of mold. There was a small refrigerator in the corner that had beads of sweat on its door, no doubt contributing to the issue. The air conditioning was off, so I used the remote control to turn it on. Giselle had been in the bathroom for several minutes. I was concerned, but then, she'd been through hell and probably needed some space, so I sat on the loveseat and waited. I wanted to hear what it was she'd remembered at Myett's after seeing her husband on television.

A very distinctive sound emanated from the thin wall separating me from the bathroom: the sound of throwing up. Once, then again, then silence. Good grief. I heard water running, then more silence.

When she emerged, her hair was down, her sunglasses and hat were gone, and she had a steely look in her eyes.

"There are toiletries in the bathroom," she said. "I brushed my teeth."

I remained seated. "I'm more interested in what you remembered. Do you feel up to talking about it?"

She inhaled a deep breath, held it for a moment, and let it out with measured control. She came and sat next to me on the loveseat, forgoing a wooden chair next to it.

"Yes, but it's hideous. Even so, I'm not sure it would be enough to have me killed."

"Do you really think François tried to kill you?"

She shrugged and leaned back deep into the loveseat. Our shoulders and hips touched. I considered moving to the chair, but it might make her feel more alone. And I liked the way she smelled. When our bodies brushed against each other, it sent tingles through my limbs.

"Why else would he lie at the press conference?"

"You don't think he could have been duped? Maybe someone else lied, told him your body was on the helicopter?"

She shook her head. "We both saw his limousine follow the black van to the morgue. He would have identified me himself." She shook her head with fervor now. "No, after what I caught him doing, he would be ruined back in France if anyone found out. As I said before, his popularity is already at an all-time low. My supposed death would give him a sympathy bump. But if I were alive and told anyone what I saw, then his popularity would plummet further."

I waited. She sat quietly and then glanced at me.

"If they were willing to kill me to keep it secret, then they'll certainly kill you if they find us." Her eyes welled up as she spoke. "I'm sorry, Buck." She leaned her head on my shoulder. The gash across her head from the helicopter crash peeked through her brunette hair.

I put my arm around her shoulder. She was a tall woman, but at six-three, I was still a half foot taller, so my arm rested comfortably on her shoulder.

"I'm not afraid, Giselle. I know these islands pretty well and have a lot of friends here. We can stay under cover until we decide what to do next." I gave her shoulder a squeeze. "But I need to know what you know so we can best decide what to do."

After a minute, she sat forward and faced me.

"Okay, Buck. I trust you, and damn it, I need you. I'd be lost otherwise."

Just then there was a knock on the door.

14

I SAW THE PROPRIETOR THROUGH THE WINDOW. He was holding a bottle of Champagne. This guy was starting to irritate me.

I opened the door and stepped outside to block him from entering.

"Sorry to disturb you, Mr. Reilly, but I forgot to give you the courtesy Champagne that comes with the room." It was in an ice bucket, and there were two glasses on the tray, along with a hibiscus flower.

"Thank you," I said. "That's very kind."

"Is there anything else you need?"

"We're just here for the one night to take a break from the boat, so no, we'll be fine. Thanks again." I stepped back and closed the door in his face. Whether it was curiosity or hospitality I wasn't sure, but his timing sucked.

I placed the Champagne bucket on the table.

"Moët et Chandon," Giselle said. "French."

I sat in the wooden chair and pulled it forward to face her.

"Okay, Giselle, please. I'm dying to know what the heck you saw that caused all of this."

She smiled sympathetically, but the smile faded quickly to a frown. She eyed the Champagne.

"A drink would help."

Dear God.

I popped open the Champagne and poured us each a glass. The bubbles seeped over the edge of her glass. Once they settled down, she took a long sip.

"Okay," she said. "I'd been out at an all-day event with the other first ladies here for the summit. But just before lunch I started getting dizzy and felt flush. I wanted to lie down, so I returned to the hotel that the French contingent is using."

She polished off the Champagne and wiped her lips. I refilled her glass.

"Security does not stop me, of course, so I walked straight to the floor cordoned off for François and myself. Oddly, there was no guard outside the door, so I walked in, and, well …"

Another sip.

"I have always been a quiet walker. I frequently surprise François, but this time I walked in on him—in the bedroom—with a …" She bit her knuckle for a moment, wincing at the recollection. She swallowed and then sat back. "I walked in and he was in the bed, naked, on his knees behind a young local girl. Having sex with her."

Well … that was brutal, but I didn't see—oh. Something about her tone, the disgust in it, suddenly registered.

"You said a local *girl*?"

She nodded quickly. "No older than thirteen. A young island girl. Her eyes popped wide when she saw me. François looked right through me, but that wasn't even the worst part."

It got worse?

"His head of security, Alphonse Zidane … he was holding a video camera. He was filming them! The sick bastards! I ran and Zidane followed after me."

She guzzled her second glass of Champagne.

"I jumped in the elevator. He took the stairs but I beat him and jumped back into my car for the airport. No way I could face—would even want to see François after that—and Zidane has always made me uncomfortable. Now I know why. Who knows what other perversions he arranges."

Grisly indeed. Children are over the line in any civilized country. And taking advantage of a local American island girl would be an international incident.

But one worth killing his wife to conceal?

She shivered and I moved from the wooden chair to sit next to her on the loveseat. She fell into my arms and I held her tight. She continued to quiver and again felt warm from raw emotion, shaking and crying.

"Had you ever suspected him of this type of thing before? Did he have … other affairs?"

"No! I don't believe so, at least none that I'm aware of, but Zidane has been his head of security for over a year now. I never trusted him."

"Did Zidane follow you? To the airport?"

"Not as far as I could tell, but the security team is substantial. They track my every move on my phone, and the phones of my assistants and bodyguards, so they know my location at all times. When I demanded the helicopter, with orders to have the presidential plane readied, it would have immediately been brought to Zidane's attention."

I imagined the sequence of events. It would have caused an explosion of logistics for their team to make happen, all on an unexplained and unplanned basis, which was the opposite of what well-planned security agendas are based on.

"How long before you took off on the helicopter? From the time you left the hotel?"

She poured herself more Champagne.

"Forty-two minutes. I was pushing everyone like a crazy woman. Nobody knew why, but I kept tapping the face of my watch and complaining how long it was taking. Twenty minutes, thirty minutes, forty minutes. Finally we departed."

All that being said, I still had difficulty imagining how the French president or his head of security would have access to a rocket, especially one originating from the Virgin Islands. Something didn't seem right. Then I remembered the three men who came to search Soper's Hole. They didn't seem like professional security officers, and certainly not members of the Groupe de Sécurité de la Présidence de la République. So what was their connection? How were they so well-informed?

Something smelled rotten.

Dead rotten.

"Affairs are common in France," Giselle said, "and not unexpected by men in power. But *children* ... that is detestable, and François' presidency would collapse under the pressure of such news. Even his best friends would condemn and abandon him—they'd have no choice. And with me as a witness? God knows what those pigs would do with Zidane's video, but that would ruin François—it would put him in jail."

I took a sip of Champagne, though it felt odd to be drinking something so celebratory under these circumstances.

"Did you tell your assistant or bodyguard what you saw?"

She shook her head. "I was too upset. I would have told her on the flight home, but I never got the chance. She knew it was something terrible, though, because I have thick skin. I'm not prone to outbursts or crying."

"Would your bodyguard be loyal to you or to the head of security?"

"Robert was new, came in at the same time as Zidane. I liked him and treated him with respect, but it was not a close relationship. We are counseled not to get too close to the bodyguards. They have a job to do, and friendship dulls the edge needed for vigilance."

"So Zidane could have been in communication with him. Not that the man would have wanted to be blown up, but his boss would have understood your entire plan and known your exact location. They were probably terrified you'd tell the world once you'd gone back to France."

Giselle lowered her face into her hands. She sat that way for a couple minutes. When she looked up, her eyes were again sharp.

"At the press conference, when François said they'd found my body, I saw Zidane standing next to him. That's when I remembered everything."

It was now clear that we had to remain in hiding and that nobody could be trusted, aside from people I knew here in the islands. But even then, word would eventually get out. Giselle's being alive was just too big. What was the end game? How could she be safe? And me, for that matter. I didn't want to raise that yet. I needed to come up with a plan, and worrying her over the lack of one wouldn't help. She was a smart, tough woman. Hell, it was just as likely she'd come up with a plan, but either way, we had to control when and how we came out of hiding.

Giselle stood. "I need to shower, and eat. This room smells like blue cheese. Can we eat early in the restaurant, before other guests arrive?"

I had an idea. A radical one for me, but under the circumstances, it could be the best one possible.

"Okay, you shower. I'll go for a walk. Is thirty minutes okay?"

"An hour, please. I need a long hot shower to feel human again."

"I'll come back then."

She dropped her chin and glanced up at me. "Don't feel like you can't be here in the room—our suite." She laughed quickly to herself. "My marriage is over, and your friend Scarlet abandoned you here. We are both outcasts."

The sentence hung in the air. After a moment, she left for the bedroom and swung the door shut, but it didn't close all the way.

15

I FOUND A QUIET OVERLOOK BEHIND THE HOTEL and held my cell phone with both hands. They were shaking. I'd been in my share of difficult situations, but never one with such international magnitude. I wanted to keep my name out of it but also wanted to help protect Giselle and find a quick resolution that would prevent either of us from getting killed. If François' goal was to make her disappear and he found out she wasn't dead, he'd send his men to hunt us down, with the intent to kill.

I stared at my phone. A debate roared inside my head.

I scanned the directory. I rarely used a cell phone, and for years I'd sworn them off, but eventually, when my failure at e-Antiquity faded to old news, I bought one and used it sparingly. The number of names I had in my directory was minimal, so I quickly found the one I was contemplating calling.

T. Edward Booth, special agent, Federal Bureau of Investigation.

Booth had haunted me for years after e-Antiquity crashed. He'd claimed to have evidence about me warning my parents to dump their e-Antiquity stock before it collapsed—which I had indeed done. And then, when they were killed crossing a street in Geneva after opening a numbered bank account for me and depositing valuable maps and clues to yet undiscovered treasures before the creditors could seize them, the FBI accused me of killing them for the inheritance. But my parents had left everything to my brother, Ben.

Bottom line, Booth had made me his bitch. I'd done recon, research, and dirty work on cases outside his jurisdiction. My successes had propelled him up the federal ladder and further away from me.

Would he take my call?

Was this a crazy idea?

Would Giselle freak?

I pressed "send."

One ring, two, three—damn—four—

"You'd better be butt-dialing me, Reilly," Booth said. "I told you to lose this number a long time ago."

"You'll be glad I called."

"That would be a first," he said.

"I assume you're still the same ambitious pain in the ass you've always been?"

Silence followed for a moment. "I'll take that as a compliment, kid."

"Not a kid anymore, Booth. And what I have to tell you is the biggest news you've ever handled."

His laugh was sharp, maybe too sharp. I let my statement sink in.

"Okay, Reilly, enough foreplay. What have you got for me?"

"I need your help in the Virgin Islands."

"You get arrested again? Don't you ever learn?"

"I haven't been arrested, but I might get killed."

"Very dramatic. What's the story?"

I bit the side of my mouth for a few seconds but still believed this was a good gambit. Booth's greed for recognition made him easy to play, and this situation would be a major carrot.

"Let's not use any names—"

"My phone is encrypted with the most sophisticated—"

"Mine isn't."

"Got it. Proceed."

"You're familiar with the big news down here, I presume."

"News?" A second's pause. " You mean the, ah, unfortunate accident—"

"That's the one, but it wasn't unfortunate. It was intentional."

A heavy exhale caused static in my ear. I could imagine his ever-stale coffee breath.

"Hang on, hotshot. What are you saying? Terrorists?"

"Worse. Inside job—from very close within, in fact. Can't get any closer."

Booth processed the bomb I'd dropped on him. I gave him a moment but wanted to get off the phone quickly in case anyone was monitoring it.

"How in the hell could you know that?" he said.

"Because I saw it happen. I was first on the scene and rescued someone."

"Who? Don't be coy, Reilly."

"*The* someone."

"Wait a minute—are you saying that all this ... news ... is bullshit?"

"Way to go, Booth. You're getting faster in your older age. And to anticipate your next question, I have *the* someone stashed for safety."

"Where? I can help!"

"Keep your phone handy. I may need you at a moment's notice. But don't trust anybody from their camp—all the way to the top and all around him. Don't say a word."

"I'll have a team there in—"

"I'll call back."

Click.

He'd send a team in fast, and hopefully he'd keep his trap shut or the French hunters would come after us with a vengeance. I sat still, looking out over the placid blue waters to the south of Roadtown. I wasn't betraying Giselle, I was trying to protect her—us—from the shit storm that must be secretly brewing over her missing body.

Giselle trusted me.

But that trust would vanish if she knew I'd called Booth.

And, well ... I was trying to be mindful of the situation. That was something Scarlet said I was incapable of doing the night before she left. She said I was always planning, thinking down the road, working on some kind of big idea. Guilty. It was how I was wired. But sitting here now, I tried to keep my thoughts planted in the moment, and what I felt worried me.

Giselle was intelligent, hurt, afraid, and … beautiful. It wasn't her looks, though. We had the beginning of a bond—a unique bond. Was that some kind of syndrome? Stockholm syndrome is when a captive falls in love with the captor. Florence Nightingale effect is when a caregiver develops feelings for a patient. What is it when people share heightened emotions when on the run for their lives?

Buck Reilly syndrome?

I stood up.

"You're an idiot, Buck."

I glanced around to see if anyone had heard my whispered epiphany. All I had to do was get the woman to safety, do my part, and fade back into oblivion. That should be my plan. That *was* my plan.

I walked back to our suite, glanced around, and saw nobody, not even the proprietor. The door was locked, but I had the key. I knocked anyway to let her know I was here.

"It's me, Buck." I spoke loudly so she could hear me through the door.

When I pushed it open and stepped inside, I noticed that the bedroom door was open. There was no sound—I rushed forward into the room.

"Giselle!"

The bathroom door was open, and there she was. Standing in front of the mirror, wrapped in a towel, combing the fingers of one hand through her dark brunette hair. She held the hair dryer in her other hand.

She jumped.

"Buck, you scared me."

My heart raced, but as she assessed my concern, a smirk bent her lips. Relief passed though me.

"Sorry. I'll let you finish up."

"Are we set for dinner? I'm famished."

"All set," I lied, knowing my next act would be to call the front desk.

I closed the bedroom door, mindful to not forget whom Giselle was and that I needed to stay on my toes and out of fantasyland.

16

I'D ASKED FOR THE TABLE IN THE BACK CORNER of the dining room, close to the door to the patio. I now sat facing out to the dining room and had positioned Giselle to face me on the back wall. She had pinned her hair up tightly in a French braid—go figure—and we both still had on the same outfits we'd arrived in. She had ironed hers, but I was a wrinkled mess and worried that I smelled like low tide.

My attention scanned the room as another couple arrived. They were elderly, probably in their seventies, wore hearing aids and thick glasses. American, Canadian, I wasn't sure, but they spoke English. A waiter walked the length of the room to our table. He wore dark pants and the same type of Polo shirt that the proprietor had on earlier.

"Can I get you something to drink?" he said.

"A glass of Bordeaux for the lady, and I'll have dark Cruzan rum with one ice cube."

He nodded once and sauntered away. I spotted the proprietor behind a small bar near the kitchen door. There were three stools, but nobody sat there. He saw me look his way and waved.

"Crap."

"What's wrong?" Giselle said.

"Sorry, the hotel manager just spotted us. Looks like he's pouring our drinks."

"We just need to act totally comfortable with the situation, Buck."

I smiled at her. Her eyes sparkled in the waning light that cast long shadows inside the open patio doors. Her ability to roll with the punches was impressive. "What's our story?" I asked.

Giselle lifted her eyebrows. Somehow she had rallied away from pain, anger, and fear and for the moment seemed to be enjoying this crazy situation. I was terrified, and I was just the guy who'd found her.

She leaned closer. "We are dating, but only have been for a few months. You took me sailing around the Caribbean to sweep me off my feet, and"—she lowered her voice—"it's working."

"Where have we been so far?"

"We started here in Tortola, sailed over to St. Thomas, and were then headed to Jost Van Dyke but the wind and current didn't cooperate, so we changed course to Cane Garden Bay." She smiled.

Impressive. "The best deceptions are always kept close to the truth," I said.

"So you are practiced in deception?"

The proprietor approached our table carrying a tray with our drinks.

"Here he comes," I said with a smile.

Giselle let loose a loud laugh as if I'd said something hilarious. She caught me off guard but then pumped her eyebrows. Deception. Got it. I laughed, too, but it sounded wooden, even to me.

"Your drinks, Mr. Reilly and Ms.?" he said.

"Ms. Lyon," she said. "Claire Lyon." She beamed when she spoke.

"Thank you," I said. "We'll both have the snapper special you have on the chalkboard out front."

His eyes lingered on Giselle, but she turned to face me and angled her face away from him. "Can we make it to Peter Island tomorrow, dear?"

The proprietor turned abruptly and walked quickly toward the kitchen.

"He's gone."

"You didn't answer my question." Her ability to rise to the occasion was amazing.

"Were you an actress?" I said.

"As a matter of fact, I had been studying drama at the University of Grenoble before I met François."

"You're a natural. And your English is very American."

"I lived in Aspen, Colorado, for a winter working at a hotel."

Then, because she'd mentioned his name, I asked, "Where did you meet François?"

"My parents own a small hotel in Courcheval, a ski area in the—"

"*Trois vallees*—three valleys. I've been there, it's beautiful."

"*Tres bien*. He was a young, ambitious politician from the region, and I was a senior at the university. He stayed at our hotel for a civic meeting. It was his first election. My parents invited him to dinner with us—he's ten years older than me." Her expression wavered, but she pulled it together. "We all stayed up late into the evening listening to his ideas for the future of France. He was progressive, passionate, handsome."

"Love at first sight?"

"Close. The next night, my parents and I attended his town hall speech and he placed us in the front row. Nearly a hundred people came to hear him—his reputation was one of a rising star." She paused, shrugged, and shook her head. "He chose to come back to Courcheval on election day, and when he won, my parents threw a victory party. I didn't realize it at the time, but aside from him becoming the municipal councillor, I was his prize."

"Things happened fast from there?"

"A whirlwind. I barely finished school, and rather than going to Paris for acting, I went to work for him in Lyon, and to sleep with him at night. His passion and vision was so consuming it sucked me in. We were married less than a year later. That was nearly twenty years ago now. "

No new diners had arrived, so I felt comfortable that nobody could overhear us. "No children in those twenty years?"

She shook her head with her lip curled. "François was unable. He volunteered to adopt, but frankly, we were moving every couple of years as he rose in the political ranks, and once we got to Paris in the Senate, life was too full and busy for children. I'd been very close to my parents and would not have wanted maids and caretakers to raise my

kids, so we focused on the next election instead, and he kept winning."
She shook her head. "Then, six years ago, he won the biggest of all."

"Sounds exhilarating, and exhausting."

She nodded slowly and sipped on her Bordeaux. I took a gulp of
rum, enthralled by her story.

"It *was* exhausting. Still is. And worse, he's changed with each new
victory. He was always consumed with winning—and with govern-
ing—but it was the hunt, the race, the strategy he truly adored. By the
time he became—you know what—I hardly knew him anymore. The
passionate young man at that town hall was gone, reshaped by political
parties, donors, corporations, and foreign interests."

I spied the waiter emerge from the kitchen with our food. I hadn't
studied him closely before but did now. He was either a mix of
Caucasian and black, or Middle Eastern. He didn't smile when he put
the plates on the table, and I sensed an immediate change in Giselle's
expression. Her eyes fluttered and she covered half her face with her
hand.

"Anything else, madam?" the waiter said.

She shook her head and didn't look at him. He squinted toward
me.

"Thanks, we're all set," I said.

He walked back to the kitchen, glancing once back toward us
before rounding the corner.

"You okay?" I said.

She took a gulp of the wine. "I feel like someone just walked on
my grave." She pushed her seat back, but I reached fast across the table
and put my hand on top of hers.

"Stop, please."

Her eyes were wild. "I want—I need to go."

"We have to eat—remember what I said about anomalies? We can
eat fast, but—"

"I'm not hungry. That waiter reminded me of our security detail."

"He looks like he might be North African. Are members of the
security detail—"

"Several are Algerian, some are Muslim. I'm indifferent to their religion, but his facial features and coloring, they reminded me of Zidane's men."

"Let's eat fast and go."

She didn't argue but inhaled the fillet of fish with beurre blanc and the accompanying mixed vegetables and rice. I ate quickly, and within minutes we'd cleaned our plates.

"Can I have the key?" she said.

I killed my rum and handed her the key to Room 12. "I'll go pay the bill—wait, here comes the manager again."

To my surprise, Giselle stood, stepped toward me, bent down, took my chin in her hand, leaned in, and planted a delicate kiss on my lips.

"Don't be long, my dear." She spoke loudly and turned and walked out the open patio doors without looking back.

The proprietor had arrived and stood aside awkwardly as she departed.

"No dessert?" he said.

I smiled. Part acting, but there was a good chunk of spontaneous infatuation in there, too.

She'd kissed me.

Granted, it was an act, but it was still … a kiss.

"No dessert, here at least," I said. "Please bring me the bill—oh, and how about another bottle of that Moët et Chandon you'd brought us earlier?" I winked at him.

My acting may not have been as good as Giselle's as I could see something unsettled in his eyes.

"Of course. I'll be right back."

It took nearly ten minutes, but he returned with our bill and another bottle of Champagne on ice. I signed it to the room.

Had he put the pieces together and recognized Giselle, or did he still think she reminded him of someone else? Curiosity was known to kill the cat, which reminded me of the fear I'd spotted in Giselle's eyes when she saw the waiter, but my money was on the fact that we were in a tiny hotel high atop Tortola and that the people here cared little about European matters.

What could the proprietor do to cause us problems anyway?

He was the least of my concerns. After the kiss from Giselle, I was going to have a hard time being anything but mindful tonight.

Scarlet would be proud.

17

THE CHAMPAGNE WAS MEANT TO BE PART OF OUR COVER, but I couldn't help feeling an odd sense of excitement. The door was again locked, so I knocked, announced myself, turned the key, and walked in. Once inside I heard the television on in the bedroom. The door was open, so I walked to the doorway and stopped.

Giselle was seated on the bed, staring at the screen with faraway eyes.

"President François Huibert will be returning to France tomorrow before the conclusion of the G8 summit to accompany his wife Giselle Huibert's remains back for a state funeral," the newscaster said. I noticed a small red "CNN" in the bottom corner of the screen.

Giselle hadn't budged since I walked in. Her attention was fixed on the television.

The newscaster continued, "No further explanation of why the helicopter suddenly lost power and crashed into the Sir Francis Drake Channel, but authorities in St. Thomas reported that there will be a news conference about that tomorrow."

Giselle shook her head, stabbed her thumb on the remote control's power button, and threw it down on the bed.

"Unbelievable. What body are they saying is mine? Even if it was burned terribly, which from what you said none of them were, don't they have DNA here? Dental records? It's absurd!"

I placed the tray of Champagne on the dresser.

A tear streaked down her cheek. She wiped it off and flung her hand toward the bed as if disgusted by her own feelings.

"It's not weakness to let your emotions run their course," I said. "It's healthy."

She rubbed her eyes and they cleared. She stood rigidly and took two long strides to the ice bucket. "You brought Champagne?"

"Seemed an appropriate encore to your acting when you left the restaurant."

"I wasn't acting, " she said.

My heart skipped a beat. The kiss?

"I was terrified. That waiter—he looked like the men on François' security team. I had to get out of there."

"Right, the waiter," I said. "You covered your fear pretty well."

She took the Champagne bottle in her hand, peeled off the foil, and pulled the cork like an expert.

"You do that well, too," I said.

"I'm French."

She poured a glass.

"I feel bad for my people," she said. "François is using my popularity to gain sympathy for himself." Her face twisted into a scowl. "He disgusts me. After what I walked into at our hotel, we were finished, but now, this assassination attempt—my assistant murdered with two others—followed by this fiction? No. I want to hurt him *and* his henchmen."

She'd only poured one glass of Champagne, and after she took another sip she handed it to me.

"I have some ideas about who can help you, Giselle."

"You mean us, Buck Reilly. I'm afraid you're in this up to your neck."

She reached up and placed her hand around my neck. Her palm was hot and my skin was aflame beneath it. Our eyes held. She slowly pulled me toward her and licked her lips as my face came closer to hers.

"You rescued me, kept me safe. And you've been a gentleman all along."

Her breath was hot on my face.

"But I want more from you."

She got on her tiptoes and pulled my head down until our lips pressed together. My hands fell to her waist and grasped her hips. What began as a delicate kiss quickly became more urgent.

I pulled back and her arm slipped from around my neck. Now her hands clutched my hips. She was breathing heavily, her eyes half-lidded, and my body responded so quickly—and obviously—I leaned away.

"Giselle, this is a bad idea."

Her eyes remained narrowed, and her hands slowly slid up my back. My heart was thudding in my chest, and what little resolve I had left was fading fast.

"You're married …"

"I'm French, remember?" she whispered. "And I'm never going back to him."

She pulled me toward her and our hips collided. I felt the stiffness between us—her groan told me she did, too.

Her hands lifted my shirt and I bent lower so she could pull it over my head, and then her lips were on my chest. I fumbled with the buttons on her shirt—Scarlet's shirt. She'd worn it, what, a day ago? More like a lifetime. Giselle pulled her shirt off with one hand and pushed me onto the bed.

We each pulled off our own pants and were then naked in a hot embrace atop the covers. Our kisses alternated between delicate and hard as we rolled over and over until we nearly fell off the bed, our lips locked and our hands probing. We rolled back to the middle and I was on my back with Giselle on top of me—her hands massaged my chest and then slid lower.

She hovered over me and I opened my eyes.

Hers were open, watching me, her lower lip clenched between her teeth but still able to smile. She lowered herself slowly—a short-breathed gasp sounded from her parted lips. I squeezed her thighs—another gasp, mine, then together. Her back arched and my hands cupped her breasts as we found a rhythm of pressing, pushing, lifting…

"Oh," she cried. "Oh, Buck …"

I arched my back and pressed deeper. She shuddered, her hands clutching at my chest, her nails digging in. She squeezed her legs into me—my heart skipped. I sucked in a breath and held it as our bodies froze in intense pleasure.

A moment later, she fell on top of me, our chests moist with sweat, her hair flung across my face. My arms were wrapped tightly around her until I began to rub her back. She shuddered again, but this was different. A salty drop landed on my cheek, and I extended my tongue and licked it off. It was a tear.

"Are you okay?" I said.

She nodded quickly, and I wiped the tears from her cheeks.

"I haven't been with another man since I fell in love with François."

Whether she wanted this for release or revenge, I didn't care. All I knew was that she was as sensual as she was smart and beautiful. And I was a lucky son of a bitch.

"I didn't do this to thank you, Buck, or to break myself free from the bond of my relationship. We have had nothing for years, and after seeing him in the hotel … I could no longer play the charade."

"I understand."

"No, let me finish." She got up on her elbow, brushed her hair out of our faces, and looked me in the eyes. "I feel so connected to you—practically a stranger, but these past couple days have been unlike any in my life. Our connection is so, so …"

I pulled her back down onto my chest. "I feel it, too, Giselle."

And I did. So much that it scared me.

Buck Reilly syndrome.

18

WE MADE LOVE THREE MORE TIMES THAT NIGHT, each different from the last. Once tenderly, followed by urgent, and finally crazed from exhaustion, our desire just barely eclipsing our fatigue.

We awoke in a ball of sheets. Only getting a few hours of sleep would have been enough to leave me tired anyway, but the physical effort we'd exerted had me sore, chafed, and scratched up, too.

"*Bonjour, monsieur.*" Her voice was a whisper.

"*Madame.*"

"*Non. Mademoiselle, s'il te plait.*" She giggled. "I am no longer married."

She tickled me and I leaped from the bed. My feet landed hard on the wood floor.

"You're so ticklish." She giggled again. "I can't remember if I discovered that during the night or not." She stacked pillows behind her and sat up. "You are so tall and muscular. I just want to look at you."

I laughed and then assumed the position of the Greek sculpture called *Discobolus*, commonly known as the Discus Thrower, and flexed my muscles for all they were worth.

She howled with laughter. "Grr, come back to me, you Greek god."

"As much as I'd love to, one, I'm too sore for you to touch me, and two, it's eight fifteen and Valentine is picking us up at nine sharp. We need to get out of here early—our friend the proprietor was getting awfully curious last night."

"Hence my acting when I left the restaurant."

I frowned and put my hands on my hips. "I thought you said you weren't acting."

Her teeth glistened in the light that sneaked past the window shade and lit her face. "Only a little."

We both showered—separately, or we'd never have gotten out the door—and having gone first, Giselle toweled me off when I got out. Her long dark hair was a bird's nest after last night. I turned her to face the mirror and ran my fingers slowly through the knots in her hair while using the blow dryer on a low setting to straighten it out. I watched her in the mirror as she watched me. She smiled the entire fifteen minutes it took to dry her hair.

When finished, she turned around and slipped into my arms. We held each other for a long moment, not saying a word. If my head was swirling, hers must have been a tornado. Somewhere in the middle of last night, I'd stopped thinking of her as the first lady.. Now she was just Giselle—my lover. We'd been together three days nonstop, which is a lot for adults, especially when you start out as total strangers. There was still so much to learn about each other, but we'd developed a sense of trust that normally took weeks, if not months, to earn in a relationship.

I couldn't kid myself, though. It was a complicated road ahead for Giselle, and my role for now would have to be as an adviser on how she should best reappear—provided she'd listen to me, of course. I hoped Booth and the FBI could assist with that, and although I'd not told her about my connection to him yet, I planned to at breakfast. The hotel put out muffins, croissants, and fresh juice each morning, per the dining guide here in the room, and we still had ten minutes before Valentine was set to arrive.

With one last look around the ruins of the bedroom, I shook my head. "We trashed this place."

Giselle patted me on the behind. "Bravo."

At the door, I had a moment of clarity. "Before we leave, let's make a plan for the day."

"Your friend is picking us up—"

"Are we going to the airport, or the police—"

"No police, Buck."

"Giselle, you can't hide forever."

"Why not? I'm dead. The president of France said so. My ashes were shipped to Paris overnight. There will be a state funeral in a couple of days, and Giselle Huibert will soon be buried and forgotten."

I knew my mouth was hanging open because I was breathing through it.

"I am Claire Lyon from Montreal now. I may look familiar, but that's just because the world is infatuated with a dead Frenchwoman. Inconvenient, yes, but I tolerate it out of sympathy for my distant cousins in France." She finished with a smile and a nod.

"Wow," I said. "You were able to make love to me repeatedly and still had the energy to come up with a plan to reinvent yourself. Very impressive."

"*Merci.*"

"But wishful thinking, I'm afraid."

Her smile disappeared and her brow arched. "Why? We're in the Caribbean. You have many friends here, some of who have questionable repute—you told me that yourself. Don't you know somebody who can get me a fake passport?"

"Ah … yes, I probably do, but—"

"But what? I just want to sail on your boat for a month and move on with my life."

"It's not my boat, Giselle. I told you it's a rental. It's due back in six days."

She flung a hand at me as if to dismiss such a simple thought. "So we'll rent it longer, or better yet, buy it from the company. I have money—"

"But you're dead, remember? You can't use your credit cards or go to the bank for a withdrawal. You don't exist, not in the world you're contemplating."

She took a step back and crossed her arms.

I stepped toward her and took her shoulders in my hands. "I'm just being pragmatic, thinking of the big picture." I bit my tongue. So much for keeping my thoughts on the present.

"Pragmatism is boring. I want my own life."

"You *can* have all that, but first you have to deal with reality." I paused. "I can help with that. I have friends in the United States government—"

"No, Buck." She brushed my hands away. "I will not face the man who tried to kill me—killed innocent people—and be lost into the morass of public fascination, being followed everywhere by news teams and broadcast to every television on the planet!"

That description triggered a flashback of my demise after e-Antiquity. The press had been relentless, and while I was notorious, Giselle was not. But she was far more of a public figure. She was right, though: it would be a long grueling process of constant attention. A normal life could take tears to regain. I remembered wanting to flee, to hide and disappear, but it wasn't possible. It wouldn't be for her, either, but she wasn't ready to hear that yet.

I glanced at my ancient Rolex Submariner. It was 9:05. Valentine would be waiting out front. There was no sense in pressing her—she'd only run away and end up in worse danger.

"We need to go," I said. "I'll have Valentine take us back to Cane Garden Bay. We'll sail to Jost Van Dyke, or maybe Puerto Rico."

Giselle reached for my arm and clutched it close. "Thank you, Buck. For understanding."

I kissed her and my thoughts turned blank and I lost myself in her lips, in the smell of her hair, cheap hotel soap or not. She was a bouquet of tropical scents. We embraced, not out of passion but out of what I felt as faith.

"Ready?" I said.

She nodded quickly and took my hand in hers. I pulled the door open and we stepped outside.

A half dozen people stood twenty feet away—flashing lights blinded me.

Oh no!

"Mrs. Huibert, you're alive!" a man yelled.

I squinted into the flashing lights—camera strobes. Next to them were two men with video cameras and three men with microphones.

A cacophony of yelling followed—questions.

"What happened?" one man said.

"Does your husband know you're alive?" another said.

"Who is this man?"

"You're holding hands—is he your lover?"

I realized we were still holding hands—shit!

A horn honked repeatedly above the din of reporters. I shielded my face but looked past them to see Valentine waving wildly from the road, next to his Crown Victoria.

"You are mistaken!" Giselle shouted. "My name is Claire Lyon. I'm from Montreal!"

I pulled her forward. "Let's go!"

"Mrs. Huibert!" A reporter stepped into our path. "What are you doing—"

I shoved him aside like I was a fullback bursting through the line. A video camera was shoved in our faces, and I swatted it. It fell to the ground with a clatter.

"Run!"

I pulled her along the full fifty yards to Valentine's open door and pushed her inside. When I turned I saw the reporters running in pursuit. I dived into the backseat and the old Crown Vic burned rubber as we tore away. The last thing I saw was the proprietor smiling widely, standing in the doorway. He must have called the press. Every person in the western world would know the name of his dumpy little inn, and he'd be famous.

And Giselle was exposed.

SECTION 3

WELCOME TO THE FISHBOWL

19

"DAMN, BUCK. IF TROUBLE DON'T FOLLOW YOU LIKE A SHADOW," Valentine said.

I was staring out the back window, and sure enough, multiple cars raced after us. Damn.

"Where can we go?" I said.

"Ain't nowhere to go if these buzzards gonna follow us all day. Can't outrun 'em on these island roads. Too many switchbacks for this old car."

A motorcycle passed the pursuing vehicles and sped up behind us. A cameraman hung on behind the driver, determined to photograph us fleeing.

"What do we do, Buck?" Giselle said.

In the mirror I saw Valentine roll his eyes.

"Let's go back to the boat at Myett's—"

"We can't outrun them in a catamaran," Giselle said.

Valentine was already headed that way. We'd have to turn around if I could persuade her to go to the police.

"They know who you are," I said. "There's no point in running. You haven't done anything wrong."

Valentine was staring at us in the rearview mirror. A hairpin turn was coming up fast.

"Watch the road!" I said.

"I know the damn road."

"No, I can't do it, Buck. Not like this, chased in by the press—"

The motorcycle raced up on the driver's side of the vehicle and the cameraman aimed his camera into the backseat.

"Get down!"

Valentine swerved toward them and they fell back, but if the cameraman was worth his salt, he'd definitely got a few photos of us. Valentine swerved back the other way into the hairpin turn—the Crown Vic skidded in the gravel on the shoulder and nearly spun out.

"I don't want to die like Lady Diana!" Giselle said.

"Myett's is up ahead," Valentine said. "What do you want me to do, Buck?"

"Drive down as close as you can to the water. Our dinghy is tied to a palm tree there. We'll run for it. These cars can't chase us on the water."

Valentine nodded but then glanced back at me in the mirror again. "The lady was right. You can't outrun nothing in a catamaran."

"We have no choice—"

"Want me to call Detective Bramble? I'm guessing he'd drop everything and be here in a flash." He nodded toward Giselle.

"He'll know soon enough, thanks to the press, but no, Gis—ah—Claire refuses to come forward. He'll come looking for you, though, Valentine, and he'll recognize me from the photos."

"No doubt."

"So tell him we'll need help and we'll contact him through you."

Valentine nodded again. My old friend was wise and knew we needed a plan. This wasn't much, but at least it was something.

"We'll sail east toward Beef Island. Maybe we can arrange for a plane."

Giselle shook her head. She was pissed and I couldn't blame her.

We took a hard left into the small parking area by Myett's and sped past the restaurant—heads turned in our direction—and Valentine nearly drove through the fence that separated the lot from the beach. Our dinghy was still tied to the tree by the beach. He hadn't come to a full stop yet when I grabbed Giselle's hand.

"Let's go!"

I threw the door open and we jumped out.

"Be careful!" Valentine said.

After I slammed the door he threw the transmission into reverse and backed up fast toward our pursuers, causing them to swerve wildly out of the way. The motorcycle lost control—the driver laid it down and it slid into the sand.

The tide was falling, so the dinghy was a good fifty feet from the water. I yanked the rope free and Giselle and I each grabbed a side of the inflatable boat.

"Madame Huibert!" A reporter shouted as he ran toward us.

Four other men followed him.

"Hurry," I said.

Giselle stumbled and lost a shoe but stayed upright. Her face was contorted like that of a Navy SEAL training at Coronado.

"Why are you running?" another reporter said. "How did you survive the helicopter crash?"

"Why did the president report you dead?" another said.

We reached the water's edge and shoved the dinghy in and out from the beach. Giselle dived in and kept her head down. A light surf worked against us, but I waded out farther before I climbed aboard. I saw the paparazzi lined up on the water's edge now, cameras raised like rifles—which they might as well have been, considering that their coverage could get us killed.

The engine started on one pull—thank you, Moorings—and I gunned it out toward the boat. The bow lifted and then settled down quickly and we were up on plane.

Giselle rolled over and lay flat, staring up into the sky like she'd done the day I rescued her.

"Are you okay?" I said.

She gave me a thumbs-up followed by a petulant smile.

Quite the woman, this one.

"When we get to the boat, get onboard quickly and go inside. Their cameras will still be able to see us clearly at this distance."

"Will they follow us?"

"What do you think?"

The sky would be full of helicopters in no time. With the G8 summit still in session on St. Thomas, there would be a ton of foreign press in the area, with helicopters, boats, long-range cameras, everything. No story coming out of the summit would be as tantalizing as the French first lady on the run with a strange man, and why her husband had lied about her death.

The stern of the catamaran faced the beach, so it was impossible to come in from a different angle and use the boat itself as cover from the cameras.

"Ten more seconds," I said.

I reduced power, but the velocity of our speed had us come in hot. "Grab hold!"

Giselle sprang up and rolled onto her knees. She grabbed the rope I'd left hanging off the swimming platform and tied it quickly to the cleat on the bow of the dinghy. Without further prompting, she stood, grabbed hold of the rail, and pulled herself aboard. Her feet had no sooner touched fiberglass than she ran into the salon. With the motor off, I checked the rope on my way past the bow—it was snug. I climbed aboard the cat and kept my back to the beach as I made my way toward the bow.

Who could blame the son-of-a-bitch proprietor for calling the press? Giselle could run, but she wouldn't be able to hide for long. And she wouldn't be able to run for long, either. These islands were just too small to avoid an all-out womanhunt.

Using the boat hook, I grabbed the line connecting us to the mooring buoy and pulled us closer, ever so slowly, until I was able to disconnect us from the floating ball. Set free, we were adrift. I shielded my face as I walked back down the side and took the steps up to the helm. With the kill switch disengaged, I started the engines, which again fired right up—a novelty to someone used to operating airplanes that are seventy-five years old. I put the boat in gear.

We headed east, as I told Valentine we would, but I had a different plan. With autopilot engaged, I hurried down into the salon.

"Giselle?"

She emerged from the aft port cabin. She'd changed into shorts and a T-shirt. Smart. Her eyebrows were arched. "Damn those bastards!" she said.

"Pack a small bag of clothes, and grab some for me, too."

"Where are we going?"

My smile softened her features. "I have a plan."

20

WE MOTORED THE LENGTH OF CANE GARDEN BAY, and the crowd on the beach followed our progress, led by the news teams. A huge rock bluff marked the end of the beach, and for a fair distance beyond that there were no roads or vantage points where we could be observed. Catamarans under power aren't slow, but they're certainly not fast. I was totally exposed on the helm for the cameramen to shoot, but as soon as we passed that bluff, I breathed a sigh of relief. Temporary, yes, but even that felt like a minor victory.

Giselle had been monitoring our progress from inside, and as soon as we were away from Cane Garden Bay, she came up to the helm.

"All ready below," she said. "Are you sure this is a good idea?"

I turned to face her. "If you're not ready to confront the situation head-on, we don't have many options."

After another mile, a broad and relatively undeveloped cove surrounded by high hills came into view. There were no roads leading to it or dwellings around it, only a white sand beach. I steered the cat into the center of the cove. Fortunately, none of the press had a drone as far as I'd seen, so this would be a safe place until they figured out we'd never come back into sight down the coast. By then helicopters would be scouring the waters, so time was of the essence.

Ecological groups seeking to protect the limited coral here had set two mooring balls in the cove. Both were empty. I steered for the closest one and asked Giselle to stand on the bow with the boat hook and try to grab the line to the floating buoy. She immediately grabbed the hook, positioned herself on the bow pulpit, and glanced back at me. I reduced power, angling slightly up from the buoy as a strong current pushed against us and threatened to have me miss the mark.

"Get ready!"

I pushed the throttle into neutral and we slowly floated up to the ball. Giselle bent down, extended the boat hook, and caught the line on the first try.

Good job.

I steadied us in the current by alternating from forward to reverse while she tied us off. Another thumbs-up lit even greater admiration for her in my heart. I killed the engines, flicked the kill switch, closed and locked the control panels on the bridge, and went down to the salon. I found Giselle in my stateroom with my dry bag half-packed out on the bed.

"I took some of your friend's clothes," she said. "Is this enough for you?"

"Sure." I looked past her to the bed and leaned over and slapped the top of the headboard. The secret compartment opened and Giselle's eyes locked on the 9mm Sig in there.

"Are you bringing that?" she said.

I hesitated. Irritating reporters were one thing, but if the people who'd shot Giselle's helicopter down came after us, protection would be key. But my past trouble here in the BVI—being accused of a murder I didn't commit—was like acid reflux in my mind. I pushed the compartment closed.

"No, I think we'll be okay."

Her eyes lingered on the closed compartment. With the dry bag over my shoulder, we exited the salon and I locked the door.

That done, I turned around to see her with her hands on her hips.

"Ready?" I said. "We need to get out of here."

"Wait a minute."

I glanced down, and what I saw in her eyes stopped me in my tracks. She stepped into me and wrapped her arms around me. She held me tight, and I reciprocated even though the need to get moving was churning like a hamster wheel in my gut.

"Thank you," she said. "You have been amazing. I am so grateful."

Though I was tempted to pop her bubble and remind her that we couldn't run for long, that we should call the police as I'd been suggesting, I held my tongue. One thing at a time.

"You're pretty amazing yourself. Now let's get out of here before they find us."

I took her hand and led her down to the swimming platform. She held the dry bag while I pulled the rope attached to the dinghy, drawing it right up to the stern of the cat.

"Climb aboard."

She hunched down, took hold of the side of the rubber-coated dinghy, and scooted aboard. I handed her the yellow dry bag and climbed on as well. Without delay, I scurried past Giselle, holding on to her shoulder for balance, and sat down on the wood seat.

Once the engine was started, she untied the line connecting us to the catamaran, and I put the outboard in gear. Rather than aiming toward the center of the sand beach, I steered us in a half circle and aimed us straight out into the Caribbean Sea.

"Where are we going?" she asked.

"To see a man about a fox." I grinned at her.

21

WE MOTORED FURTHER OFFSHORE, BACK PAST CANE GARDEN BAY, just two people out on a pleasure cruise. I studied the shoreline, but the throng of people who'd chased us here were gone. The paparazzi are a predictable herd—once cut off at the end of the beach, they'd have rushed back to their vehicles to continue pursuit down the coast. So far so good.

The dinghy was an uncomfortable watercraft for longer distances, and once we were out in open water, the seas swelled higher and made the ride rough. Giselle sat in the center, scanning in all directions, whether for pursuers or looking at the beautiful waters, I wasn't sure. Aside from keeping an eye on our course, my attention was through my binoculars aimed off the back of the boat. There were no fewer than three helicopters buzzing around Tortola, and before we were too far away to see them any longer, I was pretty sure one was hovering over the cove where we'd ditched the catamaran.

"What's that ahead?" Giselle said.

My heart jumped as I looked forward. What I saw was another old friend.

"That's called Sandy Spit."

The tiny island had been wiped clean of the once-plush vegetation that had covered most of its land. A favorite among boaters for anchoring off its shore and swimming in to walk the pink beach, picnic or snorkel, the island was now largely stripped down to sand and man-made coral pyramids thanks to the hurricanes of a couple of years ago.

"It's beautiful," Giselle said.

I had the feeling she wanted to stop, but there was no way we could do that with helicopters on the prowl. They could get from Tortola to here in moments, which they no doubt would once they'd exhausted their search there. We continued past with the throttle on full, bouncing in the waves, the spray soaking us as we continued toward the dark silhouette of the island ahead.

Giselle pointed toward the dark hilly mass ahead with her eyebrows raised.

"Jost Van Dyke." I had to shout to be heard over the engine and churning water.

She nodded once and hunkered down, with both hands holding tight to the line tied to the front cleat.

We came in from the east, heading straight to the coast near Sidney's Peace and Love in Little Harbor. If anyone were to track our course using satellite images, which was likely, I wanted to make it as hard as possible to find us. Sidney's was open, and we continued southwest along the coast, as close to shore as the depth, wake, and surge would allow. The rocky shoreline was jagged and slowed our speed by half compared with open water.

"Not very populated here," Giselle said.

"Only about three hundred people live on Jost, but thousands of tourists visit Soggy Dollar, Ivan's, Sidney's and Foxy's every year."

She glanced back at me, her brow furrowed. "Is it smart to come here then?"

"We don't have many choices of places we can run in a dinghy. I used to have friends here, hopefully still do, and fingers crossed that they'll help us."

I wasn't smiling, and neither was Giselle. This was no tourist visit, and we both knew it. Looking at her back in the Green Parrot T-shirt she'd taken from Scarlet's clothes, I thought of her naked in bed last night. Daylight had cleared my fantasies of our running away together. No matter what she'd told me, the reality was that she'd needed release from the life she was seeking to escape, and I happened to be there. Yes, I'd saved her from drowning and kept her out of harm's way so far, but this job was too big for me. I needed help. Hopefully, my friends would be on-island and willing to stick their necks out. I wondered whether we should come up with a cover story to facilitate their help. What would Giselle think?

We puttered farther along the coast out to the point at the end of Little Harbor, then turned north to continue along the coast into Great Harbor.

"I have a suggestion," I said.

She turned to face me. Her shirt was soaked, her hair wild, her nose sunburned, but she looked alive and her brown eyes sparkled. "I was counting on that."

"Unfortunately, I'm pretty well-known in these islands. And every one of my friends will know who you are at this point, especially if my name surfaced in the news of your resurrection and they see us together."

"So?"

"So we have three choices. First, we can get the help of the FBI and turn ourselves in to the police."

"No. Next?"

"We can explain the truth to my friends and make it clear we may be hunted by the men who shot your helicopter down. If they find us, they will kill us and probably anyone who's helping us."

She sneered. "Not very compelling."

"The third is a stretch but may get us some temporary grace. We play the part of lovers on the run."

She smiled. "The truth?"

"But we need some backstory. Buck Reilly syndrome won't hold up."

"*What* syndrome?"

"What I'm calling a syndrome—the victim temporarily falling for her rescuer."

Her smile vanished. "That's what I am? Simply a victim of your charms?"

I held up a hand. "I'm just coming up with ideas to buy us some time—don't take me literally."

Her lip trembled. Truth be told, that was how I saw it. "Hence the need for a backstory, something more believable. I was thinking we could say we met in Paris, back in the days when my company e-Antiquity was still on top of the world. We actually did an exposition of the Mayan Serpent King's treasure at the Musée D'Orsay—"

"I remember that. I'd told François I wanted to attend, but he refused."

"Perfect. So let's say I gave you a private show and a spark erupted between us. You were married, I was engaged—"

"I remember hearing about you now, Buck. Some of my friends saw you. They gushed about the handsome American millionaire archaeologist."

"All the more perfect. So our connection dates back, well, seven years now."

"Were we lovers then?"

"We don't have to share all the details of our long, ah, friendship."

She nodded once, quickly. "Yes, we were lovers. We snuck off and met in several other places over the years, but this trip to St. Thomas was our chance to run away together." She smiled.

I felt my face flush—or was it the sun? I had to be sunburned, too.

"How do we explain the helicopter crash then?"

After a moment, she sat up straight. "I was never on it! I'd sent my assistant ahead to Tortola to ready my plane to depart, and sadly the helicopter crashed. You and I had already run off together on your boat."

I didn't like it, but we needed sympathy and didn't want the authorities to be alerted until we were safe and Giselle was ready. It was flimsy, but it could buy us a little time and discretion.

"You said you'd been married?"

My grimace made her eyes go wide for a moment.

"Didn't last long, but I was indeed married."

"Since you were here with Scarlet, I'm guessing she was not your ex-wife?"

"No, Scarlet and I worked together at the peak of my career. She was instrumental in a lot of our most important finds. But she never really got the credit she deserved. We were lovers."

"And?"

"After we discovered the tomb of the Serpent King in Guatemala, I was the toast of the archaeological world. I received a bunch of awards and at one such event met the then-top supermodel in the world, Heather Drake."

"Of course I know her. We saw her many times at Fashion Week in Paris." Giselle puckered her lips. "Very beautiful."

"Very crazy, too. And deceitful." I spared Giselle the details of Heather's running off with my partner, Jack Dodson—I didn't want her pity. But after what she'd found her husband doing, I guess we were on par in the relationship department.

She reached back and squeezed my calf. "Neither of us were lucky at marriage, but at least yours was brief."

And my spouse didn't try to kill me.

Up ahead, our destination came into view.

"We're headed to that beach up there." I pointed toward a long swath of white sand.

Giselle smiled. "I brought the green bathing suit bottom."

Good grief. What would it take to scare this woman into appreciating the peril she—*we*—were in?

22

WE BEACHED THE DINGHY ON THE WHITE SAND on the far right side of the shore. In the middle of the beach was a police station. Foxy's bar and restaurant was to our right. I nodded toward the police station. Giselle glanced at it, frowned, and pointed to Foxy's.

The sun was bright and straight overhead. A light breeze whisked sand along the beach and provided some relief from the mid-eighties heat, but it still felt hot after a couple hours of stronger wind aboard the boat. My legs were stiff as I looked up and down the beach. A few tourists were scattered around on chairs and towels, but nobody paid us any attention.

Had the news that Giselle was alive made it here to Jost Van Dyke?

Hopefully not.

Giselle had pulled her hair up into a ponytail, and with her sunburned nose and cheeks, shorts, and Green Parrot T-shirt, she looked like an island girl.

"Okay, cross your fingers," I said.

We strolled down the beach. When she wrapped her hand around my arm, I glanced over and found her smiling. Whether it was for disguise or because she felt more comfortable, I again marveled at her poise and calm. She'd been declared dead, then spotted alive with a man who wasn't her husband while her actual husband was probably trying to find and kill her, and she was as calm as anyone on this beach.

I must have smiled back, because she gave my arm a squeeze.

Foxy's had been almost entirely rebuilt since two hurricanes last pounded these islands. The floor plan had changed, but the ceilings and walls were already half-covered with knickknacks, photos, and island junk, just like they had been for decades before the storms. A cacophony of people and music filled my ears. It was lunchtime and the bar was crowded. We walked inside and I steered Giselle into the store behind the bar.

"Hello, sir." A large woman in a colorful sarong greeted us from behind the register. "Here for some T-shirts, or maybe some of Foxy's Island Rum?"

"We'd like a couple hats, please," I said.

The woman pointed toward the back wall. I chose a red one and Giselle took a blue one. We adjusted the headbands and donned them. I paid the woman in cash.

"Is Foxy here?" I said.

"I believe so. Does he know you?"

"We go way back. Could you tell him Buck is here?"

"Okay," she said. "Just wait in the bar."

Two stools were open at the closest bar, which we took. A tall skinny bartender with crooked white teeth stepped forward.

"Welcome to Foxy's. What can I get you?"

"I'll have a Carib," I said.

"Strawberry daiquiri, and can we get lunch?" Giselle said.

"Chicken roti is the special, but we also have burgers, fish sandwiches—"

"Chicken roti is perfect," Giselle said.

"Make that two."

Another crooked smile and moments later our drinks arrived. The beer was ice-cold and refreshing. Giselle moaned in appreciation at the taste of her daiquiri. We'd been on the water for hours with nothing to drink and hadn't had a thing to eat all day. The roti would be—

Motion caught my attention.

Somebody was waving from back by the entrance to the store. Gray hair, salty white goatee, red Make America Great Again hat—it was Foxy.

Giselle spotted him, too. "What's going on?" she said.

Foxy waved us over.

"Come on, let's go."

"But our food, I'm starving."

Giselle followed me. Foxy looked from me to Giselle and back and shook his head as we got closer. He waved us over between the store and another building and waited for us in a large backyard edged with flowering bushes, palm trees, and a couple of beached sailboats.

"Buck Reilly. Son of a bitch."

"Foxy, good to see—"

"So the news is true." He looked right at Giselle.

She stuck her hand forward. "Hello, I'm Claire Lyon."

He took her hand, bowed, and kissed it. "Claire what? Shoot, nice to meet you, Ms. First Lady."

Giselle's mouth fell open. Did she really think people would buy the Claire Lyon from Montreal shtick? He let go of her hand and gave me a hug.

"When I saw you on the news getting on that catamaran, I wondered if you'd come here. Can't believe you made it. Must be every cop, Coast Guard, Navy plane, helicopter—you name it—all out searching for you two."

I glanced at Giselle and her wide eyes. Maybe her denial was finally hitting the wall.

"Has my name been mentioned on the—"

"News?" he said. "Not at first, but guess who had his own press conference? Your old buddy Detective Bramble. He revealed your identity and shared a brief history of your past exploits here in the British Virgin Islands."

"Perfect," I said.

"Hell, nearly been as much talk about you as, ah, the lady here."

"Please, call me Giselle." Her face was now devoid of surprise or fear.

"Nice to meet you, Giselle." Foxy again shook her hand. "None of my business what you two are up to, but you're going to have some 'splaining to do at some point, no doubt about that."

The crooked-toothed waiter appeared down the same path we'd followed and held two plates of chicken roti. He put them on a small table, smiled, and disappeared the way he'd come.

"Might as well eat," Foxy said. "You'll need the energy."

"What we need is your help," I said.

We all sat down, and Foxy watched my face, waiting.

"Giselle is in danger—guess I am now, too, since the world knows we're together."

"*Together?*" Foxy said.

Our cover story seemed a lot thinner now than it had on the open water, so I decided to stick to the facts—at least with Foxy.

"Giselle's helicopter was shot down. I happened to be spearfishing nearby and raced over to see if there were any survivors. There was only her, and she was unconscious."

"Damn. News ain't said nothing about getting shot down."

"And my husband—soon to be ex-husband, that is—lied to the world about my death," Giselle said.

"What the hell?"

"It's a long story and we don't have all the details, but we believe that someone—obviously—is trying to kill her. Mercenaries, assassins, take your pick, but before I even knew who she was we sailed to Soper's Hole, and the next morning three dark-skinned men were searching boat to boat for her."

"You mean dark-skinned like me?" Foxy said.

"No, like Middle Eastern or Northern African, maybe."

"Probably Algerian," Giselle said. "France has a large Algerian population."

"Anyway, the BVI government had given them tracking information on all the boats in the vicinity of the crash, and they'd tracked me down and knew my name. Scared the hell out of me, to tell the truth."

Giselle placed her hand on mine. Foxy's eyes opened wide.

"Anyway, we tried to hide out on Tortola for a night and make a plan, but the hotel manager recognized her and the rest is history."

"Sounds like a fine mess to me."

"These men won't stop looking for us—"

"Police station right down the beach—"

"No," Giselle said.

Foxy's eyebrows lifted.

"Giselle, we can't outrun this. It's too big," I said. "We need help—"

"Not the police."

"Why?" I said.

"I don't trust the police here."

Foxy leaned forward. "They're good people."

"I'm sure they are, but our security team, the Groupe de Sécurité de la Présidence de la République, met with all the heads of police in the islands before we came down. Policemen and security people—Secret Service types—always stick together. We go to the police, then they will call the Groupe de Sécurité, which means Alphonse Zidane will immediately be alerted to our location. No, Buck, it is not happening."

Well, at least I finally fully understood her reluctance. She was right—there was no way local police wouldn't call the French security apparatus. Nobody would believe there was some type of conspiracy going on. And they'd want attention and credit for finding her—us—at this point.

"So you want to stay underground?" Foxy said.

Giselle smiled.

"My *grand-pére* was in the underground in the Second World War." She looked from Foxy's face to mine. "It's in my blood to fight back covertly. So, yes, we must stay underground. I want answers."

After a several-second delay, Foxy howled with laughter. "Damn, Buck, you got your hands full now, brother."

Giselle placed her hand on mine and squeezed it.

That was an understatement.

23

"WE GOT PLENTY OF UNDERGROUND TYPES IN THESE ISLANDS, don't you worry about that," Foxy said. "Shoot, Buck, you know some yourself."

My mind swirled back to previous trips here, times of other challenges, issues beyond the law where help was required on a no-questions-asked basis. The ragtag collection of men I'd assembled had been capable against better-equipped adversaries, but this was different. The world was searching for us, including the governments of France, the United States, even Great Britain, given the fact that we were in their territory.

It was too much.

I shook my head and rubbed my eyes.

"What's wrong?" Giselle said.

Unless we had some help. Intel.

I glanced up, my eyes clear.

"What?" she said.

"We can try to get you answers, and I think we can pull together the help we need to do it, but we do need intel," I said. "Serious intel."

Giselle stared at me, her eyes slowly closing to a squint.

"Where the hell you gonna get that?" Foxy said.

"Are you suggesting the FBI?" Giselle said.

"I've got a guy there—"

"No—"

"He cares more about his own success, believe me. He'll help, provided he gets to play a part in the endgame."

"Why wouldn't he just capture us and take the credit that way?" Giselle said.

"Because this is a bigger story than just you disappearing—"

"Buck?" Foxy said.

"And based on what you saw—"

"Ah, Buck?"

"And given the murder of everybody on that helicopter, and the cover-up—"

"Buck!"

Giselle and I turned to face Foxy.

"One thing you two need to know." He paused. "The spin on TV is you two ran off together. Broke the French president's heart. Really pissed off all the governments, not to mention the French—least that's what they been saying on the news."

The spin.

Giselle's pallor went a couple of shades whiter.

"Bastards," she said.

"That's fine," I said. "We can work with that. Let the world think that's the case. François—or his security people—certainly the killers know that's bullshit, but it might give us space to operate."

Giselle's jaw was rigid, her eyes icy. "You're right. It can help us." She glanced at me and then leaned in close and kissed my lips, tenderly. "And partially true anyway."

Foxy slapped a hand on the table. "Holy mother of God. Buck-ass Reilly and Giselle Huibert. Don't that just beat all."

We laughed. I squeezed her hand.

"As soon as I call Booth at the FBI, we'll need to get out of here, just in case." I held my breath, but Giselle didn't argue.

"I'll get you set up in a villa above Soggy Dollar. And I can get you off-island, too."

Giselle smiled. "You're not the only one with influential friends, Buck. I know a few people here, and I think they'd help me."

I studied her face for a long moment, but she gave no further indication of what or whom she was referring to.

"We'll pool our resources, but we'll start by getting some intelligence briefings set up." I patted my pants pocket and felt my cell phone. "Anybody sell cheap phones here on Jost?" I said.

"Burners?" Foxy said. "Sell 'em myself. They's still pirates around here, Buck, you know that."

At the end of the long boat dock, I held my phone to my ear.

"What the hell are you thinking, Reilly?" Booth said.

"I told you what happened. She—now we—are on the run. The press is being manipulated—"

"Where the hell are you? I already have a team in place in San Juan and can have them anywhere in the Virgin Islands within an hour."

"That's great, but we don't want to be rescued yet."

"Why the hell not?"

"Giselle wants to find out what happened—"

"*Giselle*? She's the first lady of France, Reilly! Don't do anything stupid!"

I smiled. This was going to torture Booth.

How fun is this?

"What I need from you is information."

"Information?" Booth said. "What the hell? You're not trained—"

"For which I promise that you'll be in on the climax."

"Rescuing her is the—"

"No, Booth, that's only the surface issue. There's a conspiracy here and we're going to get to the bottom of it. Giselle is determined. Look her up, study her family history. It's in her blood."

Only the sound of heavy breathing sounded from the other end of the phone. I had him.

"I need intel from you, starting with the French head of the Groupe de Sécurité de la Présidence de la République, Alphonse Zidane. His background and potential allegiances. He may be the rat here, and we need to figure out how to flush him out."

"I know some of his history already. Former French Foreign Legion. Dirty operator—that's his reputation."

"Find out more. Where he served, who he served with—"

"I don't work for you, Reilly!"

"That's right, Booth, you work for yourself. The FBI is just the vehicle. You've ridden my back to solve some petty bullshit in the past, but this is the big time. We work together on this, you'll be in the winner's circle at the end."

Silence. Heavy breathing.

"Director Booth?" I said. "How's that sound?"

"Shut up, Reilly. Fine, I'll do some digging, then I'll call this number—"

"This phone's going in the ocean the minute we hang up. I'll call you. Now, get to work."

"Don't tell me—"

Click.

Splash.

24

THE VIEW OVERLOOKING WHITE BAY WAS
BREATHTAKING. Giselle and I sat on the porch of the cottage
that Foxy had provided for us until safe passage out could be arranged.
No other homes were close by, and the golden grass served as a perfect
foundation for the brilliant blue waters stretching back out toward
Tortola and the U.S. Virgin Islands, barely smudges on the horizon at
this distance.

"What time is it?" Giselle said.

"Thirty minutes since the last time you asked." I smiled at her.
"Foxy said a boat would come at dusk. It's better if we leave without
being seen."

"But who will come?"

"He didn't say. Only that we could trust them."

There was no television at the cottage, so we had no insight into
the latest news. We had no food but were equipped with bottled water,
ice, and a bottle of Foxy's Spiced Rum, compliments of our host. The
sun was on its downward arc and I estimated it would be another hour
until sunset.

There was a small gas-operated generator to power the lights, and
inside the cottage was a bathroom, a shower, and a sitting
room/kitchen/bedroom all in one open space. Not much larger than an
efficiency apartment, and it was all one needed here on the highest peak
of Jost Van Dyke.

I sat on the floor of the outdoor deck, my legs hanging over the side. Giselle paced on the wood planking behind me. Each time she got to the far end, the same loose board would squeak. I was used to being alone, so the solitude didn't bother me, but the stress of waiting was clearly gnawing at her.

When she next walked past me, I reached out and grabbed her ankle. She tripped, and I caught her as she stumbled.

"You startled me," she said. "My mind was a thousand miles away."

"More like four thousand miles away, I imagine. What do you think is happening in Paris right now?"

Cradled in my lap, her whole body shrugged. "I'm sad for the people who worried over me, but that's it. I'm starting to think about whether or not to resurface, though."

"Finally."

"But not until we can try and learn who blew up my helicopter, and why."

"And you think we can do that on St. Thomas?"

"The summit doesn't end for two more days. Part of the French contingent remains there."

"François?"

Another shrug. "He said on the television that he would accompany my body home—lies, of course. So perhaps he stayed." She'd been twirling her hair with her fingers, but now she flung her wrist to the side. "But he is the least of my concerns." Then she squared her eyes on mine, reached up with the hair-twirling hand, and let it settle on the back of my neck. "Here we are in paradise, Buck, at least for a couple more hours. Alone, in this lovely abode overlooking the Caribbean Sea."

"Beautiful, isn't it?"

She massaged the back of my neck with her fingertips. "Yes, but so am I, and I've been pacing, waiting less and less patiently for you to notice me."

"Notice you?"

She pulled me close, and her lips were moist against mine. The delicate kiss increased in pressure until she slowly parted her lips and our tongues collided. Bent at an awkward angle, I scooted back a foot from the edge and lay down on the wood planks of the porch, with Giselle nestled close to me, her hands now up and inside my shirt and pulling it over my head.

Hers followed, and our shorts came off easily. We were naked in the warm afternoon air, surrounded by natural beauty, no other sign of humanity in sight.

She rolled on top of me, and our moist bodies slicked together with a suction sound that made us both giggle. I opened my eyes and found that hers were open, too. We locked gazes as she straddled me and slid down my torso until I gradually engulfed her. We made love slowly, with no urgency, and without inhibition in the plein air art of pure pleasure.

Finally she sat erect, her back arched and her thrusting halted, pleasure spreading through her body in spasms that held me tight until I, too, felt release, which pressed my eyes closed and curled my toes.

Giselle lay slowly upon me and we held each other. My hands traced the contours of her spine, down to her hips, and gripped her firm buttocks.

A breeze passed over the porch and she shivered atop me, so I squeezed her close. A rustling sound caught my attention and I rolled her toward the cottage.

"Hello?" a voice sounded.

"Shit!" Giselle said.

She rolled toward the door as I fumbled for my shorts, my heart thudding in my chest. Who the hell could it be?

"Who's there?" I said.

"Buck Reilly, that you?"

Shit!

"Who is that?"

"Sorry, mon. It's Benji from Foxy's. I have news for you."

It was the snaggletoothed bartender from Foxy's. Once my shorts were on, I sat forward and saw him standing in the middle of the golden grass on the path we'd taken to get here. Still shirtless, I slid off the porch and walked barefoot over loose coral rock and dried grass. *Ouch*—a burr stabbed my heel.

"Hey, Benji. What's the news?"

He was holding a cell phone. Had he taken pictures?

"Didn't mean to interrupt you there, boss." He cleared his throat. "Ah, Foxy says he'll pick you up on the beach by Soggy Dollar right before dark. Most people be gone by then, so you shouldn't have any trouble."

Had Benji recognized Giselle? I guess everyone had seen or heard the news by now, so whether he'd recognized her or not, he'd know who she was.

"This path here, one you took from the road above Foxy's? Keep taking it down that way and you'll find another path that leads up behind Soggy Dollar. Can't miss it, mon."

"Thanks for walking up here to tell me, Benji. And thank Foxy for me."

He winked at me and said in a lower voice, "Sorry again, mon."

I watched him walk away. He looked like he was typing a text for a quick second, then pocketed the phone as he disappeared down the path toward the east end of Jost Van Dyke. Well … I decided not to worry about it. If Foxy sent him up here, he must be trustworthy.

"Was that the bartender?"

Over my shoulder was Giselle, on the porch, now wrapped in a towel. I walked slowly back toward the cottage, trying to place my bare feet on patches of grass—ouch! Another small burr wedged into the arch of my foot.

"Yes. Benji." I plucked the burr out and it pierced my finger. "Foxy is picking us up at the end of this trail at dusk."

Giselle looked statuesque on the porch above me. Her hair was down and around her shoulder, and she leaned on the rail watching me. Her cheeks were lifted from her smile.

"I'm going to shower then," she said. "Join me?"

I glanced back to where Benji had disappeared. I was certain he'd spied on us as we were making love on the porch, maybe even taken pictures. Little bastard.

"No, I'll keep watch. You go ahead."

Her smile turned to a frown, and then she laughed. "Suit yourself."

Back on the porch I pulled my shirt on and put on my shoes. I was a fool for letting Benji sneak up on us. Something about his words bothered me. Apologetic for disturbing us—because he was watching? Or something else?

The sound of water running from Giselle's shower was evident through the screen door behind me. I stood, hands pressed against the railing, looking down at White Bay below and across the darkening blue water toward the rest of the BVI and beyond to the USVI. Lights were starting to flicker on the distant hillsides and the bows of boats approaching Jost. Another peaceful evening playing out in this remote corner of the Caribbean Sea.

A red light flickered above the water, moving faster than the boats. It was coming straight toward White Bay. I grabbed my binoculars from the dry bag, turned, and propped my elbows on the railing to steady my hands. Before peering through, I searched for the red light—there—still coming toward Jost, as if on a string.

A sick feeling fluttered in my gut.

I adjusted the binoculars until a black orb came into view.

A helicopter.

Coming toward us in a straight line.

Shit!

25

"GISELLE! GET OUT OF THE SHOWER. WE NEED TO
GO!"

The water was turned off.

"Buck? What are you saying?"

"Get dressed and fast. A helicopter is headed straight for us!"

She leaped from the small shower, toweling her long, lithe body as she moved toward her clothing folded neatly on a wooden chair.

"What happened—who could it be—the press?"

"That snaggletoothed asshole from Foxy's must have told someone. And the press is the least of our worries."

I walked the interior perimeter of the small cottage searching for a weapon, but there was nothing. The utensil drawer held spoons and forks but no sharp knives. Another drawer had a mousetrap and a lighter. There was a black cast iron pan on the two-burner stove, salt and pepper on the counter, and a candle—nothing else.

Giselle jumped into the middle of the room, her clothes on and her hair soaking her shirt. "I'm ready. What are we going to do?"

Good question.

The sound of helicopter rotors could now be heard below us. The pilot was staying low to work his way over the bay and up the valley, searching. Daylight was waning, but we'd still be seen if we ran.

"Buck?"

Behind Giselle was a small closet. I rushed past her and pulled it open. Cleaning tools, broom, mop and bucket, a spool of fishing line, and a five-gallon gas can. I grabbed the broom, broke it over my knee, and handed her the half without the bristles.

"Go out the back door, get to the trees, and stay under cover. When the helicopter comes, make sure they can't see you—"

"What about you?"

"Work your way down toward the trail, get hidden, and wait for me!" I grabbed her arm. "If something happens to me, go straight to Soggy Dollar. Foxy will be there to get you—"

"No!"

"Go, now!"

Giselle hesitated for a second. Then she grabbed her small bag and hurried out the back door. I cinched my dry bag up on my back and glanced around for any signs that we'd been here.

A plan formed in my mind.

Outside, next to the back door, was the generator. It was full of gas. I pulled the choke and pumped the rubber ball to prime the carburetor, and it started on my first pull of the cord. Back inside I flipped on the bathroom light and closed the door, got the spool of fishing line from the closet, tied it to the front door handle, and uncoiled enough to get to the wooden chair by the bed, nearly in the center of the room. After pulling off another section of fishing line and laying it on the floor close to the back door, I ran it to the chair, broke off the line from the spool, and tied it to the chair's leg. The cushions from the small couch fit under the bed sheets, and I moved them around until it looked like people were under the covers.

Back in the kitchen area, I grabbed the candle and retrieved the lighter from the drawer.

The sound of the chopper grew ever closer. It made me think of someone coming at me with a weed wacker. I hoped Gisele was safely hidden.

I placed the candle on the chair next to the bed. The lighter flicked but only sparked. No flame. I shook it and could hear fluid inside.

Another flick—nothing.

"Come on!"

I adjusted the flow of lighter fluid on the front of the lighter and flicked it again and it lit. My hand was shaking as I lowered the flame to the wick of the candle, which lit right up.

Nice romantic scene.

Back at the closet, I grabbed the five-gallon gas can, which felt nearly full.

What if the helicopter did have press on board?

No—my gut said otherwise, and my intuition had got me out of more tight situations than I cared to remember.

I carefully dumped gasoline all around the bed, soaking it, and made sure there was a pool under the chair. I soaked a hand towel with gas and tucked the can behind the bed with the rolled-up towel inside its open mouth. A glance out the window—the helicopter was approaching fast, no doubt headed for the cottage, and flying way too low to be legal. Another argument against the likelihood that it was full of zealous newshounds.

At the back door, I gently pulled the fishing line taut from the chair and through the door, which I closed before tying the line to the outside handle. The line tucked into the space between the handle and the door. It was practically unnoticeable in the fading light.

If someone peered inside the windows, would they notice the lines to the chair? The windows had gauze curtains, so you couldn't see clearly inside. The generator was fairly loud, and if spent lovers were asleep in bed, maybe they'd sleep through the sound of the approaching helicopter. I sniffed hard but didn't smell the gasoline.

The helicopter hovered over the open area down by the path. If it circled the cottage, there was nowhere for me to hide in the back. I banked on our pursuers' assuming Giselle and I would be unarmed and vulnerable. Through the gauzy windows I saw the helicopter set down hard in Benji's golden grass.

Now was my chance—with the helicopter close to the cottage, it blocked their view of the back. I sprinted toward the trees as I heard the power reduce on its engine. Fifty feet to go—I held my breath the entire way. I glanced once to my left, but the angle was just right to cover me. Once among the trees, I stumbled my way another fifty feet in and stopped.

Where was Giselle?

My heart pounded in step with my rapid breathing. Adrenaline coursed through my bloodstream like it was shot from a fire hose. I looked around the woods and down the hill toward the path. I saw a speck of color a hundred feet down—Giselle's bag was blue. I started working my way through the thin copse of trees, staying low.

Movement back toward the cottage caught my eye. Three men had emerged from the helicopter. Two carried what appeared to be automatic rifles—or camera booms? Couldn't be. But even if they were, reporters wouldn't break into the cottage.

I stepped on a stick—it cracked. I froze.

The men in the open space continued toward the cottage, crouched low and moving quickly. Between the generator and the helicopter, they couldn't hear me. I increased my pace toward Giselle's blue bag. She spotted me and waved once but kept low.

Smart lady.

I was twenty feet from Giselle—

BOOM—WHOOSH!

A loud explosion knocked me off my feet. The cottage erupted into an orange ball of flames.

"*Mon Dieu!*" Giselle said. "What happened?"

"Let's get to the trail and down to the shore before they search the perimeter."

The sound of a man screaming caught my attention and I glanced back over my shoulder to see one of the men run toward the helicopter, his clothes a ball of fire. Another man tackled him and must have rolled him around. I didn't see the third man.

We continued cautiously down the hill until we found the trail. To the left was Great Harbor and Foxy's. To the right was White Bay and Soggy Dollar.

A sudden burst of machine gun fire tore into the evening sky.

"Buck Reilly! Where are you?!"

The voice was distant and had an accent. I was certain it was the man who'd boarded our boat in Soper's Hole: Jacques.

Another burst of gunfire.

Giselle grabbed my hand.

"Welcome to the underground," I said. "Let's get the hell out of here."

26

THE PATH WAS ROCKY BUT WE MADE FAST PROGRESS. A few men had come running up the hill past us, but they were locals rushing to see what had happened to the cottage. We said we didn't know but were afraid of the fire, so we were running away.

The burning cottage was visible during our entire descent. A loud roar sounded—the helicopter—as it took off and made a beeline south back toward Tortola or St. Thomas. At least one of the men onboard required immediate medical attention. Had others stayed behind to hunt us? I wasn't going to wait around and find out. It was already past dusk and I was worried Foxy wouldn't wait, so I kept as quick a pace as the dim light and uneven footing allowed.

The trail ended in a wide patch of sea grape just above the beach. We waded through the low plants until we stood on the white sand. Small groups of people were scattered around, all staring up the hill at the cottage still aflame. Dry arid islands like Jost Van Dyke were always vulnerable to fires, and I hoped and prayed the coral field around the cottage would keep the fire from spreading.

Giselle and I walked down to the water's edge.

"Now what?" Her voice was a whisper.

I took her hand and continued slowly toward the far end, where I knew Soggy Dollar to be. Several boats filled the harbor, and there were nearly a dozen dinghies beached on the sand, some of which had people standing near them. We walked toward them as if we belonged—just another couple out for an evening stroll after a day of cruising the local waters and beach bars.

On one beached dinghy, a man with a big smile caught my attention—what the heck? I knew him. It was Nick Norman, a friend and my favorite singer-songwriter from Key West. The pretty woman in the bikini next to him was his wife, Kelly, her long, wavy hair the color of summer wheat and her skin tawny and gold from the sun. Coincidence, or had our luck changed?

Nick saw me and nodded as we approached.

I bent my head toward Giselle. "These are friends of mine ahead. They've seen us, we can't hide."

She squeezed my hand tighter.

"Hey, man," Nick said. "You looking for a ride?"

Kelly gave me a hug. "Funny seeing you here," she said, and then smiled at Giselle and hugged her too as if they were old friends.

They'd certainly have seen the news, but they paid Giselle no special attention. My mouth must have been hanging open because Nick patted me on the shoulder and nodded toward the dinghy.

"Did an old gray fox send you?" I said.

He laughed. "That's right, brother. Climb aboard."

Finding friends from home here was surreal. I didn't even know they knew Foxy. Nick and Kelly pushed the dinghy deeper into the water.

"How far are we going on that?" Giselle said.

"Just out past these other boats to Foxy's," Kelly said. "Only take a couple minutes."

Nick climbed aboard and lowered the outboard. Giselle boarded and I followed. With a twinkle in her eye, Kelly pushed us out waist deep and then pulled herself onto the boat over the bow. The engine started right up and Nick swung us around and pointed the dinghy out to sea. As he weaved his way slowly around anchored boats, he nodded back toward the island.

"Where's Foxy?"

"He was afraid he'd attract attention on the beach." Nick nodded back toward the island. "Hell of a fire up there," Nick said.

"Ah, yeah, pretty crazy," I said. No need to put them in greater danger by telling them what happened.

Bioluminescence swirled around the dinghy as we passed slowly through White Bay. The moon was bright on the horizon, and the stars had already begun to emerge.

"Beautiful night," Giselle said.

"Almost every night's like this," Kelly said. "No place I'd rather be."

There were sails in silhouette, a sailor's sky turning red. I could imagine toasts being made all around the harbor.

"Adios, Jost," I said.

"You mean, until we meet again," Giselle said.

I exhaled a long breath as we passed the last of the boats in the bay. The ball of flame on top of the hill had subsided, but red ashes and a column of smoke still rose into the night sky. I scanned the horizon ahead and saw only one other boat. It was a sleek silver center console with a small forward cabin, maybe thirty-four feet long. Nick must have read my thoughts.

"That's where we're headed," he said.

The name on the transom was Silver Fox. Giselle squeezed my hand, told me she saw the same thing.

"Ahoy there!" a voice came from the back of the ship. It was Foxy. He waved to us.

Foxy tossed us a line, which Kelly grabbed and pulled us in.

"Said I'd get you back to St. John," Foxy said.

He reached out and helped Kelly aboard and then did the same for Giselle.

"You have a lovely boat," she said.

"Gets me around."

The boat was unlike any other center console I'd ever seen. Long and broad, there was a row of four seats behind three other seats at the helm. A small cabin was below the helm and the bow was open. He must use it to transport supplies and people. Nick and I pulled the dinghy onto the back deck.

"Nick's doing a show on White Bay tomorrow," Foxy said. "You both being from Key West, I thought he might know you. Go below so you can stay out of sight."

Giselle and I followed him inside the salon, where reggae music played—Ziggy Marley. Foxy came down, opened a cupboard and poured some of his own brand of rum over ice in a few glasses.

"What happened up the hill?" he said.

"Pretty sure your bartender ratted us out for a reward."

"Benji?" Foxy's pervasive smile turned cold.

"Helicopter came in fast and men with guns stormed the cabin." I paused. "Had to improvise."

Ziggy sang about love being his religion. Foxy's face showed no love at the news.

"I'll deal with him," he said.

"Benji knew you were coming to get us. The helicopter may return," I said.

"Let's go," Foxy said.

Within moments we were aimed out to sea and moving at speed across the wake, slicing calmly through. We stayed below. Foxy took the helm, and Nick and Kelly came down.

"What's the latest news?" I said.

His big smile returned but his eyes were serious. "A ton of speculation over you two: why you disappeared, your relationship, when you'll reappear."

"Any statements from the French government?" Giselle said. "Like maybe why my husband said I was dead?"

Nick nodded. "An official statement that your body hadn't been recovered, but since everyone else had died in the crash, they assumed you'd been killed, too."

"How convenient. Even though they'd said I'd been cremated."

"Any more news about why the helicopter crashed?" I said.

"Just that it had had mechanical problems," Nick said.

"Mechanical problems?" Giselle said.

I put my hand on hers. "Let's not go there, okay? Out of respect for our friends' well-being?"

Nick looked from me to Giselle and back.

"There are people hunting Giselle—and me, actually—who could do us harm." We'd already put them in danger, so they deserved to know the situation, but too much information would increase their risk. "It's best we don't share all the details."

He nodded, his eyes still serious, but he smiled, too. "I'm not worried about it. We have a lot of friends in these islands, and we'll help you any way we can."

Giselle smiled broadly. "Thank you."

"We'll get you on-island as fast as possible," Kelly said. "I have a friend with a guesthouse in Peter Bay where you can stay and regroup." He paused. "Do you have a plan?"

I turned to Giselle. "We do have some options but need to finalize how to proceed."

Nick nodded. "We'll leave you two alone. I'll let you know once we're nearly there."

"What about clearing Customs?"

"Not a problem. Foxy said he can call it in."

With that they left us alone.

Giselle's eyes narrowed. "You told them we have options."

"I didn't want to tell them what we really had in mind." I paused. "Is that still what you want to do?"

"Yes. As soon as possible." There was no smile on her face now. "Will Foxy and your friends help us with that?"

"We can't ask them. I have people in mind who are more appropriate for that kind of work."

"Not your friend at the FBI?" she said.

"He's not my friend, and no—the people I'm thinking of are on the opposite end of the spectrum from the FBI, believe me." I studied her eyes, which were gravely serious. "Are you sure you're comfortable going down that road?"

She nodded slowly. "I've been cheated on, lied to, shot down. Now we're being hunted and these men will kill us if they get the chance." Her jaw quivered, but it was out of anger, not fear. "I'm already down that path, and I want answers, not a bureaucratic inquiry through the French courts that will take months and produce nothing but lies."

I held up my glass of Foxy's Firewater rum. "Cheers to that."

27

"MY FRIEND SAID YOU COULD USE THE HOUSE ON THE POINT AS LONG as you need to," Kelly said.

The Silver Fox hovered in neutral, a hundred yards off the shore near Peter Bay.

"Can't thank you guys enough," I said.

Giselle hugged Foxy and kissed him on each cheek. When she stepped back, I saw him smiling widely. "We owe you and won't forget," she said.

"Together in good times, together in need. I know you'll be here to help us when we need you, too," he said.

"Count on it," I said.

Kelly gave us each a hug, and then Nick loaded us into the dinghy and took us to the beach below Peter Bay Estates.

"There's a key in the conch shell by the front door," he said.

We thanked him, agreed to connect when—*if*—we got back to Key West, and the moment Giselle and I were off the dinghy, Nick put the engine in reverse, swung around, and headed back to the Silver Fox. Giselle took me by the arm, and rather than rushing up the rocky path toward the West Indian-styled home built into the boulders above the shore, she spun me back to face the water and blackness of night.

"Have you ever seen so many stars?"

Her ability to enjoy the moment amid all she'd been through and still faced continued to amaze me. She was more able to live in the moment than anyone I'd ever known. That reality tugged at my heart and I put my arm around her waist.

She leaned her head against my shoulder.

I turned and kissed her slowly. The sound of waves lapping onto the beach was mixed with the breeze that rustled palm fronds behind us. Our kiss lingered and she squeezed me closer.

I no longer thought of who she'd been—I was now lost in who she was.

She pushed me back. "Did you see that?"

"My eyes were closed."

Her giggle gave me a tingle down my spine.

"I like to watch you when we kiss," she said. "There was a huge shooting star!"

There was a light on in the home on the bluff, and it beckoned as a place of refuge. "Come on, let's go."

Steps were carved into the gray coral pathway that curved fifty feet above the beach. A gate blocked our entry to the walkway beyond it, but it wasn't locked. Another hundred feet up the landscaped path was the front door to a beautiful cut-stone two-story home. Giselle tried the handle.

"It's locked."

Among the planters with red firecracker bushes and red crotons was a large conch shell, and as Nick had said, there was a key tucked inside. Once the door was open, we stepped in and walked around the house. Giselle marveled at the furnishings while I checked to make sure the windows and doors were locked.

"Simple yet elegant," she said.

"And secure."

There were three bedrooms—two on the first floor and one on the second, where we dropped our bags on a chair. A lot of Caribbean homes have separate freestanding bedrooms with a central kitchen/great room, but this one was more self-contained.

There was a large-screen television on the wall, which Giselle turned on and tuned to CNN. Once commercials for St. Thomas car rentals, a restaurant, and a boat charter company were finished, Anderson Cooper's face filled the screen. I had an instant sense of foreboding.

The initial story was an update on the increasingly muddy political landscape surrounding the upcoming American election. We suffered through that to see what was next—which turned out to be a photograph of Giselle and me as we fled the hotel on Tortola, hand in hand.

Crap.

Giselle turned up the volume.

"The first lady of France, Giselle Huibert, and her companion Charles Reilly III were last seen aboard a catamaran registered in Reilly's name, leaving Cane Garden Bay on Tortola shortly after these photos were taken. The boat was later found abandoned, and authorities believe Huibert and Reilly left aboard a dinghy that had been the catamaran's lifeboat."

Giselle sat on the end of the bed. I sat next to her.

"There's been no sign of them since that time and it's unclear whether they remain on Tortola in hiding, fled the island by some other means, or have sought government assistance."

"Not the latter, that's for sure," Giselle said.

"President Huibert has released a statement grateful to learn that his wife is still alive and apologizing for the incorrect announcement of her death, citing Coast Guard officials' belief that she was lost in the Caribbean Sea when her helicopter sank. No information about why the helicopter crashed has yet been made public, with authorities stating that it's an active investigation."

"Charles B. Reilly III, better-known as Buck Reilly, was a world-renowned archaeologist and treasure hunter who, although his company e-Antiquity went bankrupt several years ago, is credited with major finds including the tomb of the Mayan Serpent King in Guatemala, where aside from vast riches, the most detailed codex of Mayan history was discovered. These documents, dubbed the Reilly Codex, have proven invaluable to scholars, filling in wide gaps in heretofore unknown details about Mayan history.

"Reilly was briefly married to supermodel Heather Drake, seen here with Reilly's former partner, Jack Dodson, who served five years for fraud and criminal activity that led to the demise of e-Antiquity. Drake and Dodson, now together, declined to be interviewed."

"Good grief," I said. "They'll leave no stone unturned, Giselle. I hope you know that."

She grunted and flung a wrist toward the television. "After living in the public eye for almost twenty years, I have nothing to hide." She glanced at me.

I held my hands up.

"Yes, I was a treasure hunter, and I do have a few skeletons in the closet, I'm afraid."

Her scrutiny of my face lasted several seconds.

"But you're not a criminal, Buck, I'm certain of that."

"Some may disagree, but no, I have never been convicted of a crime."

She shook her head. "It's not like we planned this and ran off together. You saved my life, and now we've fallen for one another."

"Buck Reilly syndrome."

She slapped my shoulder. "My feelings for you are not because you saved my life!"

Feelings?

"I see in you a man of action, honor, integrity—former treasure hunter or not—a man that I trust and have come to care for, deeply."

A flood of emotion laid me back on the bed. I rubbed my eyes.

"I'm sorry if that upsets you—"

I sat back up. "It does *not* upset me, Giselle. It's just all been so sudden. This is the first moment I've felt we were safe in the past few days."

She scooted away from me. "So you're saying this has happened too fast."

"Whoa, whoa, whoa, I'm not saying anything like that." I edged over next to her and brushed the hair off her forehead. "I care for you, too. It's hard to believe we didn't even know each other until a few days ago. But we have to stay sharp, vigilant—we can't let our guards down."

She stood quickly. "Of course we cannot—"

KNOCK, KNOCK, KNOCK!

The sudden knocking on the front door downstairs froze the words in Giselle's throat. I jumped up and glanced out the window but could see nothing.

"Maybe it's Nick and Kelly checking to see if we need anything," I said. "Wait here. I'll let them know we're good."

Giselle crossed her arms as I hurried down the stairs. My gut was twisted, from both our conversation and the sudden knocking on the door.

I peered out through the peephole, and what I saw nearly caused me to pee my pants.

SECTION 4

TURNABOUT IS FAIR PLAY

28

KNOCK! KNOCK! KNOCK!

The pounding grew more insistent.

Son of a bitch!

I looked up the staircase. "Stay upstairs!" My voice was an urgent whisper.

"What's the matter?" she said.

KNOCK, KNOCK, KNOCK, KNOCK!

"I'll take care of it," I said.

"Buck?"

I went back to the front door. Thoughts raced through my head as I reached for the handle.

KNOCK, KNOCK.

I pulled the door open.

Special Agent Edward T. Booth of the Federal Bureau of Investigation stood in front of me with three other men, all dressed in dark slacks, white shirts, and blue blazers.

"Well, well, well, look what we have here," Booth said. "The man of the moment, international playboy—"

"What the hell do you want, Booth?"

He stepped toward me, but I held my hands up to block his entry.

"You know what I want, Reilly. Where is she?"

"I've broken no laws here. You can't just walk inside—"

"The first lady of France is missing, hotshot, and was last seen with you of all people, fleeing a seedy hotel in the British Virgin Islands. I'm authorized to do whatever needs to be done to ensure her safety."

I heard a commotion behind me and watched Booth's eyes go wide.

"How dare you barge in here barking insults!" Giselle shouted from behind me.

A rat could have hidden in Booth's mouth, it was opened so wide.

"I'm sorry, ma'am."

She was now next to me with her fists balled on her hips. "Who are you and what business do you have here?"

I almost laughed at her in her shorts and T-shirt, suntanned, hair down and looking quite sexy as she dressed Booth down.

"Excuse me, ma'am, but I'm Special Agent—"

"I heard your name and will convey it directly to the president of the United States if you don't change your tone immediately."

Booth held his hands up and stared at the floor as if he were trying not to provoke a vicious dog—was that federal training in how to kowtow to a foreign dignitary? The other agents shuffled in place and glanced at each other.

Booth cleared his throat, stretched his neck taller, and lowered his hands slowly.

"I'm terribly sorry, Madame Huibert, but this is an international incident of the utmost concern to our government—"

"I would certainly hope so!" Giselle said.

"Once we determined your location—"

"My helicopter was shot down—innocent people murdered, my friend and assistant Jennifer Gascoin included!"

"Shot down?" Booth said. "You're certain?"

Giselle stepped forward and I thought she might slap him, but she leaned in close to him instead.

"I was on the damn thing! I saw a rocket flash through the air, strike the front of the helicopter—then all went black. I'd say I'm quite certain."

The agents shuffled around again, one glancing over his shoulder.

"May we come inside, ma'am?" Booth said. "We don't want to draw attention to you here."

Giselle stepped aside. "You have five minutes."

Once they were inside I closed the door. We made no move to go sit on the pair of couches twenty feet away. Booth caught the grin I was trying to hide, and his lips pressed thin until they turned white.

"This is incredible news, Madame Huibert—"

"Has there been no forensic analysis of my helicopter? Your experts could not deduce that the front had been blown off?"

"As a matter of fact, representatives from the United States have been denied access to the helicopter because you were supposedly killed on it."

"Denied access?" she said. "By whom?"

I recognized the smug squint in Booth's eyes before he spoke. "The French government, of course. Your husband has forbidden any access to the warehouse where your helicopter has been stored, claiming it as sovereign ground."

Giselle's lip quivered and her eyes welled up.

"How the hell did you find us here, Booth?" I said.

He turned toward me. "You're not very good at being an international fugitive, Reilly."

"What's that supposed to mean?"

"Foxy's? Soggy Dollar? Your usual haunts? Seriously? All we had to do was monitor phone traffic until a call was made this afternoon and your names were mentioned. We didn't have time to get to Jost Van Dyke, but we monitored all boats coming and going—and true to your MO, you enlisted the help of another musician to save your skin." Booth glanced quickly at Giselle. "So if we could find you, I'm guessing others could, too."

Damn.

Booth turned back to Giselle, no doubt anxious to maintain the upper hand but also hesitant. "And once your helicopter crashed into the Caribbean Sea, how did you come to meet Mr. Reilly?"

Giselle bit her lip. She didn't do this out of fear. I'd already come to recognize some of her mannerisms.

"He saved my life. If it weren't for Buck, I would have drowned."

"So you are here voluntarily, of your own will?" Booth said.

Giselle laughed. I felt her hand reach around my waist and pull me close. She kissed my cheek.

"Your five minutes are up," she said.

Booth's eyes nearly popped out of his head. "Madame Huibert, please!"

"We've done nothing wrong."

"Your life is at risk—both of your lives! Why would someone shoot you down? We can't just walk away—you're the first lady of France, for goodness sake! What am I supposed to tell the director of the FBI, who's already briefed the president?"

Giselle stepped toward Booth again. "You tell them nothing!"

"I can't do that—"

"Giselle, please," I said.

"Your president will call François—"

"Giselle—"

"And his men will come—"

"Honey, wait!" I said.

She stepped back, glanced at all of us, and nodded. "I'm going upstairs. Please tell them what happened, on the condition of complete and total confidentiality. Nobody can call my husband, his security people, or report anything about finding us."

With that she stormed back upstairs.

"'Honey'?" Booth said. "What the fuck is going on here, Reilly? Are you kidding me?"

"She says her husband and Alphonse Zidane, his head of security, blew up the helicopter."

"Why the hell would they do that?"

I looked at the other agents, who stood silently listening to our every word.

"Please have them wait outside," I said.

All eyes turned to Booth.

"Fine. Go ahead, guys. Wait for me outside."

They filed out, doing their best to keep straight faces, but one shook his head in disbelief. Once the door closed, I turned back to Booth.

"Per her wishes, do we have your word for complete confidentiality?"

"Are you freaking kidding me? Yes, sure. I'll have to tell the director, but depending on what you tell me next, we wouldn't call a suspected murderer, now would we?"

"I don't know, Booth. Weird shit happens in diplomatic circles."

He held his right hand over his heart and held his left hand up like a Boy Scout. "You have my word, Reilly. Now—what the fuck?"

"Short story, really. Giselle was on a junket with the other first ladies in attendance at the G8 summit, but she didn't feel well, so she returned to the hotel where the French contingent and her husband were staying—"

"Frenchman's Reef," he said.

"She walked in and went straight to their suite. In the bedroom, her husband was having sex with an underage girl."

"That's it?" Booth's brow furrowed. "These French—"

"And they were being filmed by Zidane."

Booth squinted. "Kinky."

"Worse than kinky. She fled and was chased all the way to the airport, but she'd phoned her assistant, who had their helicopter waiting to whisk them over to Beef Island Airport, where the presidential plane was supposed take her back to France. Halfway to Tortola, a rocket shot the helicopter down, killing everyone but Giselle."

Booth shook his head. "And you just happened to be there?"

"About a mile away, spearfishing. I'd just climbed aboard my dinghy—saw the white streak, the explosion, watched the damn helicopter drop out of the sky. I hauled ass over, and as Giselle said, the front of the chopper was blown off. I got to her seconds before it sank."

"And she wasn't injured?"

"Big gash on her head, unconscious. Had amnesia when she came to on the dinghy and even back at my sailboat. Her memory didn't return until the next day—after people we're sure were affiliated with her husband's security team came searching for my boat at Soper's Hole on Tortola."

"I know where it is."

"They told me about the helicopter accident and that the first lady of France was onboard and missing. I about shit my pants. I didn't even know who she was until then. We've been on the run ever since."

"Why didn't you call the police?"

"She wouldn't let me. Her concern is that any local police would want to alert the French security force, or even the press. She's terrified."

Booth grimaced. "Didn't seem too scared to me ... honey."

"She wants answers, Booth. Help us by keeping this quiet and I'll keep you close, make sure you're there when she blows this wide open."

"I'm not interested in the French president being a pedophile."

"But you're drooling over nailing the French president for killing those people on the helicopter and conspiring to murder his wife—on American territory."

Booth glanced around the house. "This is a huge mess, Reilly. And again, if we could find you, the bad guys can, too. I can't just let you two stroll off into the sunset."

"Let me talk to her. I have a burner cell and I'll call you, but get the hell out of here now. If we're tailed or monitored she'll freak. It'll blow up in your face, I promise you that."

Booth chewed at the side of his mouth. "I can get satellite coverage—"

"You'd have to explain why you wanted it. Just keep your phone handy. You'll be the first call I make, and hopefully soon. I know this is over my head."

"That's an understatement."

I bit my lip. I wanted Booth to think I needed him, and I also wanted to hide our real plans from him. The fastest way to get Giselle to safety was to help her learn the truth. I had a plan and the kind of friends who could make it happen.

"I'll dig deeper into Zidane," Booth said. "I already told you about his ties to the French Foreign Legion."

"But you didn't dig any deeper when I told you to—"

"Buck?" Giselle's voice called down the steps. "Are those men still here?"

"Special Agent Booth is leaving now," I said.

"This is crazy, Reilly," Booth said.

"Do your job, Booth."

"That would be to arrest you and take her into custody."

"In the shit storm that would follow, you would take the fall in grandiose fashion." I paused. "Trust me."

He grunted. "Shit."

He shook his head again and walked out the front door. The other agents stood there waiting. He waved them down the path, and the one who'd shown frustration before stood staring at me for a long moment. I closed the door and slid the bolt lock into place.

Shit was right.

29

"WILL THEY LEAVE US ALONE?" GISELLE SAID.
We were seated on the bed upstairs. The TV was off, thankfully.

"Not for long. They can't."

"I don't want to be rescued by the FBI, Buck. Not yet. What can we do?"

"I have a plan, but it'll involve some less than stellar local citizens."

"I'm okay with that if it helps me prove that François is a sick murdering bastard."

"I can't promise that. And even if I can persuade these guys to help, it won't be out of the goodness of their hearts."

"I have money—now that I'm alive again. François can't freeze my accounts."

"We'll see." I turned to face her. My palms were clammy. I hated to go this route but knew no other way, given Giselle's refusal to work with the authorities—any authorities.

"I'm sorry for getting you in the middle of all this—and for being so difficult." She scratched my back.

"I'm going downstairs to make a couple calls. I'd rather not have you know the details or be involved with what I'm going to set up."

She stopped scratching but leaned over and kissed me. I kept my eyes open this time, as she did. Hers fluttered.

Back downstairs I checked all the windows and doors again. Would Booth be using microphones to eavesdrop on us? While I was sure he'd have liked to, I doubted he'd have come to Peter Bay with that type of equipment. I scrolled through names and numbers on my personal phone, found the ones I hoped would be of assistance, selected Diego Francis, and dialed his number on the burner.

Diego was a St. John-based drug and arms smuggler I'd met a few years ago while helping Crystal Thedford search for her kidnapped husband. Diego had wanted to use my flying boat, but when a Russian competitor moved in hard on his territory, Diego helped me as a way to get to him.

After three rings, a voice answered. "Hello?" It was a woman.

"Is Diego there?"

"Who is it?" Her voice was less than friendly.

Based on how Booth had tracked me, any of my former acquaintances—I'd never considered them friends—might also be monitored. I decided not to take chances.

"Tell him it's the guy from a few years ago that took him on a Russian billionaire's yacht."

"Say what? Is this some kind of—oh, wait, you're the guy in the news."

"Yes, but don't mention my name, please."

"Hang on."

A rustling sound caused me to hold the phone away from my ear. A male voice registered a second later.

"You gotta be kiddin' me."

"Long time no talk to, Diego. How you been?"

"I been better. Lucky you caught me now, man. Seen your shit all over the place here, brotha. What the hell? You always chasing married women around, eh?"

His reference to Crystal Thedford made me smile. When a body was found and misidentified as her husband, we'd shared a bed and nearly made love. But then we found the missing husband, Diego and I got shot, and Matt Hoggatt wrote a song about me called "The Ballad of Buck Reilly." What a life.

"So it seems," I said. "But this married woman is different."

He laughed. "It's always different. Mine, too, right baby?" His voice was muffled as he said something to the woman who'd answered the phone. Then he came back on the line. "So I'm guessing you need help again—something that'll get me shot up like last time?"

"That's why you're so good at what you do," I said. "Your intuition is always spot-on."

"Nah, lost my touch, brotha. After our little adventure few years back, Babylon made it their mission to get my ass, and they did. Red-handed with a load of guns and blow. Sentencing is next week. I'm out on bail, lookin' at fifteen to twenty, so don't count on me doing anything to make that worse."

Babylon, meaning the police. Damn.

"I'm sorry to hear that. Local matter?"

"Nah, man. Feds. Hell of a sting in international waters. Must have been fifty of the bastards."

"Ouch. Been to that amusement park, got the T-shirt," I said.

"Yeah, but *you* got off."

An idea popped into my head that sent me pacing around the living room. "Well, maybe you can get off, too."

"The hell you sayin', boy? Game's already over, guilty as charged. Just waiting on the other shoe to drop on my prison sentence."

"How about if I could arrange a presidential pardon?"

"The fuck?"

"You've obviously seen the news. The black jackets are on the case here, and there's a whole lot more to the story than what's been on TV, trust me. You help me—us—they'll owe you, *brotha*."

For a moment, the only sound on the other end of the line was breathing.

"That's rich, man, but how the hell you think you gonna deliver?"

"We have a plan and need help, but it'll require a few more people, too. We can keep you out of the middle, but I'll make sure you get credit if we're successful."

"You got the others lined up?"

"That's one of the things I need you to do," I said.

"Shit. Nobody'll help me now, man, scared I'm setting them up to save my own ass."

"The beauty is that you won't be doing anything illegal. Just working logistics."

"Logistics, huh? You know the guy flying the plane or driving the truck gets busted, too. Who else you got in mind?"

"Assuming you still have a few guys under your employ, like maybe Brass Knuckles, who cold-cocked me? Few more on your team, and same on the other team."

"Yeah, he's still around, but he's waiting on sentencing for the same shit, too."

"So he gets the same deal as you if we succeed."

"What do you mean about this other team?"

This next step was as delicate as tiptoeing through a minefield—blindfolded. The other guy I'd met here before who stepped up to help—thanks again to the Russian billionaire who came down hard on his operation—was St. Thomas-based Boom-Boom Burke. But Boom-Boom and Diego had been sworn enemies, competitors who reluctantly came together to help me help them get rid of the Russian. Whether that détente had survived, I'd soon find out.

"I was hoping you could reach out to Boom-Boom."

"You crazy, man? He's still my chief competitor here. Our alliance went up in smoke once he got back to St. Thomas. We'd sooner kill each other than work together."

I thought about it for a second. "Maybe Boom-Boom could use a get-out-of-jail-free card, too. And I need him to get three other people to help as well." I paused. "And we'll pay both of you guys for your time."

"My time? Shit, man. The time I got left out of stir is worth more than all the money in the world."

"Unless you help my lady and get that pardon."

Diego laughed into phone. "You got me curious, man, I'll give you that. Tell me what you have in mind and we'll see."

So I did.

It took a few minutes of double-talk and guarded description, but to his credit, Diego got it. He'd made a living out of being a high stakes gambler. Any smuggler did, whether they ran drugs, guns, whatever. He was smart—he'd just chosen to use his brains in illegal efforts. Even I could appreciate the draw of fast cash, and for a poor kid from Charlotte Amalie who'd never have a shot as an entrepreneur, it was probably as good an option as any. Until he got nailed.

"That is rich, man," he said when I finished. "You just as crazy as ever—worse even. Didn't think that was possible."

"Simple yet effective, no laws broken on the front end—"

"Keep me outta that back end, brotha. Let Boom-Boom stick his thick black neck out on that." Diego paused. "You really think you can get me that pardon?"

"My lady will help make the case, guaranteed."

"You're *lady*, huh?" He paused a long minute. "Okay, I'm in. What the hell. Might as well use the time I got left to try and do what my lawyers couldn't. Pardon, huh? Shit yeah."

I pumped my fist like I'd just thrown a touchdown pass in the Super Bowl.

"Call Boom-Boom, make nice, and I'll hope to see you like we discussed. If you don't show, I'll know it didn't work out."

"I'm on it." He paused. "Tell your lady I'm looking forward to meeting her."

"You got it."

We disconnected. With that piece of the puzzle in place, I had to get others set up or we'd be leaving half-cocked. I smiled before making the next call, knowing it would be met with astonishment.

The phone rang twice, and the familiar voice answered.

"Hello?"

"Ray, it's me—don't say my name!"

"Bu—what the fuck? What the hell is going on?"

I'd put Ray Floyd, my aviation mechanic, partner, and friend, in more difficult situations over the years than I cared to admit, but I was convinced he secretly enjoyed it.

"Too much to explain right now."

"Is it all true?" His voice was breathless.

"I don't even know what they're saying. Some yes, but if there's any speculation that I, er, we did something wrong, that's bullshit."

"Ah, yeah, there's plenty of speculation to that effect."

"Okay, we need to make this quick. Everyone I know is being monitored by either the feds or the Frogs, and the latter definitely mean us harm."

"What can I do?"

God bless Ray.

"Need you to make some calls for me, set up a few things."

I gave him the details of what I needed to have done, and he took it all down without question.

"I've got the Beauty gassed-up and ready to go. Just been waiting on you."

"They'll be watching the plane, and probably you, but yeah, get down to St. Thomas and wait for instructions."

We discussed that in a little more detail, and again he was champing at the bit. No bitching or admonitions, which was rare for him. The news must really have been bad on television.

"Be safe, Bu...rother."

"Thanks, friend. That's the goal."

We hung up, and for the first time in days I felt like I was finally getting ahead of the curve. I'd much rather have been on attack than on defense, even if I was outgunned: one nuclear superpower vs. Last Resort Charter and Salvage's two antique airplanes. Plus I had Giselle Huibert, the granddaughter of a World War II French partisan, a couple of drug smugglers, and a promotion-hungry FBI agent.

How could we go wrong?

30

GISELLE AND I HURRIED DOWN THE PATH in the predawn light. Either Diego would be there and we'd move on to the next stage of the plan or Booth would show back up with his ass freshly chewed out and demand to take us into custody. His thirst for success would buy us time, but those other blue blazer boys would eventually go over his head, sell us out to CNN, or turn us over to the French.

I stopped at the gate, which was a good vantage point, and searched up the hill to the luxury community of Peter Bay Estates to our right, then down to the beach and over the water to our left. There was no sign of anybody, friend or foe.

Damn.

I hoped Diego didn't let us down.

"Looks clear." Giselle's voice was a whisper.

I smiled in the darkness. She was as game as they came and her motivation undeniable. I'd finally explained the plan over coffee thirty minutes ago and she loved it.

"Let's get to the beach," I said. "Be careful, a twisted ankle would ruin everything."

I continued through the gate and walked slowly down the cut-stone path. Giselle walked behind me with her hands on my shoulders. We took our time, still ten minutes early for the rendezvous. Stars were fading and an orange line lit the eastern horizon as the sun prepared to rise.

No sooner did our feet touch the sand than the sound of a boat caught my attention. No, not *a* boat—several boats. Giselle squeezed my biceps and pressed her body close to mine. She was shaking—was it from the cool air or nerves?

"No matter what happens, thank you, Buck." Her voice was a whisper.

I spotted four boats approaching the beach, side by side, no lights.

It was either Booth, Algerian assassins, or an arms and drug smuggler hoping to save his ass by saving ours.

At a hundred feet away, I couldn't see any detail. Fifty feet away I saw a lone man in each boat. My heart raced.

A flashlight lit from the center boat and slashed through the air until it settled on us. The boats drew closer, their engines producing a quiet rumble. I held my hand up to block the light and it was extinguished. We took a step back as the boats—none more than thirty-five feet in length—coasted onto the sandy shore.

One man stood up in the boat that had shone the light in our faces. His dark silhouette climbed over the side and splashed into the light surf. My stomach clenched—there wasn't enough light to discern features.

"Right on time, Reilly."

Diego Francis.

I exhaled with a whistle. I'd forgotten how short he was, but muscular and with a smile so big it lit the dark beach.

He walked up to us and lit the flashlight but kept his palm partially over the lens. Once he was in front of us, Giselle squeezed my biceps harder.

"*Madame Huibert, enchanté. Je m'appelle* Diego Francis." He extended his hand, and she let go of my arm to accept it.

"*Enchanté.*"

"Is everything as we discussed?" I said.

Diego now extended his hand toward me and I shook it. "Did you doubt me?"

"Boom-Boom?"

"Getting in position now." Diego glanced back toward Giselle. "*Nous devrions partir, maintenant.*"

"*Bonne,*" Giselle said. "*Allons.*"

French was the one foreign language I knew fairly well. Go figure.

"Yes, let's go," I said. "Which boat should we get in?"

"Mine," Diego said.

"Thought you wanted to stay out of the middle."

"Always ready to help a beautiful woman in peril." His teeth gleamed in the early light.

He led us to his boat, which when I got around its side I realized was a thirty-five foot Contender with triple three hundred-horsepower engines on back. Diego sat on the port gunwale and climbed aboard first and then turned to take Giselle's hand. I helped boost her onto the boat and then jumped aboard and swung my legs onto the deck.

Giselle sat on the bench seat in back and pulled a blanket folded there over her. I stood next to Diego as he signaled his associates—all had dreadlocks. We backed slowly out until Diego could spin the boat around, and then we waited for the others to turn around as well.

"See you at Woody's tonight," he said to his men. With that he pressed the throttle forward, as did his associates. One quickly turned his boat to the northwest, another turned north, and one followed us to the east.

If Booth—or anyone else for that matter—was monitoring our location with drones or eyeballs, there was no way they could keep track of four boats all leaving at the same moment.

A state-of the art display of electronic gear, GPS, radar, tempera-ture, oil, depth—everything you needed—glowed a subtle orange that was visible but didn't hurt the eyes in low light. The boat sliced through the water with ease and I hoped the light wind and surf portended a mild crossing. I had questions for Diego but didn't want to scream over the roar of the nine hundred HP behind us. Giselle was smiling, so I sat next to her, crawled under the blanket, and slipped my arm around her shoulder. She pressed in tight. I could feel the chill of the morning on her skin.

Diego glanced back and smiled.

Once we passed between Mary Point and Whistling Cay, the third boat cut northeast, probably heading for Tortola. Fifteen minutes later we rounded the East End Point of St. John into a blazing orange sun.

Giselle and I donned sunglasses. Diego then changed course to the southeast—that left St. Croix as the only possible destination. After an hour, I could see it on the horizon.

Details of St. Croix began to come into focus. Diego's Contender took the bigger waves with grace, thanks largely to his deft handling of the throttle as we climbed over larger walls of water. Resort hotels lined parts of the beach, while other areas remained green or were dotted with modest homes. St. Croix was the largest of the U.S. Virgin Islands, with a population of fifty thousand and a far less robust flow of tourists.

In twenty more minutes, we were idling slowly as we approached a small hotel dock on the eastern end near Buck Island—no relation. No people were visible, but a four-door sedan was parked on the road near the end of the dock. I moved to the bow of the boat and took a line that had been spooled on the deck. Diego coasted slowly up to the wood-planked dock and subtly manipulated between forward and reverse until we sidled up right next to a cleat. I wrapped the bowline, and when I looked back I saw that Giselle had secured the stern.

When Diego turned off the engines, the numbing sound of the three massive outboards finally went silent. I glanced up and saw that a man had gotten out of the car—a huge man, black as night, his shaved head glistening in the morning sun.

Diego beckoned me back to the helm and the three of us huddled together.

"Thanks for making this happen, Diego," I said.

"As promised." He paused. Diego was anything but shy, but we weren't his usual business colleagues, and the terms were vastly different. "Everything else is in motion, too."

When he turned his gaze to Giselle, his brows lifted slowly. She radiated beauty in the soft light. I saw his Adam's apple bob as he swallowed.

Giselle stepped forward. "Buck told me about your situation."

Her eyes caught mine for a second. She'd not been happy about helping a convicted arms smuggler, but when I reminded her that the French underground had been full of rogues and villains as well as thought leaders, artists, and other people of questionable repute, she backed off.

"If we're successful, I will speak to the president of the United States on your behalf," she said.

"And my men?" Diego said.

"Of course—"

"And Boom-Boom and his men, too."

"Boom-Boom?" Giselle said.

Diego nodded toward the huge human moving slowly down the dock toward us. He looked larger than I remembered. He wasn't smiling.

"You all should jump off now, though, 'cause, ah, Boom-Boom and I are silent and very distant partners on this matter."

Giselle hugged Diego. "Thank you."

"My pleasure." He nodded toward me. "Watch this one. Gotta lot of heart, a ton of guts, but tends to get a little crazy when shit goes down."

Giselle smiled. "I'm counting on it."

31

BOOM-BOOM DROVE WEST TOWARD CHRISTIANSTED, ST. CROIX'S most populated city. The coastal road offered a beautiful panorama out over the Caribbean Sea to the north and lush verdant hills with flowering trees and vegetation to the south. Conversation had been minimal. What had I expected, a hug?

"Have you heard if anybody followed any of Diego's boats that picked us up on St. John?"

"No," Boom-Boom said.

"Does 'no' mean you haven't heard, or you did hear and nobody followed any of them?"

"Yes."

Giselle and I exchanged a glance.

"You got a lot to be nervous about, eh, brudda?" Boom-Boom said. "You, too, Queenie."

"I'm not a queen," Giselle said.

"Not no more," he said.

"Can you touch base with Diego and ask?"

"No. Dis be an operation. Need radio silence."

I didn't disagree, but I'd have liked to get a comprehensive report on our situation.

"That's smart," I said. "You've been luckier than Diego."

"Nothing to do with luck, brudda. I pay a lot of people for information. Gotta stay ahead of trouble. Know when to check in and when to stay low. Right now we stayin' low."

It reminded me of my e-Antiquity treasure hunting days. I'd paid lobbyists and informants all over the place who kept me apprised of political climates, changing winds, competitors, and sometimes even the whereabouts of police. Everyone wanted a piece of the action, whether from a treasure hunter or a smuggler. As an archaeologist, I liked to tell myself I was doing research in ancient cultures, but I knew that was bullshit. We always kept a huge chunk of our find, which, because we were a public company, was critical to showing growth and profit. At least Boom-Boom didn't have a board of directors, or investors whining about a return of their capital when stock tanked.

"Where are we headed?" I said.

"Meeting spot just before Christiansted."

Would Boom-Boom turn us in? Or kidnap us for ransom? Lord knows he was capable and had the connections. According to Diego, his empire had grown since I last saw him a few years ago. Had he branched out to more than weed? Was he into guns now—or, worse, human trafficking? I swallowed hard.

"Appreciate you helping us out—"

"Twenty-grand, Reilly."

"What?"

"Diego said you'd pay me twenty grand."

"He ..." I bit my tongue. As pretty as the view was, I didn't want to get dumped on the side of the road here. Giselle squeezed my hand and gave me a subtle nod. "That's the deal," I said. "Provided we get to our destination safely."

Boom-Boom laughed once. Then he popped a joint into his mouth and flicked a lighter, and the car quickly filled with smoke. I lowered my window. He handed the joint back toward Giselle.

She accepted it without hesitation and took a hit.

Good grief. "Pass," I said.

"More for me and Queenie," Boom-Boom said.

As he finished the joint, we pulled into a small marina by the Buccaneer Hotel. Palm trees lined the shore, sailboats dotted the horizon, and an old stone sugar mill reminiscent of the island's past stood nearby. Long waves lapped at the curved bay.

Boom-Boom parked the car in a small lot by the marina and opened his door. There were wires hanging out from under the steering wheel.

"This your car?" I said.

"Nope."

A stolen vehicle. Perfect.

Tied to the dock were four boats, different from the ones from this morning, but the plan was the same. If anyone was following us, we'd improve our odds by forcing them to choose one of four targets.

"Who are we riding with?" I said.

"Me," he said. "First boat on the right."

Were these boats stolen, too? If so, what if the police or the Coast Guard spotted us? The reality was we didn't have any choice.

Giselle had been quiet since we got in the car with Boom-Boom. I could feel her uneasiness. And even though Boom-Boom had been quiet, I was grateful that Diego had persuaded him to help. The plan I'd devised was playing out well, so far.

Boom-Boom's boat was a trawler. The other boats were a mix of center-console fishing boats, a speedboat that looked like it belonged in an offshore race, and a cabin cruiser. If they weren't stolen, they were probably part of Boom-Boom's smuggling fleet. They certainly were today, anyway.

"Get onboard," he said.

There was a gangplank, which I crossed first before reaching back to help Giselle. The trawler was probably thirty-six feet and at least forty years old but in decent condition. Once Giselle stepped onboard, a flash in the distance caught my eye.

Uh-oh. It was a police car with its lights on. The car stopped at the dock, near Boom-Boom's stolen car.

"Buck?" Giselle said.

"Get below, Reilly," Boom-Boom said.

"What are you going to do?"

"Spend more of your money," he said.

I followed Giselle into the cabin, which included a small galley, a head, and two staterooms. I steered her toward the forward stateroom.

"In here."

We entered the stateroom, which had a double bed and no decoration or personal touch. It smelled musty. There was a small porthole covered by a sun-faded blue curtain. I peeked out and saw a police officer walking up the dock toward the boat. Boom-Boom stood with his hands on his hips, waiting.

"Can we trust him?" Giselle said.

"Shouldn't, but he did help me before. And we have no choice."

I peeked outside and saw the men talking. The policeman smiled and nodded. He turned to look at the boat we were on. Boom-Boom said something else and the man nodded again.

"What's happening?" Giselle said.

"He's talking to the cop. He's handing him something—looks like a wad of cash. The cop looked both ways … He took it."

Boom-Boom said something else and the cop laughed. When Boom-Boom turned toward the boat, he was smiling, too.

A moment later we felt the Caterpillar diesel turn over and the deck vibrated below our feet. Once we'd cast off from the dock, I turned to Giselle.

"Wait here. I'm going to speak with the captain. Lock the door. I'll knock twice and then you can let me in."

Giselle's lips were pressed tight. She was a cool character, but we'd already covered a lot of miles, some of which we were about to backtrack. Before we got out to sea, I wanted to talk to Boom-Boom about the plan. From the stair that led to the deck, I saw the boats from the dock behind us in a line.

"Whatcha doin' up here, Reilly?" Boom-Boom said. "You get spotted, all this runnin' around's been a waste of my time and your money."

I stayed in the stairwell. "Can we talk about the plan?"

Boom-Boom turned to me, and a long few seconds played out.

"One a' dese boats is headed to Tortola, another to Virgin Gorda, another to Love City and we's goin' to Rock City."

Love City was St. John and Rock City was St. Thomas.

"And then? On Rock City?"

"We's getting picked up, then heading to a meeting place for next steps. Isn't that what you wanted?"

I wanted to call the police, but Boom-Boom wouldn't want to hear that.

"We're going to the hotel where the French delegation is staying," I said.

"Queenie going home?"

"Not exactly." I paused. "She wants answers—ones we can't get easily."

Boom-Boom arched his eyebrows. "Sounds like you need more than just a ride, Reilly."

"True, but I don't know what we'll be walking into, so I don't know what the hell we'll need."

Boom-Boom shook his head slowly. "I'll stick with you in Rock City. I'm good on the fly."

A warm sensation spread through my arms. "Thanks, Boom-Boom."

Now outside the channel from the marina, Boom-Boom added throttle. The bow of the big boat lifted momentarily but settled down on plane quickly. She wasn't fast, but she was steady.

"Now stay outta sight," he said.

"Roger, captain."

32

GISELLE AND I HAD BEEN LOCKED IN THE STATEROOM FOR AN HOUR, out in the middle of the Caribbean Sea. We were reclined on the bed, as there were no chairs in the room and the galley was uncomfortable.

"How much longer?" she said.

"Could be another hour. We're only doing around eight knots."

She rolled over to where I lay on my back and placed her hand on my chest. "So we have time?"

"Time for what?" I said.

Her hand moved slowly from my chest, to my stomach, to my crotch.

"Seriously?" I said.

"I'm antsy. It will stop me from worrying."

She nuzzled closer and buried her face in the side of my head. I felt her take my ear between her teeth. She gently chewed on it while her hand rubbed slowly over my shorts, which were getting tighter by the second. Was Giselle an insatiable lover due to her long stale marriage, because she was French, or because she found me irresistible? Or was this just how she suppressed anxiety?

I rolled toward her and our lips pressed together. My hand massaged her side over her shirt, then underneath it. She pulled at my belt, which came free, and then at the top button of my shorts—

BANG-BANG-BANG!

Someone was beating on the door. I sat up quickly, jumped to my feet, and pulled my belt tight.

At the door, I leaned closer to it.

"What's up?" I said.

"Open the door!" It was Boom-Boom.

I glanced back at Giselle, who sat on the edge of the bed, her hair wild. I unlocked the door and pulled it open.

"What's the matter?"

"One of Diego's guys called. Two of their boats were intercepted, including Diego's, as he returned to St. John."

"By who?"

"One by the FBI, and Diego by some French security people."

Damn!

"What did Diego say about the security people?"

"No way to know. They still got him."

"How did Diego's people know then?"

"Because one a' dem assholes called 'em. They're threatening to torture him. They know he helped you, but who knows what else."

"Shit!"

"The FBI stopped the other boat at Jost Van Dyke."

"Any issues?"

"Lots of questions from some fed named Booth who was cussing your name. These French assholes, they for real. Said they'd kill Diego if he didn't talk." Boom-Boom squinted. "Some serious shit, Reilly."

"None of them know where we're headed," I said.

He nodded. "Good, that's what I wanted to know."

"What else did the French people say?"

"Said they was taking him to St. Thomas. They want a swap—you and the queen for Diego."

I stared into Boom-Boom's impassive eyes. "And?"

"I don't give no shit about him, man. And you owe me money."

"What about his men?" Giselle said.

"They'd trade you in a heartbeat."

"We'll get him back," I said. "Can you tell them?"

"Sure."

Damn. Zidane's men were getting closer. Diego was supposed to get sentenced for smuggling in a few days. If he didn't show, they'd assume he ran and he'd be up shit's creek—if he were even alive at that point. And he helped us hoping for a pardon. Damn.

"How much longer?" Giselle said.

"Another twenty minutes we'll be at Red Hook. Good and busy there, so we can blend." He glanced back at Giselle, then at me. "I'll leave you two alone."

The door closed and I could hear his heavy feet tromp through the galley and back up the steps to the helm. I closed and re-locked the door.

"So the FBI was watching us," Giselle said.

"Good thing we left early. Poor Diego. We have to help him."

"François must be wondering why I haven't called my own news conference yet." Her eyes were aimed toward the floor, but I didn't have to see them to know they burned with the inner turmoil raging in her head.

"That's a good question."

She jerked her attention up toward me. "And you know the answer—I have no evidence, nothing." She paused. "He'll never expect me to go back to question people at the hotel, but they'll be leaving today, so we don't have any time to spare."

"And we need to help Diego."

"If we succeed they'll have no reason to hurt him." She jumped to her feet and began to pace the small cabin. I sat down and watched her, waiting to hear what she was spinning her mental wheels on. She finally stopped in front of me. "With Diego out of the picture, will we have help there?"

"We were supposed to. I told Diego the very rough idea you and I had discussed, but we didn't have any specifics yet. Boom-Boom will help, but we'll need to pay extra."

She surprised me with a fleeting smile. "I want everyone to be surprised so they don't overthink their roles."

"Are you going to tell me?"

She smiled wider until her teeth shone brightly. She straddled my legs and lowered herself onto my lap, her arms wrapping around my shoulders.

"As soon as we finish what we started."

33

THE SOUND OF THE ENGINE CHANGED PITCH.

"We must be closing in on Red Hook," I said.

Giselle jumped up and peered through the window. "You're right, we're close to land."

"I'll check with Boom-Boom."

I opened the stateroom door. If some crazy bastard fired a rocket at our boat, I wanted to make sure Giselle could escape. Halfway up the steps I looked up toward the helm.

"Anything new?"

Boom-Boom glanced down in the passageway. "I killed the radio. Don't want nobody finding us."

"What happens on arrival?"

"We got a ride waiting. Stay down there and I'll let you know when it's safe."

The smell of the fresh salt air made me realize how musty it was below deck. Back in the stateroom I found Giselle watching the island pass through the small porthole.

"We'll be there soon," I said.

She didn't look away from the window.

"Are you sure about this, Giselle? Now that they have Diego, we need to consider his safety, too—"

"We only need a few hours. After that, I'll do whatever you say."

Finally, light at the end of the tunnel. But there was no way of knowing how long this would take. I just hoped Diego would be okay.

He knew we were headed to the hotel where the French mission was billeted on St. Thomas, which could get us all killed if he talked. And even if he did tell them what they wanted to hear, these were serious players. They'd have no compunction about dropping him overboard with his hands and feet bound.

The weight of Giselle's operation was settling in on me. Her husband was a murderer who she was dead-set on exposing. Her need for answers wasn't just to settle their personal score—she wanted to make sure he was dealt with quickly and with certainty. Otherwise, like most politicians of his stature, he'd play rope-a-dope long enough for the matter to be pushed aside by more urgent news.

Now that we'd been exposed and exploited by François in the press, who swallowed the juicy gossip with unquenchable thirst, Giselle had become the villain. With me. And in the court of public opinion, it was nearly impossible to prove innocence after being condemned on television as guilty. She refused to accept that.

The engine slowed further and I felt the direction of the boat turn. We had to be at Red Hook.

"We're at the marina," Giselle said from the window.

"Let's go to the galley," I said.

She took my arms in her hands and stared up into my eyes. Her face was serious. Deathly serious.

"I'm sorry about your friend Diego. He was kind to help us. Let's do this now, and hopefully we can help him later today."

I was going to respond that Diego wasn't really my friend, but I bit my tongue. Friends were few in this world, and he'd been there for me more than others who'd describe themselves as my friends. And Diego had indeed helped us.

"Just promise me that once we get to the hotel, if it seems impossible or blows up in our faces, we get the hell out and call the FBI." I paused. "And let's make sure nobody gets killed."

Her eyebrows lifted at the last part. "We'll see."

"Reilly!" Boom-Boom's voice sounded through the galley. "Need some help up here."

I hurried up the steps and shielded my eyes until I got my sunglasses on. We were halfway into a slip at the marina. I rushed to the bow to cleat us off. Boom-Boom expertly guided us into the slip, and once I'd tied the bow tight, I hurried back to the starboard corner and pulled a line there to bring us in close and then tied us off there, too.

Boom-Boom shut down the engine and we met on the deck. He was holding the hats Giselle and I had brought onboard.

"That was easy," he said. "I'm used to running boats at night. Here, put your hats on."

"Nice job."

I took the two Foxy's hats and donned the red one. Giselle waited below deck and I tossed her the blue hat. The sound of Boom-Boom hailing someone on shore caused us both to look up. An unmarked white Ford van was at the end of the dock, its passenger doors open.

My heart was in my throat.

"All clear," Boom-Boom said. "Let's go, brudda."

Giselle went first and I followed closely behind her, scanning every direction. Another large man with dreadlocks stood by the open back door of the Ford van. Boom-Boom was already in the passenger seat. He glanced over his shoulder at us.

"Where to?"

Giselle sat forward. "Our target is at one of the buildings at Frenchman's Reef Hotel."

"Go figure," Boom-Boom said.

"First need you to stop at Bluebeard's Beach Club, near Frenchman's Reef," I said.

"Again, go figure."

The driver looked back at us. "Most of that area's closed off 'cause of the foreign politicians there."

"I have a room booked at Bluebeard's," I said.

"There are politicians at the target hotel," Giselle said. "French politicians."

"French security, too," I said.

"This is my island," Boom-Boom said. "They can kiss my ass."

34

THE RIDE THROUGH THE HILLS OF ST. THOMAS WAS A PLEASANT DISTRACTION. The van had two captain's chairs in the back and curtained windows. The curtains were tied open for now. We all stared out at the passing shanties, odd freestanding retail buildings, people on the streets, and scrubby vegetation broken up by the occasional lush landscaping of a resort hotel. As we descended toward the resorts near Charlotte Amalie, we had to switch to the back roads—there were security checkpoints on all the major thoroughfares to protect the G8 summiteers. Fortunately, Boom-Boom's driver knew every back alley, gravel road, and dirt track toward our destination.

Downed trees and piles of wrecked homes were still evident two years after the hurricane. Tax dollars and FEMA assistance had been scant here in the islands, and a lot of the inhabitants merely pushed the rubble aside and continued with their lives, something their ancestors had done for generations.

The setting changed as we got closer to the tourist area. Homes were nicer, streets wider and freshly coated with concrete, and there was no sign of trash or dead vegetation.

"Few more blocks," the driver said. He drove on what I realized was a service road, behind working-class houses, but we could see the backs of some large hotels ahead.

"You ain't using your name, are you, Reilly?" Boom-Boom said.

"Nope. Should be all set." Provided Ray had done what I asked him to do.

"I know Bluebeard's. There's a back door that leads right to reception," the driver said.

"We'll wait in the van," Boom-Boom said.

Paranoia seeped back into my brain. Would Giselle be safe? Would Boom-Boom try to claim whatever bounty was inevitably on our heads by now? I forced those thoughts away. He could have already done that if he wanted to. Like with Diego, we weren't friends, but we had history. Guys like these were loyal to their people because they were the only ones they could trust. Somehow I'd been granted that designation, and right now I trusted them more than anyone else on earth.

The driver braked by a row of dumpsters and rolled to a stop in front of a narrow concrete driveway that led to a few white stucco buildings. I swallowed, hard. Showtime.

"Good luck," Giselle said.

"Meet me out front," I said.

A maid did a double take as I passed her in the back hallway that led to reception. Unlike at the La Concha Hotel in Key West, entering through the back door must not be common here. The lobby was small, with a pink tile floor, white stucco walls, and a blue macaw on a stand behind the counter.

"Hello," the bird said.

"Hello," I said and immediately felt foolish.

The woman behind the desk smiled.

"How many people respond to the bird?" I said.

"About 50 percent." She spoke with a grin. "Do you have a reservation?"

"Yes, it's all prepaid. Name is Jonas. Tony Jonas."

"One minute please." The woman pushed buttons on her computer and a fresh smile appeared on her face. "Here you are, Mr. Jonas. Can I have a credit card for incidentals?"

"Just use the one on the reservation if you don't mind. I left my wallet on the ferry from St. John. My girlfriend is taking a cab back to Red Hook to retrieve it."

"Was your driver's license in your wallet, too?"

"Afraid so, but I can come back later if you want a copy of it." I smiled and held my breath as the receptionist paused to process this hiccup in the hotel's routine.

"Okay, that will be fine. How many keys do you need?"

"Three if you don't mind. One each for me and my girlfriend and one extra since I'm prone to losing things."

The woman laughed. She busied herself processing keys and finalizing my paperwork and then held up a pink sleeve with the keys inside.

"Room 223," she said. "You can either use the stairway in the front lobby or the elevator."

"Thanks." I picked up the keys and started to pivot away.

"Please return with your driver's license when you have it." Her smile had faded to efficiency.

"Will do."

I walked into the front lobby, where the elevators were, as well as some architect's attempt at a grand staircase. The stairs led me straight up to the second floor. Room 223 was at the end of the hall, on the corner and across from another stairway. Perfect.

Inside, the room was basic. King bed, television, floral chintz sofa, and sliding glass doors that led to a small balcony facing the water but too low for a view. In the bathroom I considered myself in the mirror. My beard had several days of growth, my hair was askew, and there were dark circles under my eyes. I looked like a man on the run. No surprise there.

Back out in the hallway, I descended the staircase and walked out through the front door. The white van was there and I jumped inside.

"Now what?" Boom-Boom said.

"One of Diego's men is supposed to meet us behind the hotel where we're headed," I said.

"How he gonna know we here?"

I pulled my remaining burner phone from my pocket and dialed a preset number Diego had given me.

"Yes?" Brass Knuckles answered in a whisper.

"On the way. Are you okay and, ah, ready?"

"Yeah, mon. You close by?"

"We'll be there in five minutes. White Ford van. Meet us out front—"

"No, out back. I have garbage for you."

"Garbage? What about security?"

Brass Knuckles had already hung up.

We drove out to the main road and turned toward the larger, more palatial-looking hotel a few blocks away. The driver turned left again just before the hotel and then right onto the same service road we'd been on before. There were guards with guns roaming the sidewalk, but no checkpoint. When we pulled up outside, we found a man throwing bags of trash into a pair of dumpsters: Brass Knuckles. I'd called him that ever since he'd used a pair to cold-cock me a few years ago at the Beach Bar on St. John.

"That Diego's man?" Boom-Boom said.

"Yep."

We rolled up and stopped. Brass Knuckles grabbed one of the bags off a pile and brought it to the van. I rolled down my window and he handed it to me. The bag was heavy.

"Any word on Diego?" he asked.

I noticed he was wearing an official hotel nametag with his photo on it. These guys had accomplished a lot in a short period of time. Hopefully, that meant Diego hadn't shared what he knew of our plan with his captors. If the enemy had broken Diego, though, we could be walking into a trap.

"None that I've heard," I said.

The man shook his head. "Damn." He paused. "I got everything I could. It's all in there."

"We'll find him," I said.

"There's security everywhere but only one dude up on the fifth floor near the presidential suite when his boss ain't there," he said. "But there's been a lot of French people in and out of here all day." He held up a walkie-talkie. "I'm on Channel 3."

"How will we—"

"Get out of here before someone asks questions. I'll be working around the loading dock, so call me when you come back."

"We won't be long," Giselle said.

Brass Knuckles stared at her long and hard. Diego was in deep shit because of her, and me.

With that, we continued back down the service road for Blue-beard's Beach Club to assess what we had in the bag and decide if it would be sufficient to advance the plan.

35

I SPREAD THE BAG'S CONTENTS OUT IN THE BACK OF THE VAN. I smiled at what I saw, but everyone else was looking perplexed.

"The hell's all that stuff, brudda?" Boom-Boom said.

A few outfits were inside the bag. I held one up—it was a maid's uniform, which had a security badge on it. The photo was of a white woman with dark hair. Giselle was brunette, but there was a cheap dark wig, too. The second outfit was a green one-piece landscaping jumpsuit. That had a photo of an older black man, bald.

"Gotta be for you, Boom-Boom," I said.

"Better be double-XL," he said.

The third one wasn't really an outfit but a sexy black camisole.

"That must be for you, Reilly," Boom-Boom said. Everyone laughed.

There were also a few rolls of duct tape, some towels, and an empty gallon milk container, and wrapped inside another bag was a machete, a steak knife, four walkie-talkies, and a pair of brass knuckles. The latter made me smile. *Must be an extra pair.*

"Not much there," Boom-Boom said.

"You men clear out and I'll change into the maid's uniform," Giselle said.

The van doors opened and Boom-Boom and the driver got out. I exited the vehicle to discuss the plan with them. We huddled in front of the vehicle, which was pressed close to some red bougainvillea.

"See if that jumpsuit fits," I said.

Boom-Boom grimaced, took his black sneakers off, kept his jeans on, and slipped a leg inside the jumpsuit. I glanced around but didn't see anyone.

"Here's the plan," I said.

As Boom-Boom pulled the jumpsuit up over his clothes, I explained. His forehead wrinkled the more I spoke. I finished as he pulled the zipper up on the front of the lime-green outfit with the resort logo on the back. If circumstances were different I would have laughed. The legs on the jumpsuit were six inches too short, and the top barely contained Boom-Boom's massive torso. If he took a deep breath the outfit would explode.

"You call dat a plan, brudda?"

"It's gotta happen fast and requires a fair amount of luck. Sounds like there's always one security guard that stays at the suite whether anyone is there or not, so that's what we're banking on."

"Luck might not be enough," he said.

"You take the machete and play the part of landscaper, but let's try not to hurt anyone, okay? Right now we're innocent parties trying to uncover what the hell happened here. But if we hurt someone, we'll all be guilty too. No get-out-of-jail-free cards."

Boom-Boom smiled. "You do things your way and I'll do mine, brudda."

The side door of the van opened and Giselle stepped out. The maid uniform was baggy on her, but the wig fit well. It may have been cheap, but at a glance it was believable. My heart bounced at her transformation.

"Are you sure about this?"

"Yes," she said. "And we're running out of time. The conference ends in a couple of hours and what's left of the French contingent will clear out quickly. Let's get moving."

"What she said," Boom-Boom said.

My head spun with the impossibility of what we were about to attempt, but I was counting on her still having clout even if we did get caught—provided we didn't get caught by Alphonse Zidane, who would make us disappear.

We climbed back inside the van and moved out.

36

WITH THE VAN BACKED IN PAST THE DUMPSTERS NEAR THE LOADING dock, we climbed out. I'd keyed the mic on the walkie-talkie to let Brass Knuckles know we'd arrived. The loading dock door opened and he stood there waiting. He nodded at Giselle's outfit, but when he saw Boom-Boom he shook his head.

"Anything new?" I said.

"Couple more people back here now. Seems like they're packing up." He paused. "And I had to deal with this guy." He turned and pointed toward the corner. A hotel security guard was tied up and partially covered with garbage bags.

"Is he alive?" My voice squeaked.

"Yeah, mon, just taking a nap."

"We need to move fast," Giselle said.

Brass Knuckles took a piece of paper out of his pocket and unfolded it. He'd drawn a crude map. "This square is the first floor. We're here."

The loading dock was a small square on the bottom of the drawing.

"They got stairs in three places." He pointed to three boxes inside the square. One was close to the loading dock. "These lines are corridors, and that's the lobby. The suite where the guard is posted is up on the fifth floor, here." He stabbed his finger onto the page close to the stair by the loading dock.

Perfect.

"I haven't seen President Huibert, but his security team patrols round-the-clock to keep anyone from getting inside."

We all looked at each other. Nobody was smiling now.

I handed out the walkie-talkies. "If there's trouble, say 'abort.' If you see a target, say 'target' and the room number near where you are. And if shit goes bad, scream for help." I glanced at my watch. It was 4:20.

"We need to be out of here in twenty minutes, max," I said. "Hit and run."

"What if there's no target to hit?" Boom-Boom said.

"There will be something, I'm certain," Giselle said.

I turned to Brass Knuckles. "You have what you need?"

He nodded slowly.

"Okay, have it ready, because we'll be hauling ass if we get that far."

He kept nodding slowly.

Now for the hardest part, at least to me.

I turned to Giselle. "Are you ready?"

She nodded once. For the first time since I'd known her, she hesitated.

"You are Giselle Huibert and have every right to be here, disguise or not. If you come across one of the people you think is bad, shout like hell and we'll come running. They won't—can't—hurt you here," I lied. "Okay?"

She gave me a slight smile.

"Twenty minutes," Boom-Boom said. With that he picked up the machete and the half-filled garbage bag, walked out the loading dock door, and disappeared around the side of the hotel. Landscapers were less obvious on the grounds.

"You're next," I said.

Giselle leaned into me quickly and gave me a peck on the lips. I took her in my arms for a quick hug.

"I'll be right behind you," I said. "Keep your walkie-talkie on and keep us posted."

She walked through a metal door and down one of the hallways noted on Brass Knuckles' map. The stairway she'd take was only fifty feet away. The fear I felt for her had me anxious to follow immediately after her, but I counted to sixty, like we'd planned.

Once I was inside the hallway, the sound of voices had me on edge. I had no disguise, and this wing of the hotel was closed to all but the French contingent. I was dressed in shorts and a fishing shirt but was counting on my—

A man in a hotel uniform rounded the corner at the end of the hall. The stairway Giselle should have taken was equidistant from us. Suspicion arched his brows.

He held up his palm as if to say, *Stop*. "Excuse me, sir, are you a part of the—"

"*Oui, je suis avec le delegation. J'etait fais du pescher*," I said. Would he believe I belonged here but had just gone fishing? "*C'est la notre dernier jour ici.*"

He stopped, but the tautness of his face settled. Did he speak French? Had I butchered the language?

"Okay, thanks," he said.

He continued down the hallway. Whew. If he walked into the loading dock, he'd wind up unconscious and under garbage bags, thanks to Brass Knuckles.

I pulled open the stair door and proceeded to climb the five flights up to the top floor. My heart pounded from exertion and the mystery of what awaited me at the top. The stair was very close to the president's suite. I stood at the top and listened through the door but heard nothing. Would Giselle be inside the suite? Would the guard there recognize her? Was he part of the conspiracy?

As I slowly opened the door to the corridor, the hinge creaked, and I stepped out normally since anyone would hear me anyway.

Giselle was standing by the suite door talking to a man in a suit, in English. He must not have recognized her. He pivoted to face me, another inappropriate visitor on a floor that wasn't supposed to have visitors, no matter whether the president was there or not.

He stepped purposefully toward me. Behind him, Giselle shook her head as if to tell me no, he wasn't of value. Didn't change the fact that he was coming at me. He had a radio in one hand and a bulge under his jacket near the other.

"Excuse me, sir, this floor is off limits." His English had a heavy French accent. "Please turn around and go back down the stairs—"

"My room is on this floor," I said. I continued toward him.

"This section of the hotel is closed—"

"My room is 523." I held the pink key up from the hotel next door.

He now stood in front of me and blocked my path. "That's not possible, sir. You must leave immediately."

He held the radio up and pressed a button—

"I'm going inside to clean the suite," Giselle called up the hallway, which caused the security officer to hesitate and lower the radio slightly.

He turned halfway back. "No, madame!"

In the second it took him to yell at Giselle, I'd planted my feet and dropped my fist, and as he started to turn back to face me, I nailed him with an uppercut that lifted him off the floor. He tumbled in a heap, out cold.

"The door's locked," Giselle said.

I checked the guard's pockets, took his gun and radio, and stuffed them in my pants. I found a room key in his front pocket. I grabbed hold of his wrists and dragged him the twenty feet back to the suite entry. Giselle took the key and opened the door. She glanced inside and waved me in. I dragged the man in—he was starting to come to. Once inside, I rolled him over, grabbed a roll of duct tape from my back pocket, wrapped his wrists and ankles, and rolled him onto his back as his eyes fluttered open—then spread wide.

"*Au secours!*" he yelled.

I knew that meant "help." I dropped a knee on his chest, pulled a foot of duct tape from the roll, and jammed it over his mouth as he squirmed.

"*Au secours!*"

I couldn't get the tape to stick—damn it! I pressed my weight against him and wrapped the tape all the way around his head three times. Then I wrapped his ankles to his wrists. I was breathing heavily, and when I finished, Giselle walked out of the bedroom.

"Nothing obvious in there," she said.

Damn! "Great, now what?"
"Give me his radio," she said.
"What are you going to do?"
Her smile was a thin line.
"Call for help."

38

S HE HELD THE BUTTON IN ON THE RADIO and hesitated a moment. Then her eyes narrowed.

"I need a senior security officer on the fifth floor, right away." She'd made no attempt to hide her accent. A moment passed before the radio came to life.

"Who is this calling, and where is officer Foger?"

Giselle's eyes widened. "I think I recognize that voice."

I held my hand up. "Wait—"

"This is Cheval," she said. "Come see me at my suite immediately. The guard is here. Come alone."

Only static followed her statement.

"Cheval?" I said. "Doesn't that mean horse?"

"Security's code name for me."

The voice on the radio finally broke the silence. "Madame Cheval? *Est-ce toi?*"

"*Oui. viens ici, tout de suite, s'il vous plait.*"

"*D'accord, madame.*"

The radio went dead.

"That wasn't exactly subtle," I said. My voice sounded an octave or two higher, even to me.

"No time for subtlety, Buck. You said so yourself."

"What if they swarm the fifth floor?"

"I'm still the first lady. They don't know who I've spoken to or why I'm here." She smiled. "And this will force François' hand."

"That's for sure." I held up my walkie-talkie. "We have in-bound security to the fifth floor. Report if you see activity in the lobby. Otherwise, this will go down quickly. Be ready."

Our network of ragtag criminals were successful at what they did because they stayed on top of their game. This, however, was asking a lot. Our plan was coming off the rails, and fast.

The guard I'd overpowered was awake now, staring wide-eyed at Giselle in the maid outfit. She pulled her wig off and fluffed her brown hair. When she started to unbutton the outfit, I thought the guard's eyes would pop out of his head. I bent down and took him by his bound hands and feet and dragged him across the carpet and into the bedroom.

I rolled the guard into the closet. "Keep quiet and you'll live," I said.

His head and mouth were duct-taped, but if he rolled around he could make noise.

Back in the bedroom, Giselle had transformed herself from a maid to a sexy woman dressed only in the black camisole.

"If more than one person shows up, we're in trouble," I said.

KNOCK, KNOCK, KNOCK!

Oh shit, here we go.

I rushed to the door and peered through the peephole. A lone man dressed in a suit stood there—unless others waited on the sides out of sight, that is. The man was olive-skinned and I couldn't tell through the distorted convex lens whether I'd seen him before. Giselle stood next to me, now with a bathrobe on but hanging slightly open so her camisole was visible.

I stepped to the side of the door, now wearing the brass knuckles on my right hand. My breathing was fast and my heart pumped blood double time through my limbs, making me jumpy. Giselle approached the door and hesitated as she reached for the handle. I nodded at her and she pulled the door open wide, with me hidden behind it—which was a problem, because now I couldn't see her.

"Madame Huibert?"

She took a step back and I could see her face was angry.

"*Oui,*" she said. "*Où est François?*"

I sensed movement as the man stepped inside the room. His hand appeared as he took hold of the edge of the door to close it.

"*Je ne sais pas, Madame,*" he said.

As the door began to close, I shoved it hard. It hit the security officer and he stumbled inside off balance.

SLAM!

When the door closed I leaped toward the man—the same one who'd boarded my catamaran back in Soper's Hole: Jacques. While still off balance, he managed to block my wide-arcing punch. My momentum carried me into him and he grabbed at me with his other hand—I saw the holstered gun as his jacket flew open. I had a good eight inches on him, but he was no doubt trained in close-quarters fighting, and my size wouldn't matter if this went too long.

I jammed my knee into his kidney.

"Ummpph!"

His left hand disappeared under his jacket—

With my feet planted hard on the ground, I crouched and stepped into him with a brass-knuckled undercut that grazed his chin. His hand came out of the jacket, the gun tumbled free, and he dropped like a sack of flour.

Were it not for the brass knuckles, my punch wouldn't have had the force to drop him, but they did the trick. My heart was redlined as I dropped on top of him to ensure he wouldn't get up.

"Good job, Buck!" Giselle handed me the duct tape.

I spun him over and taped his wrists in front—he rolled over! His eyes lidded like a cobra's, ready to strike, he kicked my shin—

Pain lit through my leg.

He rolled again, now toward his automatic pistol on the carpeted floor. I lunged at him just as he rolled on top of it. I pulled back my brass-covered fist and launched it toward his jaw—

BOOM!

My fist connected just as the gun went off.

His head rocked to the side and a tooth shot across the carpet. Out cold. Or dead.

"Buck! Are you okay?" Giselle said.

She knelt down next to me. I rolled the man over again and the gun fell from his grasp—a small pool of blood was under him.

"Damn!"

My walkie-talkie squawked. "Reilly? Heard a gunshot. The hell's going on?" It was Brass Knuckles.

I ripped the man's shirt open. The gun had been flat on the ground, but when he fired it, the bullet had grazed his back. A line of pink flesh bled, but not profusely.

"Reilly?!"

Giselle grabbed the walkie-talkie. "We're okay! Get ready!"

"It's just a scrape." I reached behind me and grabbed the duct tape off the floor and quickly bound his ankles and wrapped his head like I had with the other guard. "This is the man who came looking for my boat at Soper's Hole, the one who told me you were on the helicopter."

When I stood, Giselle was buttoning up the maid outfit. Her hands shook but her eyes were clear.

"You okay?" I said.

She nodded fast. "His name is Jacques Frappier. He's the number two man behind Zidane."

"Good," I said. "But right now we need to get out of here fast." I grabbed the man and lifted him over my shoulder. He had to weigh a buck seventy-five, easy, but with all the adrenaline I'd been pumping out, I felt like Superman. "Get the door. Let's go!"

"What about the other man?" she said.

"No time!"

She opened the door and checked the hall. "Clear!"

I carried the man toward the stairway door. Almost there, we heard the ping of the elevator arriving. I hustled the remaining ten yards—Giselle had the door open—and hit the steps and kept going. She closed the door quietly and was soon on my heels. Our feet clattered on the concrete steps. Fourth floor ... third floor ... second floor ...

The sound of a door opening above us pushed me harder. My breathing was ragged and my heart labored to pump enough blood to fuel my muscles and circulate oxygen. Giselle ran past me.

Finally at the bottom, she opened the door and peered out. She waved and I stumbled after her. Thank God the man was still unconscious. What if I broke his jaw? We wouldn't learn anything then.

She sprinted ahead and I shuffled after her. After caroming into a wall, I bounced back into the center of the hall and continued toward the now-open door into the loading dock. A man appeared—a large man. Boom-Boom. He grabbed the security man just as I nearly collapsed into the loading dock.

Boom-Boom carried him like a toy toward Brass Knuckles, who stood beside a crate labeled "Dom Perignon." Boom-Boom lowered the man inside.

"Check ... his ... pockets." My breath was ragged.

Boom-Boom stood up a moment later with a switchblade in one hand and a small-caliber pistol in another.

"Good call, Reilly."

Brass Knuckles dropped a wooden lid onto the crate and then hammered each of the four corners as the driver backed the van into the loading dock. The van's rear doors were already open. My two large accomplices knelt down and grabbed the crate like it was a carton of Chinese food.

"Let's get in the van," I said.

Giselle hurried to the passenger side and climbed in. I followed after, just as the back doors slammed shut. Boom-Boom and Brass Knuckles jumped in the front with the driver.

"Let's go, let's go, let's go!" I said.

The van shot forward past the dumpsters and up the short access road that led to the street behind the hotels. I was turned sideways to watch behind us, but nobody appeared. We took a hard right onto the street and Frenchman's Reef disappeared behind us.

"We got one!" Giselle said. "We got one!"

"Now what?" Boom-Boom said.

"We make him talk," I said.

39

WE CHANGED OUT OF OUR DISGUISES DURING THE SHORT DRIVE to Bluebeard's, which left no option for modesty. Giselle showed no concern about the men's open stares at her camisole as she put her shorts and shirt over top of it. The driver jammed on the brakes in front of the hotel and we all jumped outside.

"Take the steps in the lobby," I said. "Meet on two."

I took Giselle by the arm and steered her toward the elevators. Behind us, the driver held the door as Boom-Boom and Brass Knuckles carried the crate inside and quickly up the stairs.

The elevator arrived and we hurried inside. I pressed "2," and when the doors opened the men and the crate were there waiting. They followed me down the hall to Room 223.

Once inside the room we allowed ourselves a moment to catch our breath. As we all sat or stood glancing at each other, the crate began to rattle. It reminded me of a chick inside an egg trying to peck its way out. The trash bag Brass Knuckles had given us earlier was dumped out on the bed.

"You ready?" I said.

"Always," Boom-Boom said. He picked up the empty gallon milk jug and a roll of duct tape. "Grab a chair and meet me in the bathroom."

"Pop the lid on the crate."

Brass Knuckles worked on the crate as I took a chair from the desk into the bathroom.

"Put that in the tub," Boom-Boom said.

I did and then went to help get the prize.

Brass Knuckles held the man in his arms. He was now awake and his eyes were arched in anger but not fear.

"You bastard!" Giselle said. She slapped him hard across the face.

The man didn't struggle.

Giselle slapped him again, and her eyes glistened like a mad woman.

"That's enough," I said. "We'll take it from here."

"I want to—"

"No, Giselle. It's better you stay in here. I don't want you to see any of what's going to happen," I said.

She stood erect and crossed her arms. The muscles in her cheeks rippled as she clenched her teeth.

"Let's go," I said.

Brass Knuckles carried Frappier into the bathroom and dropped him into the chair. His wrists were behind his back, but we left him like that while I taped his ankles to the chair legs. Then we taped his arms to the arms of the chair. He was fully secure.

He didn't struggle, but his eyes burned like acetylene torches into mine.

"All set," Brass Knuckles said.

"Tilt him back," Boom-Boom said.

We lowered Frappier until the head of the chair rested on the tub's water nozzle. I'd never tortured a man before, and my hands were sweaty and shaking. Not that I had second thoughts or feared for Frappier's safety—just the opposite. I realized I wanted to kill the son of a bitch.

I took a step back from the tub.

Brass Knuckles laid a towel over Frappier's face. Boom-Boom held up the gallon jug, now full of tap water, and poured it slowly over the towel. After about ten seconds, Frappier started to twist in the chair. His mouth was still taped, so he could only breath from his nose, which was now buried beneath a water-soaked towel.

"You done this before?" I said.

"Relax, brudda."

Boom-Boom refilled the jug from the sink and again doused the towel to the same result. A squeal and what sounded like crying emerged from under the towel.

Brass Knuckles removed the towel.

"Take the tape off his mouth," Boom-Boom said. "You make one sound, I cut off a finger."

He took Frappier's switchblade out of his pocket and pressed a button, and the blade swung out. Frappier's eyes fluttered and he coughed for a full minute once the tape was ripped off his head.

Our prisoner was breathing again, albeit heavily. His eyes scanned from the other two men to me.

"What the hell are you doing, Reilly?" he said. "You'll go to jail for this."

"Shut up, asshole!" I said. "The only one here going to jail will be you, if you survive. Now I'm going to ask you some questions, and—"

THWACK!

Frappier had spit a wad of saliva into my face.

I slapped him hard with an open palm. His eyes wavered.

Brass Knuckles jammed the wet towel on his face again, and Boom-Boom emptied another gallon of water onto it, causing Frappier to shudder wildly. The towel was removed and I leaned closer.

"Who gave the order for Giselle's helicopter to be shot down?"

Frappier shook his head to clear his eyesockets of water. He blinked repeatedly.

I shook his shoulders. "Who gave the orders?"

Frappier smiled. "Giselle, huh? So the news is true."

"Who gave the order, Frappier?"

The man laughed. He continued laughing as Brass Knuckles replaced the towel over his head and laughed until he choked on water. When we removed the towel, Frappier spit out water in a steady stream and laughed again.

"Give me his hand!" Boom-Boom said.

Brass Knuckles pushed Frappier forward and peeled the tape off his left wrist. Frappier struggled, but the waterboarding had taken its toll. He didn't have much fight left.

"What are you doing?" I said.

"Get out of the way, Reilly." Boom-Boom picked up the switch-blade, looked at it, and pulled the machete—the one he'd carried earlier while posing as a landscaper—from his belt.

"You can't do—"

"Hold his hand, pinky finger out!"

Brass Knuckles put the towel back over his face and held Frappier's hand against the side of the tub. The prisoner started to shake violently.

The machete swished by my head like a startled pheasant—

BAM!

Frappier's pinky finger shot off the side of the tub and smacked me in the chest. Blood shot out from the stub on his hand like water out of a squirt gun. I grabbed his wrist and put a towel over his hand so it wouldn't spray everywhere.

Frappier squealed.

Boom-Boom doused him two more times with full jugs of water. Brass Knuckles and I held the chair as Frappier flailed from side to side, and when we removed the towel, he was barely coherent. The stump where a finger had been was oozing blood. I wrapped his hand in duct tape.

Frappier was soaked with cold water, pale, and hung limp in the chair. His head lolled in a circle and his eyes rolled back in their sockets. I slapped him a few times—not hard, just enough to get his attention. He lifted his head up.

"Did Alphonse Zidane give the order to have her helicopter shot down?"

He nodded slowly.

"Zidane ... sent me ... looking ... for the ... helicopter." He coughed.

I pulled the chair forward so that Frappier sat upright. "Why? Because of the girl?"

It was as if his head were on a swivel. "What girl?"

"The one I saw in this room!" Giselle said.

I turned around to see her standing in the now-open doorway.

"I told you not to come in here!" I said.

"If not the girl, why did Zidane have me shot down? Did François order him to?"

Frappier giggled. "A girl? I don't know. I follow orders. Zidane said find you, and then ..."

"Then what?" I said.

"Then he said to find your boat. It was close to the crash. But you lied to me."

"What were you going to do if you found me?" Giselle said.

A partial smile bent his lips, and his eyes were closed. "Finish ..."

"Finish what?" I said.

"Finish ... the job."

His head rolled back and he passed out.

"Bastard," Giselle said.

A collective exhale left our lungs.

"He don't know shit," Brass Knuckles said.

"He knows what he told us." I paused and glanced up at Giselle. "But I also believe the part about him being a soldier and doing what he's told. Zidane wouldn't have told him why. That would be a very small group, to maintain secrecy."

"A loyal soldier, yes, but to whom?" Giselle said.

"That's the million-dollar question," I said.

"Hundred million, you mean," she said.

"It's a figure of speech—"

"No." She shook her head. "François' and my net worth is over one hundred million Euros."

Brass Knuckles let loose a long whistle that pierced my inner ear.

"Now dat's what I call incentive, brudda."

Indeed. But the timing and circumstances didn't fit snugly together, at least in my mind.

"Not that I think that's the reason, or at least not the sole reason," she said. "Based on this man and Zidane's response when he saw me the day I walked in here."

I stood up from where I'd been seated on the side of the tub. "We're not going to learn anything else from this guy." I let my gaze rest on Giselle's eyes. "Time we do what we agreed to if this didn't pan out."

"Wha-zat?" Brass Knuckles said.

"Call Special Agent Booth at the FBI."

"Say what?" Boom-Boom said. "We gonna tell the FBI we tortured this mofo?"

"That was the deal—"

"What about Diego?" Brass Knuckles said. "What's gonna happen to him when they find out we grabbed this dude?"

Shit.

"They're right, Buck," Giselle said.

"I have an idea," I said. "We trade Frappier for Diego."

"That's more like it, brudda."

If we didn't get Diego back and I called the FBI, I'd have been the next one the machete would come down on.

"Frappier's no more use to us," Giselle said. "Let's do it."

Frappier's cell phone was on the counter. When I opened it, I found that it was pass-code protected.

"Wake him up," I said.

Boom-Boom turned on the shower to full cold. After a moment, Frappier stirred and then jumped against his restraints. His eyes searched us and stopped on me holding his phone.

"We're going to trade you for our colleague," I said. "What's your pass code?"

He pressed his lips tight for a moment. Defiance filled his eyes as if he finally had a way to fight back.

Boom-Boom held up the machete. "Or I slice your fucking throat."

The defiance vanished. "One, two, three, four," Frappier said.

"Real creative," Boom-Boom said.

I opened his recent calls. There was only one number. It was in both the incoming and outgoing list. "That Zidane?" I said.

Frappier nodded begrudgingly.

"Okay, let's do this, but we need to control the exchange and it can't be from here."

Boom-Boom smiled. "I got the spot, brudda."

"Your compound?" Brass Knuckles said.

"Yeah, mon."

A queasy feeling gurgled in my stomach. If they were talking about Boom-Boom's compound high above Magens Bay, I'd been there before. It was indeed impenetrable in all ways except one: from the air.

I pushed Zidane's number and hit "send." A moment later it was answered.

"*Oui?*"

"It's Buck Reilly, asshole. We have Frappier."

I let that sink in. There was no response, but the call was still active.

"We'll release him to you in exchange for Diego Francis."

"I don't believe you," he said.

With the phone on "speaker," I aimed it toward the bathtub where the soggy, battered number two French Security chief stared at me with half-drooped lids.

"Say something, Frappier."

He sneered. "Fuck you, Reilly."

I turned the speaker off and put the phone back to my ear. "Good enough?"

A loud exhale sounded. "You're a pain in my ass," Zidane said. "When and where?"

"Magens Bay," I said. "Be there in an hour."

"What's left of your friend will be there." Zidane hung up.

"Magens Bay will be full of tourists," Brass Knuckles said. I nodded and he smiled.

"Lets put him back in the box," Boom-Boom said.

Giselle's eyes were flinty black. No fear, just disappointment mixed with determination. We hadn't learned a lot here other than what we'd already suspected. There was no confirmation of François' involvement.

I was seriously starting to miss Key West.

40

THE RIDE TO MAGENS BAY BROUGHT BACK MEMORIES of previous trips to St. Thomas, including the one when I first met Boom-Boom. Back then I was searching for a missing person and thought Boom-Boom might have him, but I eventually enlisted him to help me. It wasn't until our mutual antagonist shot up his compound that I knew for sure we'd been on the same side.

Smoke and the smell of weed filled the van's cabin. Boom-Boom had lit a giant spliff and was sharing it with Brass Knuckles. I rolled down my window.

"We owe you a huge thanks, Boom-Boom. You too, ahh—" I didn't want to call him Brass Knuckles to his face.

"Maurice," he said.

KNOCK, KNOCK, KNOCK!

Frappier had woken up and was beating on the crate he was jammed into like a contortionist. Waterboarded, his finger amputated, shot with a self-inflicted wound, beaten up, and held captive by drug smugglers who'd probably kill him if the trade with Diego went bad.

Too bad it wasn't Zidane, but his day would come.

"The beach is up ahead," Boom-Boom said.

"See anything suspicious?" I said.

"Just sunburned tourists."

The driver slowed and turned right onto the access road that led to a small parking area at Magens Bay. The lot was full of cars and shuttle busses.

Good. Plenty of cover and witnesses.

"Crowded as hell," Boom-Boom said.

"Pull up near the beach and turn around to face out toward the road," I said.

Using Frappier's phone, I texted the number we'd called earlier to arrange the swap. "We're here."

"Now what?" Giselle said.

"We wait."

From the van we watched tourists of every size, ethnicity, and race frolic on the beach and in the water. I kept my eyes on the road, awaiting the arrival of the vehicle that would bring Diego.

"You have a plan, Reilly?" Brass Knuckles, aka Maurice, said.

"Just follow my lead when they show up."

CLICK-CLOCK.

The sound of Boom-Boom cocking his 9mm Glock echoed inside the van.

"They fuck around, be hell to pay," he said.

"With that?" I said.

Just then, two black Chevy Tahoes came down the hill from the opposite direction we'd come—up from where Boom-Boom's compound was located.

He held up his Glock. "This and my men there. They got plenty firepower."

The two Tahoes pulled up to us. One driver parked to our side and the other behind the van. Their windows were down and I counted five men in each vehicle. The barrels of automatic weapons could be seen at the ready.

I glanced at Giselle. Her attention was out toward the beach. A subtle smile pulled at her lips, and then her eyes went huge.

"There!" she pointed out toward the water. "A helicopter's coming."

Shit. What if they fired a rocket into our vehicles?

"Let's get out of the van," I said.

Giselle turned to me. "Everyone here will recognize us!"

"Exactly."

We climbed out and Giselle followed me to the beach. Given the number of people here, she and I might not have drawn much attention, but with Boom-Boom and Maurice sticking close, it looked a lot like we had our own bodyguards, which always gets people curious.

A murmur started to travel down the beach. People pointed and gaped, and some stood up from their towels. Meanwhile, the helicopter continued straight for us.

"Hello, everyone!" I shouted and waved to get everyone's attention.

More people stood up and several hurried over toward us.

"Giselle!" a woman shouted.

"Be friendly," I said.

Giselle smiled and started to wave to people. Within a minute, a crowd had formed around us, with people taking pictures, shouting questions, and cheering. The black helicopter arrived at the beach and hovered over the crowd, sand blowing everywhere. It descended at an angle toward the access road near our van.

Boom-Boom gave a signal and his men poured out of the vehicles, weapons in hand. Maurice hung back at the van with the rear doors open. The helicopter set down and the rotor kept spinning. The chopper's windows were tinted, but it was only large enough to hold maybe five people.

Its rear door popped open. Diego sat inside facing out. There was a man behind Diego, holding a gun to his head.

Maurice pulled the crate out of the back of the van and let it drop to the ground—

THUD.

The lid cracked open and Frappier rolled out. He was bloody, beaten, and disheveled, but his eyes were defiant.

Diego was shoved out of the helicopter, followed by the man holding the gun. It was one of the men from Soper's Hole.

Screams passed through the crowd at the site of all the guns. People fled in every direction. I steered Giselle toward a throng of bodies that took cover behind a stand of palm trees. We watched as Frappier and Diego passed each other on their way to their respective associates, who had their guns trained on each other. Maurice helped Diego into the van as Frappier climbed into the chopper.

If I'd had a SAM missile, I'd have blown the chopper off the beach. But at least they'd stuck to the deal.

The crowd around us refocused on Giselle and started yelling questions that were far less friendly then when we'd arrived.

"What was that about?!"

"Who are those people?"

I took her by the arm. "Let's go."

Back at the van, everyone was already loaded up. Diego was in back with us. He was bruised, one eye was swollen shut, dried blood streaked from his nostrils, and his clothes were torn, but he was smiling.

"You okay?" I said.

"Remind me to say no next time you call."

"*We* owe you, Diego," Giselle said. "I'm so sorry."

"Thanks for not forgetting about me."

Our driver pulled forward.

"Take a left on the access road," I said.

"My place is up the hill," Boom-Boom said.

"Giselle and I are headed over there." I pointed toward a boat anchored at the end of the beach.

"What?" Giselle said.

"Exit stage left?" Boom-Boom said.

"You got it."

Diego coughed. "One problem. They put this on my ankle."

He lifted up his pant leg and pointed to an ankle bracelet with a red light blinking. It was the kind of tracker that police placed on parolees.

"We gotta get that off him," Maurice said.

"I've got bolt cutters in my compound," Boom-Boom said.

We pulled up to the end of the beach, where an old friend awaited us: Captain Jay Rushing.

"Good luck, Reilly," Boom-Boom said. "You too, Queenie."

Giselle hugged each of them. "I can never thank you enough."

"Forget about thank-yous," Diego said. "Just get me that pardon."

With that, we watched the van disappear back up the service road. I heard keys jingle behind me. Captain Jay walked over to us, his key chain bouncing on his belt.

"You ready to get out of here?" he said.

"Damn straight," I said. "But first, meet Giselle Huibert."

Ever the gentleman, Jay took her hand and kissed it. We all laughed.

"The pleasure is mine," Giselle said. "Now, let's please leave. I have a bad feeling."

Just then a loud buzz echoed out over the bay. My stomach tightened. The black helicopter had returned and was making a beeline toward Boom-Boom's hilltop compound.

We hurried to the dinghy. They jumped inside and I shoved us into deeper water before climbing aboard. There was no engine, only oars.

The idyllic calm of the bay was shattered by the sound of distant gunfire.

As we arrived at Jay's boat, which was named *Helios*, I saw the helicopter hovering to the side of the hill's peak. A sudden white streak launched from the helicopter toward the ground, followed by a loud explosion and a plume of smoke. It was the same type of white streak I'd seen when Giselle's helicopter exploded.

"Those double-crossing bastards," she said.

"They must think we're still with them."

Once aboard the center console boat, Jay and I pulled the dinghy out of the water and placed it upside down on the T-top above the center console. Jay quickly tied it down.

The sound of the assault up the hill continued. Automatic weapons fire was being returned from Boom-Boom's compound. He'd been attacked there before and was no doubt prepared this time. Jay started the boat.

"Hold on," he said.

He gunned the engines and we were quickly up on plane, skipping small waves like a high velocity projectile headed to the northeast.

"How did they find them?" Giselle had to shout over the wind and the engine noise.

"That tracker on Diego's ankle."

"Bastards."

"They're intent on cleaning up all loose ends," I said.

After traveling fast along the northern coast of St. Thomas for twenty minutes, I spotted a ferry coming out of Red Hook. It, too, was headed northeast.

"Our enemies have already proven capable of tracking all boat traffic in a wide area. They must have satellite coverage monitoring the region, so stay under the T-top," I said.

"If they're tracking us, how will we get away?" Giselle said.

We had no phone and no way to contact Booth, even if she'd let me, so that wasn't yet an option. There was always a Mayday, but by then it would be too late.

Jay glanced over his shoulder at us. "Where to, Buck?"

I pointed to the ferry. "Get up close to that ferry and stay right behind it. With any luck, our radar image will appear to be a part of the bigger ship."

"But where do you want to go?" he said.

"Wherever they're going."

SECTION 5

VIDEO AT THE END OF THE WORLD

41

IT TOOK AN HOUR AND A HALF, BUT WE ARRIVED AT Virgin Gorda at sunset. We followed the ferry all the way to the docks at Spanish Town.

"Where will you stay?" Jay said.

I had no idea but wouldn't tell him even if I did, for the sake of his safety as much as ours. He must have taken my silence as uncertainty, so he spoke up.

"A lot of the nicer resorts are still closed from the hurricanes."

"Bitter End Yacht Club?"

"Closed," he said.

"Little Dix?"

"Closed."

"Biras Creek?"

"All closed."

"Been almost two years," I said. "Can't believe how much damage there still is."

"Hard to rebuild all at once. Even the big money places can't get supplies and labor. Oh, almost forgot."

He opened the plastic lid on the center console and grabbed a wad of cash. "Here's the money you asked to borrow."

I took the cash.

"Thank you, Captain Jay," Giselle said. "Where do you suggest we go?"

"Best to get away from town here. Leverick Bay Resort is open up in North Sound near Gun Point. You can take a taxi or rent a car at Speedy's on North Sound Road, straight ahead." He pointed at the road that led straight away from the ferry docks.

We thanked Jay again and set out on foot for Speedy's Car Rentals, which was only a couple of hundred yards up the road.

"Such a beautiful island," Giselle said. "All of them are, but I like Jost Van Dyke, St. John, and this one the best. Fewer people, more natural landscape." She paused. "The simple life."

"Not so simple for people trying to make a living here, but I agree."

It was harder to hide on the remote islands, though.

We arrived at the corner where Speedy's was, and down past it was a police station. A couple of police cars were there and a few officers stood out front talking, smoking, and enjoying the sunset, which burned a brilliant orange back toward St. Thomas. I worried about Boom-Boom, Diego, and Maurice. Had they survived the aerial attack? There was a strong chance they'd all been killed. The thought sent a chill through my arms that caused me to ball my fists.

Speedy's was closed. Damn. "How about the police station?"

Giselle shook her head. She had dark circles under her eyes and we were both running on fumes. I was tempted to get a room right here in Spanish Town. No resort hotels but a couple of small ones. What happened back in Tortola at the Tamarind Club had me gun-shy, though. Our faces had been on television nonstop ever since, and I was certain several of the tourists on Magens Bay would have posted their videos online by now. The odds of getting recognized had probably increased exponentially.

We'd walked past a small shopping area on the way from the docks and were now headed back that way to seek alternative transportation to Leverick Bay. I'd steal a car or a scooter, if need be. As we approached the shopping center, there was a sign that said "Buck's Market."

"Yours?" Giselle said.

"Cute."

Past that was the Bath and Turtle Pub amid a few other small buildings. We walked by a small beauty salon where a tall young woman dressed in rainbow-colored stretch pants was blow-drying an older woman's hair.

"We need food," I said.

"Order me some fresh fish, I don't care what kind," Giselle said. "I'm going to get cleaned up in this salon."

"Seriously?"

"Look at my hair. It's filthy."

She went into the salon and I went into the pub. Hardly anyone was there, so I took a small table in the back, kept my Foxy's hat pulled low, and waited for a waitress. After ten minutes, none had come, so I went to the bar.

"Help you?" the droopy-eyed bartender said.

"Couple beers and what's the catch of the day?"

"Yellowtail snapper or dolphin."

I ordered two yellowtail dinners and carried two cold Caribs back to the table. Mine was half-finished before I sat down. A television was on behind the bar, tuned to a local channel with Jeopardy on. The bartender was fixated on the show.

A lone person walked in, glanced around, and headed toward me. I lowered my hat to hide my eyes. I felt the person walk right up to my table—

It was Giselle, but she looked totally different.

"Like it?"

"I thought you were going to get a shampoo or something."

Giselle's long brunette hair was now blonde and cut into a bob. Her teeth glistened white, and she was every bit as beautiful with short hair as she had been with a full mane.

"Very sexy," I said.

She frowned.

"I'm not kidding! You look good with short hair—"

"Except for this." She tilted her head to the side so I could see the long gash on the top of her scalp before donning the blue Foxy's hat. She picked up the beer and took a long pull. Past her I saw the image on the television shift from Alex Trebek to a news team. I couldn't hear what the anchor was saying, but when the image shifted to what appeared to be amateur video footage, the scene felt familiar. It only took a second to realize it was footage of us from Magens Bay on St. Thomas.

"Oh shit," I said.

Giselle peered over her shoulder as the video changed from a shot of us surrounded by a dozen people to one that zoomed in on the black helicopter that had attacked Boom-Boom's compound. The picture was grainy, but the small helicopter was instantly recognizable to us now.

Giselle took in a sudden breath.

The bartender turned up the volume.

"… exploded, and significant gunfire followed. Three people were found dead at the hilltop property, but no names have been released to the public."

"Damn," I said.

"The helicopter fled under a hail of gunfire and was last seen speeding due east at high speed at a very low altitude."

The camera flashed back to the reporter, and behind him was a photo of Giselle, followed by one of me. "In other news, several people claimed to have seen First Lady Giselle Huibert at Frenchman's Reef Hotel today, along with her companion, Charles Buck Reilly. A French security officer was found gagged and tied up in the presidential suite, along with a hotel security person who had been knocked out and hidden in the hotel's service area. Mrs. Huibert and Mr. Reilly are being sought by police for questioning related to these incidents, as well as in regard to the shooting high over Magens Bay."

I felt myself shrinking into the seat of my chair, afraid the bartender would recognize us. Giselle no longer looked anything like her picture, but I still had the same shoulder-length dirty blond hair, and my six-foot three-inch frame was hard to hide.

"That salon still open?" I said.

Giselle nodded.

Fifteen minutes later I returned with my first crew cut since sixth grade, when my father last cut my hair on our back porch. My yellowtail was cold, but I washed it down with another beer.

"You miss it, don't you?" Giselle said.

I put my fork down. "I'm just used to it," I said and returned to my dinner.

"Hair grows back," she said.

I laughed.

"Closing time, folks," the bartender said.

I paid at the bar. "Any taxis around to give us a ride out to Leverick Bay Resort?"

The bartender's droopy eyes opened wider. "I'll give you a ride for fifty dollars."

Ridiculous. "Twenty-five," I said. Still ridiculous, but now was not the time to be stubborn.

He nodded and we all walked outside.

42

THE DRIVER HAD FAILED TO TELL US HE DROVE A PICKUP TRUCK. Rather than jamming ourselves into the cab and running the risk of conversation, Giselle and I sat in the bed of the truck. We headed away from Spanish Town and followed Centerline Road through the narrow strip of the island with Savanna Bay to the north and Handsome Bay to the south. Stars popped out like pin lights against the black sky overhead. The waning moon and wisps of Milky Way did nothing to mask the dozen shooting stars we spotted out over the Caribbean Sea as we climbed through the dark green forest of Gorda Peak National Park.

The driver didn't hurry, and Giselle and I were lost in thought out here on the eastern edge of the British Virgin Islands. We'd run out of big islands to hide on, and tomorrow we'd have to get help, whether Giselle agreed or not. With her head on my shoulder, I felt her body shudder with silent sobs. I pulled her close and tried to support her as the truck bounced over rough portions of road.

"It was all a failure," she said. "And more people died. Zidane and Frappier are free, and we found no evidence against François."

I squeezed her closer. "They're all dirty."

"But we can't prove anything. It was all for nothing."

Leverick Bay was at the end of the road, and the hotel was lit like a beacon to lost souls. I hoped there would be a room available, or we'd have to sleep on the beach. I gently shook Giselle awake as we entered the hotel's driveway, and the driver let us off out front.

"This is the first resort to open after the storms," he said. "And it's only partially open."

We had no bags. Hopefully, he assumed we'd already checked in.

The only cash I had was what Jay had lent me, and it was all hundred-dollar bills, so the driver got a fat tip. He never gave us another look as he drove slowly back toward the road that brought us here. I hesitated outside in the driveway where he'd let us off.

"What's wrong?" Giselle said.

"I have a bad feeling."

"About getting recognized?"

I nodded.

She glanced around the darkness. Behind the resort, which I now saw had only one building with lights on inside, was the blackness of ocean and a smattering of tiny lights from residences up on the hills.

"No place to run if we're spotted," she said.

I didn't want to stand out front any longer. "Let's take a walk around the grounds and check it out."

She took hold of my arm and we walked around reception and followed a landscaped path that led inside the resort. The main building had a restaurant and bar that was partially open to the outside and faced the ocean. We could see a few groups of people dining inside and at the bar, where soft steel drum music played. The path led past a swimming pool that glowed blue, then down to a beach where waves broke against the shore, their brief crests lit by the moon.

To the right of the path were the buildings that hadn't been reopened but were in varying stages of repair. The one closest to the water appeared to be nearly complete. A fence blocked access to these buildings.

"Let's walk to the beach," I said.

We took off our shoes and the sand was cool on my feet. The sounds of surf and distant laughter were a tonic that I knew could provide a false sense of security. I steered Giselle down the beach, away from the light of the resort. An idea festered in my head.

"Where we can go next?" she said.

"Next? There's no islands left. We're at the farthest east end of Virgin Gorda, which is the easternmost island in the BVI. We've run as far as we can go, Giselle." I took her in my arms. We were exhausted and the need for sleep was paramount. "Tomorrow we need to make the call. It's foolish to wait any longer, especially now that we're wanted for questioning back on St. Thomas."

"I know you're right, Buck, I do. But I don't trust the police or any security agencies. They have been at the nexus of all of this—"

"Not the FBI. I know Booth. He's a jerk and self-centered, but he's trustworthy. He'll position it to take credit for whatever happens, but he won't sell us out."

She stepped back from me and turned to face the ocean. "I have another idea."

"What?"

"François and I have a wealthy friend here in the British Virgin Islands who I think could help me—us."

"François' friend? Really? You'd trust him over—"

"He's both of our friends, and a very honorable man. He's very wealthy and smart."

"I don't know, Giselle. That seems crazy to me. If he is a friend, don't you think they'd be watching him? In case you try to contact him?"

She was quiet for a long moment, her back turned toward me as she faced the abyss of the ocean at night. "Possibly, but he's security-conscious, too."

I stepped closer and wrapped my arms around her from behind. "I have an idea, too. I'm going to check this building behind the beach here. It looks like they're almost finished restoring it. I'd much rather have a cozy king-size bed to climb into, but going to the front desk feels like a bad idea now."

She nodded once and squeezed my arm.

"You wait out here," I said. "I'll go see if I can get around that fence."

I continued slowly down the beach, glancing in all directions for other guests, employees, or security, but saw none. No wonder—the phosphorescent dial on my old Rolex Submariner showed it was nearly 10 p.m. Both buildings that faced the beach were dark and uninhabited. Between them was a gate in the construction fence. It was unlocked.

Once inside, I hurried to try a sliding glass door on one of the oceanfront rooms. It was locked. So were the next three. The fourth, however, slid open smoothly. I felt the corners of my mouth bend in a smile. Inside, the room was clean and freshly painted, and there were bathroom fixtures. I tried the faucet—water came out.

Nice.

There was no furniture and the floor was tile, but it was cool and we could sleep here and call Booth in the morning. With a fresh spring in my step, I exited the way I'd come, slid the door closed, glanced around for people, saw none, and returned to the beach through the fence gate. I jogged up the beach.

Giselle was gone.

43

WHERE THE HELL WAS SHE?
I jogged farther down the beach and saw nothing, so I returned to the path that led up to the resort. Could someone have followed us? Had the driver recognized us and sold us out to the press, or worse?

Damn!

I tried to keep a casual pace as I walked up the path. Maybe she had to use the bathroom—I hoped she didn't go to the front desk to try to get a room.

Laughter sounded in the bar and I glanced to my right. It was dimly lit, but I could see a small group having drinks. I spotted Giselle in the back of the room holding something—a phone?

I froze, staring in through the open patio bar. After a moment she extended her arm to hang it up, turned, and walked casually toward where I stood outside.

She hadn't spotted me, so I walked quickly back down the path and sat on a bench that faced the water. A moment later, I heard footsteps coming my way. A lone figure walked past. It was her.

I followed after her as silently as I could. My heart pounded hard and my mouth had gone dry. What was happening? Who had she called? How should I play this?

She stopped in the same place on the beach where we'd been standing before I went to check the empty building. Where I'd told her to wait. She must have heard me because she spun around to face me when I was still twenty feet away.

"Buck?" her voice was high. "*Mon Dieu*, you scared me. Where were you?"

"I found a way into the fenced area. There's an open room in that first building. It has running water and it's clean."

I waited.

"That's great! Let's go there. I'm cold."

Um-hmm. "Follow me."

She took my arm as she'd been doing for days now, except this time I felt foolish. Reality crashed down on me like a landslide. Had I been a complete fool? A moron? Duped by the beautiful first lady to believe she cared for me—

What an idiot!

At the gate, we entered and I closed it behind us, walked down to the fourth room, and slid the glass door open. Giselle walked inside the dark room without hesitation.

"There's no furniture, but—"

"I have news."

I stood with my feet planted wide, as if ready to take a punch. "News?"

"I went into the bar like I was a guest, asked for the phone, got an outside line, and called my friend." She was literally bouncing on the balls of her feet as she spoke.

"You mean the friend you share with François? That was very dangerous. You didn't tell him where we are, did you?" If his phones were being tapped …

"It's fine, I'm certain. We can trust him. Please don't worry."

"You *did* tell him where we are."

"He's coming to get us. Now. On his boat. We'll be safe—"

"Where's he coming from?"

"He's close by—that's what made me think of him. It's perfect."

She reached for me, but I blocked her grasp.

"I can't believe you did that," I said. "After all we've been through, you call a stranger and tell him where we are? Without discussing it with me?"

"We did discuss it, on the beach—"

"And I said it was a dangerous idea. The FBI could be here in an hour—"

"And I said no to that!"

"Ssshhh!"

"Don't sshhh me!" She took a step back.

I crossed my arms and took a couple of deep breaths. We weren't a couple, and she'd been through a hell I couldn't have imagined if I hadn't been right there with her. But her international reputation was on the line, whereas mine had been ruined long ago.

I let that realization sink in a moment longer and then inhaled a measured breath.

"From now on, you make the decisions—you don't pay attention to a word I say anyway." I paused. "I'm just concerned for your safety."

She unclenched her arms and took me in a hug.

"I know, and I love you for that, I truly do. And I do listen to everything you say, but you need to trust me on this, okay?"

Love?

I put my hands on her hips, ran them up her back, and pulled her in close. I wanted to believe that. I'd come to the Virgin Islands hoping to find love with Scarlet, and I could have never imagined all of this. But still, a nagging twitch had started to tweak my left eyelid. That was never a good sign.

I licked my lips. "I trust you."

She nuzzled her cheek into my neck. "Good, because my friend will be here any minute."

44

F ROM THE SHORE WE SAW A LIGHT FLASH, and we heard the sound of a boat's engine soon after.

"I hope that's him." Giselle said.

"Better be."

A dark silhouette materialized on the water. It was still too far out to determine the size of the boat or how many people were aboard. Her friend must have been close, because as she'd expected, he arrived quickly—less than an hour since she'd phoned him.

The lump in my throat felt like a golf ball.

"Listen, I'm sure it'll be fine." I paused. "But if not, then you run inside the hotel screaming bloody murder and I'll fight like hell to buy you time."

She extended up on her tiptoes and gave me a quick kiss. "You are gallant, Buck Reilly. Now stop worrying."

I'd been called a lot of things but never gallant.

The boat came into view, and it looked to be about thirty-five feet, maybe more. It had an enclosed cabin but was low on the water, not like a trawler but more like a launch. A big low-slung launch was an odd boat to have out on the Caribbean. The engine sound was a quiet yet solid hum. Inboard, not outboard.

How deep was the water here?

"We'd better wade out some," I said.

A man peered around the side of the cabin, and his white hair flashed in the moonlight.

"Please come out to the boat!" he yelled. "I don't want to run her aground."

I took Giselle by the hand and we stepped into the mild surf—it felt cool at first, but the water had to be eighty-five degrees. The closer we got to the boat, the more substantial it appeared. Not in length but in detail and quality. Giselle had mentioned that her friend was wealthy, but he also had the good taste to go with it. That's all too rare among the wealthy these days. I should know—I used to count myself as one of them.

"I'm afraid you'll have to swim around to the stern, but there's a ladder there and I have robes and warm beverages awaiting you," the captain said.

English accent?

Up to our waists, we lowered ourselves in the rest of the way. Giselle hung on to me and I kept my right hand running along the side of the boat. The rumble of the engine was steady but not modulating, so I could tell it wasn't in gear. We reached the aft end of the boat—maybe forty-feet long. On the transom there was a teak swimming platform with a wide ladder that he'd lowered for us.

I tried to stand but the water was too deep. I treaded water and helped Giselle to the ladder, holding her with my right arm until she took hold.

"Welcome aboard," the man said.

Definitely a British accent.

I hung on to the base of the ladder, and once Giselle was up and out, I placed my feet on the lower rung. As I ascended, I couldn't help but notice the boat was beautifully designed with rich wood on nearly every surface. At the top, I saw that the man and Giselle were in a tight embrace. She faced me, and her smile was wide. He had a shock of white hair but looked tall and fit from behind.

When I jumped onto the deck with a thud, it broke their embrace. Giselle held up her hand toward me.

"This is Buck Reilly, my savior in more ways than one."

When the man turned around, I froze as he held out his hand.

"Edward Harrell."

I'd met my share of wealthy and famous people, but few were as iconic and accomplished as *Sir* Edward Harrell.

"It's an honor to meet you, sir. Thank you for coming to our rescue."

"We'll talk once we're underway," he said.

Sir Edward moved with the deft familiarity of a man who knew his boat well. The bridge was in the front of the cabin overlooking the beautifully curved wood bow. We followed him inside. In the back of my mind I was fighting off feeling perturbed at Giselle for not telling me the identity of her friend.

"He's a very honorable man," she'd said. "He's very wealthy and smart."

Understatements, all. As a man who'd lived a life of adventure; scaling Everest, base-jumping, accomplished pilot, not to mention a world renown inventor and business man, Edward Harrell was one of my idols, and I didn't have many.

"There's a pair of robes there on the couch, and hot tea in the pot." Sir Edward pointed toward a beautiful cream-colored sofa and leather chairs inside the salon. Tea and cookies were laid out on a shiny wood table.

Giselle smiled at me. I glanced back at Leverick Bay to the dark, empty building I'd proposed we sleep in. Compared with this yacht … A pulse of inadequacy rekindled the twitch in my eye. The fortune I'd built and lost at e-Antiquity was a rounding error for Sir Edward — maybe a month's worth of interest on his billions of dollars of holdings.

We donned the robes and Giselle poured us both tea.

What else had Giselle said on the beach? "He's close by."

"Where are we headed?" I said.

"My friend Richard owns an island nearby," he said.

Of course. Sir Richard Branson owned Necker Island, a private seventy-five acre enclave that he rented out to the world's rich and famous. Branson and Harrell were some of Britain's most famous business titans. Necker wasn't far off Virgin Gorda's north end. Why hadn't Giselle suggested this sooner?

The boat moved quietly away from Leverick Bay before it acceler-ated soundly with no vibration or even a lift of the bow. Giselle and I moved forward and stood at each side of Sir Edward as he steered the ship, checking his radar, GPS, and sonar. Once on the proper heading, he turned to Giselle.

"You, my dear, have been all over the news. I'm so glad you contacted me. I've been worried sick."

"I thought of calling you a few times, but we've literally been on the run for days. And I didn't want to put you in … an awkward position."

Sir Edward glanced at me briefly.

"Nonsense. I'm just glad to know you're safe. There have been inconceivable accusations made on the news, and according to my sources there's been an all-out search for you both by the authorities— English, French, American—but also by others offering massive rewards to learn your whereabouts."

"We've used my contacts to stay a step ahead and out of harm's way," I said.

Another glance my way. "Indeed."

As if she sensed the current in the air, Giselle spoke up. "Buck has been amazing. He rescued me from the sinking helicopter—I was shot down! Has that been reported yet?"

"Dear God, no. It certainly hasn't." He turned back toward me, his brow now a landscape of wrinkles. "And why didn't you take her to the police straight away?"

"She had amnesia for the first day—"

"I wouldn't allow him to take me to the police. François' head of security is involved with the conspiracy to kill me—they killed my secretary and personal security detail. I'm not sure about François' involvement."

Sir Edward shot her a sharp glance.

"And Buck has contacts at the FBI—"

"We're in the *British* Virgin Islands, lad. The FBI has no jurisdiction here."

"True, but the incident occurred in U.S. waters," I said, "and Giselle and the G8 summit were in the U.S. Virgin Islands."

Sir Edward pursed his lips. My gut told me I'd have an uphill battle winning him over. It might not be possible at all, but I knew I'd done everything I could to help Giselle. If they really were good friends, he must have known she was a strong woman who would have chosen her own course of action.

The approach to Necker Island involved several course changes, some marked by navigational buoys and others noted on his GPS, which showed every sand spit, depth change, and, more important, a previous line of passage like a trail of bread crumbs that he expertly followed.

A lit dock appeared ahead and Sir Edward guided the boat as if he drove it every night. He probably did while he was here, but given his portfolio of mega-companies and investments around the globe, I couldn't imagine he got to spend that much time on-island.

"Man the bow line, will you please?" he said.

I hurried from the cabin and made my way up the port side of the boat, which was wide and unobstructed. A nylon rope was coiled perfectly on the dock, which I grabbed and secured to a bow cleat. By the time I hurried to the back, he'd tied it off.

"Fortunately, there are no other guests on the island, and once I got your call I sent Richard's staff home." He took Giselle by the arm. "Come, let's go inside, give you the chance to get cleaned up, put on some fresh clothing, and discuss how to fix this mess."

I followed after them, feeling like a third wheel. I was confident Sir Edward Harrell would be able to talk sense into Giselle and help me get her to safety, but it was important that he hear the whole story first.

45

W E WERE GIVEN SEPARATE SUITES, AND IT WAS THE FIRST TIME in days that Giselle and I had been apart. An unfamiliar sense of loneliness had me hurry through a shower. The hot water, soap, and shampoo felt glorious, but I was anxious to not miss any of their discussion. The closet contained white Necker Island polo shirts, and there were several pairs of khaki shorts in the dresser. I donned some that fit and glanced at the king-size bed. Whether I slept here or in Giselle's room, I didn't plan to sleep alone tonight.

The great room was decorated simply yet elegantly with original art, sturdy island-appropriate furniture, and lush area rugs that my bare feet sank into. There was a bar at the end, along with a world-class collection of rare rum and other liquors. There was a bowl of fresh ice on the counter, which I took as an invitation to make a drink. I chose Black Tot rum, placed one ice cube in a snifter, and poured out two fingers of rum. After a long gulp, I poured another finger and walked to the center of the room.

Several doors led off the great room, as did four corridors. I wasn't sure which room Giselle had been given or where Sir Edward's bedroom was, so I wasn't going to blunder around trying door handles. I sat on the side of the couch, leaving room for her to join me, and sipped my rum. My body sank into the soft cushions and I finally started to relax. After a glance at my old Submariner, I was surprised to see it was after midnight. What a day this had been.

Fifteen minutes later, Sir Edward appeared carrying a bottle of white wine and three glasses. He placed them on the table in front of me.

"Thank you so much, Sir Edward. I feel human for the first time in a week."

"Of course. I'd do anything for Giselle." He then walked to the bar and collected the bowl where I'd taken ice for my rum. Back at the table, he placed the wine in the ice bucket in the center and sat in a chair that faced me.

"Can we discuss strategy before Giselle joins us?" I said.

"I'm familiar with your history, Buck. That of e-Antiquity and its decline." His lip curled at the end of his statement as if he'd bitten into spoiled fruit.

Oh, crap.

"You made several critical discoveries," he said. "In fact, my broker acquired several pieces from the Serpent King's tomb, and I then followed your story with interest."

"It was an amazing run—"

"Quite." He paused. "And an astonishing collapse." He stared long and hard into my eyes. "Integrity is paramount amongst my friends and executives."

I winced. His left brow lifted.

"My partner ruined me and my company," I said.

"Indeed."

There would be no sympathy from him, though, which I didn't expect or deserve. I'd been complicit enough in e-Antiquity's failure, if only through ignorance and naiveté, to share the blame for its demise. I hadn't liquidated our assets or lied to analysts, investors, and shareholders—that was all Jack—but I had whisked away clues to as-yet unfound treasures when the writing was on the wall and then lied to the FBI and the SEC to save my ass. So yes, my integrity was besmirched. Some would say I'd been a pirate, born two hundred years too late.

I considered dropping Harry Greenbaum's name—he was also British, super-rich, and had been one of e-Antiquity's main investors. No doubt Harry and Sir Edward knew each other, but I didn't want to tarnish Harry's name by mentioning our former affiliation and continued friendship. It was time to blow Sir Edward's mind instead.

"Men associated with President Huibert's security team are hunting us with the intent to kill."

"That is an incredible statement. I have known François for decades. He is a loyal public servant, and while his responsibilities to France may have distanced him from Giselle, he was a more committed husband than most men of his—"

"She caught him with an underage girl, having sex in their suite on St. Thomas."

Sir Edward lowered his eyes for a moment. "Egads, how awful."

"With the head of security filming them."

That left Sir Edward speechless.

"She ran and was on her way to Beef Island to return to France when a rocket brought her helicopter down. I happened to be spearfishing nearby and saw the rocket hit the chopper. The rest, as they say, is history."

He exhaled a breath with force. "Lucky you were there."

"Indeed." I offered a slight smile.

"Apparently, it's worked out well for you."

We held each other's stare for a long second. This was not a wink-wink insinuation over a sexual conquest—I could practically hear him thinking, trying to understand how Giselle and I had become so close so fast.

He finally nodded once. "Sorry, it's all just a bit shocking. As I said, I've known Giselle and François a very long time."

"How do we get her to safety?"

He sat forward. "We have a highly qualified security team, former Royal Marine commandos at our disposal here."

"To what end? Where will they take her? How will they return her safely to France, or wherever she wants to go, and provide her the resources and podium to tell her story? She's determined to expose François, which is why we went back to the hotel on St. Thomas."

After I explained what we had done at the hotel—capturing the second in command of security, extracting limited information from him, and then the trade for Diego—Sir Edward sat back with less fire in his eyes.

"It was all Giselle's idea. I tried talking her out of it, but as I said, she's determined—"

"Talking about me?"

Giselle had entered the great room from the center corridor. Sir Edward and I both stood.

"Join us, my dear. Buck has been explaining the, ah, situation." He shook his head. "Quite grisly."

As I hoped, Giselle sat next to me. Sir Edward opened the wine and poured three glasses. I drained my rum and accepted a glass.

Giselle yawned deeply. "No wine for me. I came to say good night. I'm exhausted." She glanced from me to our host. "Thank you for sparing me the need to explain the details."

"I'm terribly sorry," Sir Edward said.

"And we cannot stay here beyond tonight, Edward. I will not put you, or Richard's island in danger," she said.

"Fear not. His man Lamont's team will be here within the hour to secure the island and ensure everyone's safety."

"Tomorrow we need to get you into protective custody," I said.

"No. Tomorrow I need to go public with my story—incomplete or not," Giselle said.

I sat forward. "We can make arrangements on St. John. We'll get Booth—"

"No. I want to get out of these islands altogether."

"I can get you to London on my jet in the morning and have my PR team ready a press conference and prepare for damage control," Sir Edward said.

Giselle's face relaxed. "I'll sleep on it. And for now, I bid you each *bonne nuit. et merci beaucoup.*" She bent down and gave me a peck on the cheek and then did the same with Sir Edward. She then disappeared down the same hall she had come from.

"We'll discuss this further in the morning, Buck. The security team will deploy silently and I'll put out feelers to trusted authorities. Get some sleep, and don't leave your room. The instructions to security will be to shoot first and ask questions later."

I took my glass of wine with me. As tired as I was, being by myself felt instantly lonely. With a glance back before entering my room, I saw Sir Edward on his cell phone.

Shoot first, indeed. So much for spending the night in Giselle's arms.

46

I SLEPT FAR DEEPER THAN I'D EXPECTED TO. When I awoke, the room was still dark. There was no clock, and the luminescence on the dial of my old Rolex had faded, so I was unsure of the time. I lay there thinking about all that had happened these past few days, concerned about these next moves. I trusted in Sir Edward and was confident he'd help us execute a safe return of Giselle into a public setting where the truth would protect her, and the sooner the better. Once her story was told, there'd be no reason to kill her.

The pressure in my bladder finally caused me to flip on a light to find my way to the bathroom. No light came from the windows. No wonder—the windows in my suite all had blackout shades.

I grabbed my watch—shit!

It was 9:20 in the morning.

After splashing water on my face, I re-dressed in the same outfit I'd had on last night, unlocked my door, and opened it slowly. I assumed the shoot-first instructions no longer applied since it was daylight. The great room was empty. No way everyone was still asleep.

I walked into the corridor where Giselle had disappeared last night. There were two rooms there, both with the doors open and both empty. One of the beds was unmade. I entered the room and smelled the pillow. Giselle had slept here. There was no sign of her limited possessions in the room or the bathroom.

An uneasy pang hit my gut.

Back in the hall, I found that it ended at a door to the outside. I pushed the blackout curtains aside and saw Sir Edward in discussion with a man dressed in camouflage military attire. He had a side arm strapped to his belt. Other camouflaged men were visible amid the manicured grounds, and they all carried automatic weapons. SA80s, standard-issue assault rifles for the British military, by the looks of them.

I twisted the bolt lock and slowly pulled the door open. When he saw me, Sir Edward waved me outside.

A glance in each direction revealed no fewer than six security men, all armed and watching me. The two men spoke no further as they awaited my arrival.

"Glad you were able to sleep, Buck," Sir Edward said.

"Where's Giselle?"

His eyelids narrowed. "We thought it best for her safety to separate you."

Perspiration beaded on my forehead. "What does that mean?"

"She left by boat an hour ago, escorted by a pair of Mr. Lamont's men." Sir Edward nodded to the man who I presumed to be Mr. Lamont.

"Their destination?" I wiped the sweat from my brow.

"Tortola. They'll be greeted near Beef Island by BVI police, then escorted to my jet at the airport. My pilot will take her to London, where British Secret Service agents will meet the plane. There will be a press conference before the day is over."

"That's *it?*"

Sir Edward had kept a straight face. He was no stranger to global threats, politics, or the need for high security, but he clearly knew there was a personal side to this situation, too. He reached into the breast pocket of his khaki shirt.

"She left you a letter."

My hand visibly shook as I accepted it from him. He bit his lip.

I cleared my throat. "What about me?"

"You can take one of Richard's speedboats and return to St. Thomas, or St. John. We'll fetch it from there later."

"One of my men can accompany you," Mr. Lamont said.

"That won't be necessary. I'll get my gear."

As I walked back to the door I'd come from, my feet felt numb on the ground.

Son of a bitch.

No doubt it was best for Giselle's safety, and it made sense to get her to London. What did I think, she'd come back to Key West with me and camp out in my suite at the La Concha Hotel?

But still, the hollow feeling in my stomach was now more like a black hole in my heart, and it hurt like hell.

Back inside my room, I closed the door, sat on the bed, and removed the note from the sealed envelope.

> *Cher* Buck,
>
> Thank you so much for everything. I feel terrible leaving without saying goodbye, and it's not goodbye, but *j'us que la prochain fois*—until the next time I see you. Richard's security experts felt it wise to whisk me off, and a professional team awaits me in London. I should be there before afternoon tea, he says.
>
> Once the news calms down, I will contact you. I want you to know I meant everything I said.
>
> Je t'aime, Giselle.

I exhaled a long breath.

Really?

Would I ever see her again?

I'd never been lucky at love, and this was no exception. Hell, this whole trip started as a vacation with Scarlet, the mother of my child and the one person in my life I should have stayed with, but I'd been such a fool at the height of my former success. Instead I'd fallen for the supermodel, blinded by success and … well, other things.

I changed out of my Necker Island polo, put on my dirty fishing shirt, and put the letter in my breast pocket.

Sir Edward had been wise and decisive, and most important, Giselle had confidence in him and agreed to leave the islands and get to safety. I'd been unable to persuade her to do that, so while my pride was hurt, my heart wasn't entirely broken. Just somewhat fractured.

Time to get off this island and back to reality. No more glass slippers or fairy tale romances. Ray would be here somewhere, and the sooner I could get inside my 1946 Grumman Widgeon and back to Key West, the better.

A shit storm of press would no doubt await.

Just what I needed.

47

E QUIPPED WITH A BOXED LUNCH AND A SATELLITE PHONE that belonged to Richard Branson, I departed alone from Necker Island on one of Necker's thirty-four foot SeaVee equipped with three 300-horsepower outboards and Edward's best wishes. A north wind had kicked up overnight, and there were now three- to five-foot seas topped with swirling whitecaps as far as the eye could see. I hoped Giselle's passage had been smooth.

The boat was one of the best center consoles on the market, and this one had every possible option and state-of-the-art electronics. I'd have expected nothing less of Sir Richard. The distance to St. Thomas was thirty-five miles, which at this pace would take about an hour and a half.

After running for thirty minutes, I needed a bio break and had a phone call to make. I'd been worried about Diego and Boom-Boom ever since seeing the helicopter attack the compound on St. Thomas yesterday afternoon. But first I needed to gut-check the situation with Special Agent Edward T. Booth.

I powered on the satellite phone and dialed Booth's cell number. After two rings, he picked up.

"Hello, who's calling please?" Booth sounded uncharacteristically formal.

"It's me, Reilly."

"Why does the caller ID say Richard Branson?"

"Long story."

"You're full of long stories, Reilly. Where's the first lady?"

"Gone to safety."

"What's that supposed to mean?"

"It means she's either on Tortola or headed there with members of a mercenary security force."

"You're shitting me."

The twitch fluttered in my left eye.

"Would I shit you?"

"Aside from the fact that you promised I'd be the one to collect her, that was a bonehead move, entrusting her to private security types."

"They're former Royal Marines. Sir Richard keeps them on retainer."

"Sir Richard, huh? This has been some adventure for you, hasn't it, hotshot?"

There was an edge to Booth's voice above and beyond what I'd expected.

"Look, Sir Edward Harrell had her whisked off while I was sleeping—"

"Edward Harrell, too? Shit, Reilly."

"Before that I tried repeatedly to get her to allow me to call you in, but she wouldn't have it." I paused. "Aside from missing out on taking the credit for her rescue, what else is bothering you?"

"Had you kept in touch with me like I'd told you, then you'd know that whoever is behind this nightmare has offered a fifty million-dollar reward for the assassination of the first lady before she goes public. A photo and a finger is all that's needed. The mercenary community's as active as we've ever seen it. Former Royal Marines or not, fifty million is a serious incentive."

Shit!

"Why Tortola?" Booth said.

"It's a British thing."

"Are British Secret Service agents there to meet her?"

"No, local authorities are meeting her boat and taking her to Sir Edward's jet, which is waiting at Beef Island."

"Local authorities? You're kidding me, right? That means your old friend Detective Bramble, who's as crooked as they come."

Bramble. Crap. Why hadn't I thought of that?

"There's nobody more senior on the Tortola police force who can handle this?"

"Not anymore."

The wind whistled past my ears and I glanced to the north. The hazy coast of Tortola was visible on the horizon. The east end was the closest point, which is where Beef Island is located.

"Can you get there?" I said.

"We're not welcome, Reilly. It's a British thing."

Damn it!

I cut the wheel on the boat and jammed the throttles forward. The SeaVee leaped ahead on the waves like a porpoise.

"I'll head to the airport there now, Booth. Do something!"

"You should have called me, Reilly!"

"I wanted to, believe me."

The east end of Tortola was maybe thirty minutes away. I pushed the boat as hard as the seas would allow. We bounced airborne over multiple large waves—the sound of her three stainless steel props churned the air.

Based on what Sir Edward had said, Giselle left an hour before me. Would they be hauling ass full out or taking their time so as to not freak her out? If the latter was the case, I could make up distance by pushing the boat to its limit.

WHHAAANNNGGG!

The props again shredded air as we lit off another wave.

The satellite phone was still in my hand. I hit the memory button Sir Edward had programmed to go straight to his private cell phone. After two rings, he answered.

"Buck? Is everything all right?"

"I don't know, but can you contact the security team that took Giselle to Tortola to check in with them, please?"

"Why, what's happened?"

"I talked to my contact at the FBI. He said there's a fifty million-dollar reward on Giselle's head. Dead, *not* alive."

"Dear Lord."

"He also said that every mercenary or hit man within a thousand miles is amped up and looking to score." I bent my knees as the boat jumped another wave and landed hard. "How well do you know those former Royal Marines?"

Sir Edward cleared his throat. "Lamont is a trusted friend. He's here now. Hold on."

The sound of muffled voices sounded over the already distorted satellite phone. After several seconds, Sir Edward returned.

"Bad news, Buck. Lamont informed me that several of his men were new, fresh in from Europe. He's dialing them up now."

I waited.

And waited.

And waited.

"No answer on their emergency frequency," Sir Edward said.

"Damn it!"

"Agreed. Where are you?" Sir Edward said.

"Middle of the Sir Francis Drake Channel headed northwest toward Beef Island."

"I'll contact my pilot for an update. My plane and flight crew should be intact unless the bloody buggers have taken over the entire airport. I'll ring you back."

Click.

My gut churned. I wasn't sure Booth or Sir Edward could do anything. I dialed another number.

The phone rang twice. "Ray Floyd here."

"Ray, where are you?"

He hesitated. "Is this Richard Branson?"

The damn caller ID again.

"It's me, Buck. Where the hell are you?"

"St. Thomas at the airport, like you told me to be. What the heck is—"

"Any word from Boom-Boom or Diego?"

Ray gave me the sobering answer to my question and I nearly drew blood from biting my lip so hard. I shared with him where I was headed and gave him specific instructions. "Rally any help possible."

I pushed down harder on the throttles and the boat leaped wildly in the rollicking waves. If I didn't capsize, I'd be there in twenty minutes.

I just hoped I'd be in time.

48

I COULD SEE THAT COMMERCIAL JETS WERE TAXIING ON BEEF ISLAND, now just ten minutes away. That was a good sign—if there'd been an assault at the airport, nothing would be moving.

The waves had settled down a bit now that the island was blocking the northerly wind, and the boat skipped across the water like a missile. Unfortunately, that image conjured up a memory of the streaking rocket that destroyed Giselle's helicopter.

From the corner of my left eye I spotted movement in the sky. A black helicopter roared overhead, maybe five hundred feet above the water. It was the exact same make and color as the helicopter that had come hunting us on Jost Van Dyke and delivered Diego to Magens Bay. It was traveling at high speed directly toward the airport at Beef Island.

Then another black chopper blew past.

Bastards.

Would they be on their way to grab her? Or maybe fire another rocket at the boat that was taking her there, or Sir Edward's jet?

Navigational buoys in toward Tortola appeared, and the channel took me wide of the island's tip. The black helicopter disappeared into the midst of the airport. It was hard to see much from the water, so I continued on at high speed, skidding around buoys to keep from running aground as I blew through the Camanoe islands.

There was a dock near the airport, but it was for airport supply ships, not public traffic. Not like that would stop me. I was seriously outgunned—hell, I didn't even have a gun. If Bramble was still the crooked piece of shit he used to be, he and the former Royal Marines could be in cahoots to make Giselle disappear.

I'd have zero clout at the airport. Booth was useless, since the Brits didn't want the FBI in their territory.

I needed a game changer.

Back on the satellite phone, I made one call, then another, connecting miraculously on both. One of my potential saviors had just boarded a plane to leave town, and the other was a permanent fixture here. Both said they'd help. They took my instructions without question.

A massive British Airways jet roared off the end of the runway, lifting into the sky just ahead of me—a shockwave of jet wash hit me in the face and I could feel the heat off the twin engines under its wings. That was another positive sign—my hands gripped the wheel tightly— or a bad one. Had they already taken Giselle away?

There was another boat tied up at the dock. It was the launch Sir Edward had used to collect Giselle and me from Leverick Bay just last night. My heart rate accelerated. I was on the right path. Now it was all down to timing—and the armed former Royal Marines, the entire Tortola police force, Customs agents at the airport, and God knew who else.

Ignoring the no-wake zone, I drove fast to the dock and then backed off quickly to pull up adjacent to the other boat. I killed the engines, tied off on its cleats, and jumped aboard the other vessel.

I had no evidence that Giselle was in danger, that the security team had double-crossed us, or even that Bramble had sold Giselle out, except for the fact that my gut was twisted tighter than a pretzel. My gut instincts had rarely let me down, and even though I'd have been happier than hell to be wrong right now, I proceeded with cautious abandon.

There was no visible sign of struggle on the launch, and the lines connecting it to the dock appeared to be tight and expertly tied. The bridge door was unlocked, so I stepped inside.

"Hello? Anybody home?"

I stood inside, listening, but heard nothing other than the remnants of the waves caused by my hasty landing as they whipped against the launch. A quick look around turned up nothing. Although I hadn't gone below deck last night, I took the few stairs down. The port door led to a small cabin. The bed covers were tight with military corners folded neatly on the end.

Nothing.

My breathing eased a hair.

Across the hall was the head. Inside, the small restroom was clean as a whistle. A scent caught my nose and I recognized the smell of Giselle's hair. She'd been in here. I stood still, soaking that up, willing her to send me a message from wherever she was, something that would ease my fears.

The toilet lid was closed, and I stepped on top of it to see if there was anything in the back of the cupboard overhead.

Nothing.

I stepped down.

Okay.

Her scent hit me again. I glanced down and felt foolish but opened the toilet lid.

My mouth fell open.

49

A WORD WAS WRITTEN ON THE INSIDE OF THE TOILET LID. Smeared, actually, with lipstick that now sat in the bottom of the dry commode.

"Help! GH."

Giselle!

There was one more door at the end of the corridor. I pulled it open—

Oh shit!

Inside were two men in the same camouflage uniforms as Lamont's team on Necker Island, but these two had bullet holes in their foreheads.

I ran up the steps to the deck and jumped over the gunwale onto the dock without breaking stride. My feet slapped hard against the aged wood planking of the short dock, which led to a concrete road on the right and up toward a storage building and a series of private airplane hangars, all of which were surrounded by a barbed wire-topped ten-foot chain link fence. A pink painted concrete wall prevented me from seeing into the airport from the dock, and had I not spotted the security camera, I would have kept running up the road toward the storage building.

Not that I couldn't use the help, but airport police responding to a security call about a fool afoot in the prohibited area was more likely to get me resistance than help. So I hurried, calmly, up the road. As it curved toward the building, the pink wall ended. I could see the tarmac beyond it.

The breath rushed from my lungs.

Both of the black helicopters were parked on the ground there, their blades spinning slowly, and beyond them was a beautiful private Falcon 8X jet with the Union Jack painted on its tail. It had to be Sir Edward's plane.

No pilots were visible in the plane's windows, and the passenger door was open. The windows were tinted on the helicopters, so it was impossible to tell if either of them was occupied. I scanned in every direction, including out toward the end of the private terminal area where two police SUVs were parked.

One big happy crooked family.

Sons of bitches.

Where was Giselle?

I did the only thing I could and continued to the end of the service road, where I found a gate with a call box and dial pad. Still nobody in sight. I pulled on the gate just as I noticed the camera under the eave of the storage building trained directly on me. The gate was locked.

Okay, now what, Reilly?

Weren't many choices. I leaned down to the dial pad and pushed in the zero button. A ringing sound emanated from a small speaker. It rang twice before someone answered.

"Yes, hello?"

"I need to get inside and to my plane," I said.

"What plane is that, sir?"

"Sir Edward Harrell's jet, there on the tarmac."

A long silence followed until it was finally broken.

"Identify yourself, sir."

I swallowed, hard.

Had Sir Edward or anyone on the Necker Island security team thought to alert the authorities that I'd be coming? "My name's Buck Reilly. You can call Sir Edward on Necker Island to confirm my access."

Another very long pause was followed by a loud click, and then the gate popped open. I entered the private area. Now what?

If Giselle were on board one of the helicopters, it would have already left. If she were on the jet, it, too, would have left, unless her captors were inside, negotiating with the pilots at gunpoint. That seemed unlikely, which left the storage building and the private aviation terminal beyond it.

The storage building had no windows but did have multidirectional cameras on every corner. Didn't matter—I was out of time. And worse, Giselle was out of time. I hurried to the door of the storage building. It was unlocked. Inside there was a small office with a man sitting reclined in a chair with his feet up on the desk. He was asleep, snoring. The rest of the building appeared to be dark inside.

Damn.

A familiar sound caught my attention.

Radial engines.

Ray.

I ran back outside just as the Beast settled onto the runway and taxied toward what I presumed to be Sir Edward's jet was parked. I smiled, briefly. Then I saw that the door on Sir Edward's jet was now closed.

Crap.

A police SUV sped from around the storage building and pulled up to where I was standing.

Four men jumped outside. All held handguns.

All were pointed at me.

"Stop right there!" The police officer closest to me yelled.

I held my hands up and gazed from man to man, trying to assess which of them were in charge so I could plead my case. Then another man stepped out from the SUV's backseat.

"Buck Reilly himself," he said.

Detective Bramble, the man who'd done everything possible to put me in prison under the false accusation that I'd killed a longtime friend of his who'd sold me a bogus treasure map.

"Didn't I warn you never to return to my island?"

"This is an emergency—"

"Spare me your drama, Reilly—"

"First Lady Giselle Huibert is here—"

"Your new girlfriend? If we can believe what we see on the tele."

"Someone killed the security guards and took her—"

"Enough!" Bramble said. Then to his men. "Bring him here."

Behind Bramble and his men, I saw that the Beast was now parked in front of Sir Edward's plane. Good job Ray. Just as I'd instructed Ray on our call.

The police officers rushed up to me. Surrounding me, they still had their guns drawn, but at least they were no longer pointed at me.

"Walk forward," one said.

I exhaled a long breath and walked toward Bramble. "If you're caught up in this, Bramble, you'll never get away with it. Your cut of fifty million or not—"

"Shut up and walk!" he said.

When I was almost to him, he abruptly turned and walked toward Harrell's jet, away from me and the SUV they'd arrived in. He slowed and I caught up to him. The men with us fanned out to our sides.

"Where are we going?" I said.

Bramble's cheeks were clenched and it looked as if he were chewing nails. He was a stout but short man, maybe five feet nine. He glanced up at me out of the corner of his eye.

Was that a smile?

The door on the Beast opened and Boom-Boom and Diego climbed outside. Their expressions appeared hard, even from this distance. I just hoped they didn't shoot anybody.

"Sir Edward called me," Bramble said.

I shifted my attention to him.

We kept walking. Bramble's statement finally registered.

His cheeks were again pressed tight. He gave me a slight nod.

Boom-Boom and Diego marched down the runway toward us. Diego gave me a thumbs-up. Bramble would no doubt know the two local gangsters, but he was focused on the helicopters.

"You ready, Reilly?" Bramble said.

"Ready for what?"

"Go!"

Bramble drew his weapon and ran forward, with two of his officers behind him, toward the closest black helicopter. The other two ran toward the other helicopter.

Holy shit!

50

I RAN AFTER THE SECOND TWO MEN TO KEEP THE NUMBERS EVEN. Of course, they were armed and I wasn't, but I'd beat the living shit out of anyone who had Giselle—

BOOM!

A shot was fired from the helicopter Bramble had bull-rushed—

BOOM! BOOM!

The left door on the helicopter flew open toward us and one of the two police officers I'd followed dropped into a firing position. A man's body fell out of the helicopter and landed hard on the tarmac. There was a bullet hole in his forehead and a line of blood down the side of his head. He had the same dark olive skin as the other men on Zidane's security team.

The rotor on the helicopter we were approaching started to increase in speed—

"Everybody out!" the lead police officer shouted.

The rotor continued faster—

BOOM! BOOM! BOOM! BOOM!

The police officer had blown major chunks off the helicopter's tail rotor. *This bird no fly*, passed through my head. The other officer had crossed to the port side of the chopper, and both of them had their weapons aimed at the pilot's compartment.

"Don't shoot!" I said. "Giselle may be in there!"

I ran forward and grabbed the helicopter's back door handle.

"Reilly!" Bramble's voice behind me sounded as if it were coming from underwater. "Don't!"

I shoved the door wide. Somebody was in back—

BOOM-BOOM-BOOM-BOOM!

Bullets rushed past my head—THWAP!

My cheek! I was spun hard toward the ground.

BANG! BANG! BANG!

Shots rang out from behind me as I hit the ground—fully conscious—my hand to my right cheek. Blood!

My eyes blurred.

Next thing I knew there were feet all around me—boots, Gucci loafers.

"Get up, Reilly."

I glanced up to see ... was it God?

He was black. And short. Angels surrounded him—Big ones.

God stuck his hand out to me. There was no white light.

"Come on, get up. You're just grazed."

Bramble.

I shook my head a few times as Boom-Boom and Diego stepped forward—my angels. Diego pressed a cloth against my cheek.

"The hell you doing here," Bramble said.

"You all right, Reilly?" Boom-Boom said.

Bramble's head nearly spun in a circle. "And you?" His eyes bulged wide. "Thought you two were sworn enemies?"

"We are," Boom-Boom said.

"It's only a graze," Diego said. "Pretty slick—maybe half the bullet deep—and not bleeding much," he said.

"So he's gonna live?" Bramble said.

"To fight another day," Diego said.

"Too bad," Bramble said.

I looked past Diego to Bramble. He was alone.

"Where are the rest of your men?" I said. "Everyone okay?"

He pointed to his right. The door on Sir Edward's jet was back open. Three officers walked down the steps, the lead man shaking his head in the negative. Another one held his palms up as if to say, *Where is she?*

I stood back up.

"Where's Queenie?" Boom-Boom said.

I saw that the fourth police officer had someone in the first helicopter handcuffed and pressed against the black fuselage. It was one of the men from Soper's Hole, when Frappier had come looking for my boat.

"I recognize him," I said.

Diego reached under his shirt to grab a gun—

"No!" I said.

Bramble tried to step in front of me. "Wait—"

I crashed between the police officer and the man and twisted his arm up at a sharp angle. "Where is she?!"

"Reilly!" Bramble said.

"Buck Reilly," the man said.

I was so surprised by his subsequent laugh that it caused me to reduce pressure.

"You remember me, right?" he said. An evil hiss escaped his lips like a snicker. "She's not here, mate."

I jerked his arm up sharply and he winced in pain. "Where is she?"

"You'll figure it out soon enough, or at least before Sunday's over." Again with the hellish hiss. Then he whispered in a voice only I could hear. "Go alone or it's over."

I shoved him so hard against the side of the helicopter that his head clunked. No snicker this time.

I stepped back to see Bramble, his men watching me. It dawned on me that he was letting me do his dirty work. Was he taking a page out of Booth's playbook?

"Before Sunday's over?" Bramble said. "That mean anything to you?"

My mind spun but came up empty. Just then another helicopter appeared from the west, at low altitude, aimed right for the tarmac where we stood.

"Watch out!" I said.

Bramble and his men fanned out, their hands on their holsters. Diego and Boom-Boom produced handguns.

"At ease!" Bramble said. "I recognize that chopper."

The small silver helicopter landed on the tarmac next to the Beast. There was only a pilot aboard—I made out Sir Edward's wild white hair in the pilot's seat. I ran to his chopper, the blade still spinning at speed.

"Reilly, wait!" Bramble's voice was distorted behind me. "What did the man say?"

I ignored him and ran to the passenger side of the sleek chopper with "Necker Island" emblazoned on its side, and yanked the door open.

"What happened here?" he said.

"She's not—"

He pointed one hand to the headphones on his ear and the other hand toward a headset on the passenger's seat of the two-man chopper. I climbed inside and pulled the headset on, and all the noise of the chopper's rotor and Bramble's screaming vanished.

"She's not here," I said. "But those helicopters belong to the bad guys—one of the men there was at Soper's Hole and recognized me."

"What did he say?"

Bramble was waving his arms at us from the front of the chopper. I closed my door and locked it.

"He said I'd figure it out sooner or before Sunday's over. That's three days from now." I paused. "And he told me to go alone or it's over."

"What did he mean about Sunday?"

Sunday? Sunday, Sunday … What the hell?

It dawned on me that Sunday was when my catamaran rental ended. Could that be what he meant? Of course they knew every detail about me by now, including the logistics of my boat rental.

"Your other boat, the launch, was at the dock here—"

"I saw it. Did you check it for clues?"

"I found a note Giselle had written under the toilet lid. It said 'help.'" I paused. "And I'm sorry, but two of Lamont's guards were there, too, shot dead. Zidane must have had another boat waiting."

"Where would they go, and what does Sunday have to do with anything?" he said.

"They must be close. The helicopters were running and ready to roll. And it may be a coincidence, but Sunday is the last day of my catamaran rental."

"Where is your boat?" he said.

"We left it a few coves east of Cane Garden Bay. I have no idea if it's still there."

Bramble had tired of being courteous and waved to his men to surround the helicopter. Boom-Boom caught my eye and held his arms wide. I pointed toward the Beast, where Ray had kept the engines running. I wondered if Sir Edward would yield to Bramble's pressure. He answered that with a flick of his wrist as he pulled back on the collective and the chopper lifted straight up.

"Should we radio that information to Detective Bramble?" Sir Edward asked.

"Hell no." Even though Bramble had acted courageously on the tarmac, he'd used me for bait and I still couldn't trust him. I reached into my back pocket and grabbed the satellite phone. "BVI or not, we need someone motivated by recognition, not money."

I dialed the number.

"Where the hell have you been, Reilly?" Booth answered like a strung-out addict waiting on word from his dealer.

"It's going down, now!"

"Great timing. I have complications here," he said.

The helicopter was fast. We were quickly eating up Tortola's northern coastline.

"I promised you the heads-up, Booth, and I need your help, now! Get your ass a few coves east of Cane Garden Bay, pronto!"

"I have company," he said. "VIPs from—"

"I don't care if you've got J. Edgar Hoover's ghost in drag. Get moving."

I ended the call, but I was uneasy about his ability to show up in time.

Shit!

"ETA is in five minutes," Sir Edward said.

I hated to put Ray and the boys in more danger, but had no choice but to hedge my bet. I called Ray.

"My catamaran's half-way up the coast here just before Cane Garden Bay." I paused. "We're going in naked and it's probably a trap."

"ETA is in one minute," Sir Edward said.

"Need your help, Ray."

"But what can I do—?"

I clicked "end."

I glanced to my left to see Sir Edward smiling.

Is everyone here crazy?

51

WE HOVERED ONE COVE OVER FROM MY CATAMARAN, which was still where I'd left her. We were far enough away not to be heard, but using Sir Edward's binoculars I could see that there was a speedboat rafted up next to the catamaran. Either someone was rifling my boat or they'd taken Giselle here to lure me in. I knew too much, so they'd still need to kill me, too.

"How do you want to play this?" Sir Edward said. "Are your friends from the FBI coming?"

I stared at the boat ahead through the binoculars. The man's voice back at the helicopter echoed inside my head. "Go alone ..."

"I don't know if anyone's coming, but I need to get down there—"

"I could land on the beach."

"Too far away."

"Or swing in low by the boat."

"They'd see us."

He turned to look into my eyes. His eyebrows were raised.

"What altitude do tourist helicopters fly around here?"

"Tours of the islands are allowed to fly at five hundred feet above sea level. Richard uses this helicopter for that purpose with his guests."

Five hundred fucking feet.

"Okay, let's get down to that altitude and fly along the coast. Before we round the corner to where the catamaran is anchored, drop us down quickly to about half that and I'll jump."

Sir Edward lowered his brows and stared at me another few seconds. He didn't say I was crazy, though, and he didn't try to talk me out of it. Eventually he smiled.

We continued forward, slowly, descending to the altitude that tourist helicopters flew around the islands, which would seem normal to anyone who'd been monitoring traffic. The rocky edge of the mountain that dropped down toward the bay at the end of the second cove got closer.

"Get ready," Sir Edward said. "I'm descending to a hundred feet of altitude. You know the water will be like concrete if you land awkwardly."

Lovely.

I pushed open the door and the wind rushed through in an abrupt wake-up call. I swung sideways and lowered my feet onto the landing strut.

"I'll gather Bramble and his men and come right back," Sir Edward said. "And I'll make sure the governor is aware of our efforts to ensure Bramble's honest. Take this."

He handed me a sheathed knife, which I placed on my belt. I pulled off the headset and edged my ass closer to the side of the seat. It still felt like we were a mile high. The edge of the cliff grew closer.

Without looking back, I gave Sir Edward a thumbs-up and launched myself out of the chopper.

I fell fast—the sound of wind whistled past my ears. The water was coming quickly—an awkward landing would be like hitting concrete. I got my angle of attack into pike position—

SPLASH!

The impact caused the wind to rush from my lungs. I speared deep into the clear water—bubbles surrounded me. Every inch of my skin burned from the impact as if I'd landed in acid.

I flailed my arms and kicked my feet to slow my descent and then scissor-kicked hard toward the surface, now twenty feet away. *Harder, kick harder, kick.* Lungs burning!

My eyes fluttered as bright light blinded me—was this the end?
WHOOSH!

I broke the surface and blasted three feet out of the water from kicking so hard. I treaded water, choking and coughing until I finally caught my breath.

Sir Edward's helicopter continued slowly up the coast, now back at tour height.

I could see the mast of the catamaran ahead. I hoped nobody was looking when I jumped or they'd have seen me plummet into the water.

How long would it take the cavalry to come?

If they came at all …

I swam toward the boat and had a flashback to the day Giselle's helicopter had been shot down.

If Scarlet and Charlie hadn't abandoned me, I wouldn't be here now.

But I would never have met Giselle, either.

In fact, she'd be dead.

I swam harder and directly toward the boat.

Images of the past several days drove me, and the knowledge that Zidane would kill us both only pushed me harder. Maybe it was blind faith—whether in Booth, Sir Edward, or even Ray, I wasn't sure, but there was no choice other than to get to Giselle and try to surprise them.

The distance was about a half mile, and after twenty minutes with no break, I was at the bow of the catamaran. I treaded water underneath the parallel hulls and listened for any sound onboard. There was nothing other than my heavy breathing and swirling water.

I continued slowly under the boat until I was at the aft swim platform. A rope hung in the water, which I grabbed and held on to to catch my breath. The water temperature was close to ninety degrees, which was hot, but colder than my body temperature. I began to shiver.

Still no sound above.

The boat tied off on the port side presented multiple choices. Should I yank its drain plug to keep Zidane from leaving? Or leave it intact with the hope of using it for our escape? I decided on the latter option.

The swimming ladder was folded up on the starboard corner of the catamaran's swimming platform. As quietly as possible, I unfolded it over the edge and telescoped it into the water. Once I'd mounted the bottom step, I hovered for a moment to recall the interior configuration of the cabin. Odds were they'd be sitting in the main salon, which would make it impossible for me to climb aboard and not be seen. If they were expecting a boat, I'd at least have the advantage of surprise.

I slowly stood up, my legs shaking from the long swim and the chill. I inched forward until I was at the transom. I raised my head until my eyes were over the edge.

Nobody was visible in the salon.

I crawled over to peek inside the boat tied to the side of the catamaran. It was another center console, with twin 250 HP engines on back. There were no weapons visible, but the keys were in the ignition. After another glance inside, I climbed over the side of the speedboat and removed the key from the ignition. I placed it in my pocket.

The boat's radio was off, so I clicked it on and changed the channel to 16, which was the emergency frequency here. I clicked the microphone—three dots, three dashes, three dots—and repeated it five times. The volume was all the way down so nobody on the catamaran could hear any response, and whether anyone heard the SOS or not I wouldn't know, but I prayed it was yet another potential source for assistance.

Back on the swim platform, I crawled slowly onto the rear deck of the catamaran. After spending several days on this boat, I knew there were no feasible weapons out on deck, but there were some options inside. I crawled forward to the sliding glass door that led into the salon, peered around inside, and still saw nobody. The door was unlocked, so I slid it open, slowly.

One foot, two feet, just a little more—

HOOONNNNNNNKKKK!

The shriek of an air horn knocked me back on my heels.

A man ran into the salon from the starboard corridor. The horn continued to sound.

HOOONNNNNNNKKKK!

He held a machine pistol aimed at my chest and kicked at the inside of the door. A broom connected to the boat's manual air horn went flying, and the sound stopped.

The man was dark, had salt and pepper hair and a tight moustache, and was dressed in black. His gun was aimed at my chest as he slid the door the rest of the way open.

"Buck Reilly. I've been expecting you."

52

A LPHONSE ZIDANE, THE HEAD OF THE FRENCH
SECRET SERVICE, ushered me inside the salon, his gun jammed
in my back. The sound of whimpering from the direction of my
stateroom hastened my step.

"Stop right there, Mr. Reilly."

We were in the middle of the salon.

"Buck?" Giselle's voice was strained. "Is that you?"

"Yes, I'm here!"

"Why did you come? They'll kill us both!"

"Quiet!" another man's voice commanded from the same direction.

"What do you want with us, Zidane?" I said.

His eyes were beady and black, and he showed no emotion on his
face at all. I guessed his age to be mid-fifties, but he was fit and moved
with the confidence of a man accustomed to success.

"You compromised our operation, Mr. Reilly."

"All I did was rescue a drowning woman. I had no idea who she
was or what the hell was going on."

"Curiosity kills. Other lives could have been spared."

"What the hell *is* going on, Zidane? Why did Huibert want to kill
his wife? Just because she caught him in bed with a minor?"

His eyes narrowed further and the tips of his teeth appeared.

"International politics are slow and futile. My people have suffered
incalculable losses—"

"The French?"

"I'm Afghani by decent but grew up in Algeria. I immigrated to France as a teenager."

Uh-oh.

"I spent my life preparing for this operation, and you, Mr. Reilly, have complicated our efforts to end the shadow war still being waged on my people."

Giselle's whimpers continued.

I balled and squeezed my fists. "What have you done to her, asshole?"

A sharp-toothed smile followed. "It is not me or my associate who will do something to Madame Huibert, sir. It is you."

Using the gun, he motioned back toward my stateroom.

"If you cooperate, we will make your deaths quick and painless. If not, we will still get what we want, but the indignities that Madame Huibert will suffer first shall be worse than anything you have ever seen. And then you will both die the most painful deaths possible." Again with the snaggletoothed sneer. "After you watch us rape her."

My hands now shook. If I could have squeezed his head, I'd have popped it like a pimple.

How long had it been since Sir Edward had dropped me? Since I'd pleaded with Booth to help?

"Walk forward, Mr. Reilly. The end we have planned for you is quite spectacular."

Son of a bitch.

With shaky legs I walked back to my stateroom. Giselle was there, seated on the bed, her hands tied behind her back, and another man—Frappier—was behind her holding a shotgun.

"We meet again, asshole," Frappier said. He held up his hand where his pinky finger had been cut off. "You'll wish I only cut off a finger."

"Buck." Her voice was a whisper. Tears streamed down her cheeks and her hair was wild. "Why didn't I listen to you?"

I sat next to her and took her in my arms. She shuddered. I pulled her closer and pressed my lips to her ears.

"Help is on the way. Stall as long as we can–"

"No whispering, please!" Zidane said.

Over my shoulder I saw that a video camera was erected on a tripod at the end of the bed. Visions of Taliban killers beheading their captives passed through my head. Was that what they had planned for us?

"That a live feed for Al Jazeera?" I said.

"France 24, actually."

"You said if we cooperated you'd kill us quick and painlessly," I said.

"And I shall, once we've filmed you together."

Zidane kept his distance but waved his wrist toward me as if he were instructing a dog to roll over. "Lie on the bed," he said.

With another glance at the video camera, I dry-swallowed and did as I was told. My senses were heightened as I listened for any sound of help approaching from land, sea, or air, but I heard only waves lapping against the side the catamaran's hull. Would my gun still be hidden in the compartment on the top of the headboard? I was so close, but there was no way I could reach it without getting myself shot first.

"Raise your hands," the other man said.

He took my left wrist and pulled it over toward the far side of the bed and wrapped a leather strap tightly around my wrist. Once that was taut, he wrapped it through a gap in the headboard. He repeated the same process with my right hand, and when he finished I was stretched tight across the bed, face up.

Blood circulated through my body at light speed, and my breath was increasingly shallow.

"Stand at the foot of the bed, Madame Huibert," Zidane said.

Giselle complied but stood there shivering. She was pale and I thought she might collapse, which under the circumstances could be a good thing.

"Remove his clothing."

"What?" she said.

"Do as I say!"

"It's okay," I said.

My circulation system suddenly felt hot, and sweat beaded on my forehead.

Giselle pulled my shorts down.

"Everything!"

Zidane ripped the wet T-shirt off me, and his associate tied my ankles to the foot of the bed. I was spread eagle on the bed, naked, exposed, and shaking with cold.

"Now, remove your clothing, Madame Huibert."

Giselle gasped. "You animals!"

She swung at Zidane, but he dodged her blow and backhanded her on the side of the head. She fell on top of me, and her elbow jabbed me in the stomach.

A subtle hum registered in my ears. I couldn't tell what it was but considered it the sound of hope.

Zidane grabbed the back of Giselle's blouse and ripped it from her body.

"Your shorts!"

She sobbed deeply, and her breaths came in quick bursts.

The hum outside grew louder. It was the unmistakable sound of radial engines.

The Beast.

Surely Zidane or Frappier must have heard it, too?

Giselle slipped out of her shorts and underwear until she stood defiantly with her hands balled in fists on her waist. Zidane snapped her bra from behind and pushed her down on top of me. Her breath was raspy from rage.

"You are a sick fuck, Zidane," I said. "Hang on—this is what you did to François Huibert, right? With the young girl?"

"Very perceptive, Mr. Reilly. But we used psychedelics with the president, along with Viagra." Zidane smirked. "He didn't know if he was coming or going."

Giselle suddenly sat up and turned to face Zidane. "You drugged him?"

"Negotiation takes on many forms, Madame. Thanks to the video, we persuaded him to vote against continued aggression in the Middle East during the summit. But when you returned early and surprised us, it complicated everything."

"That's why you shot down my helicopter?"

"Climb on top of Mr. Reilly, please."

"So François wasn't ... cheating with that young girl?"

"He didn't even know where he was."

"Bastards!" she said.

Giselle straddled me. Her face was blotchy red with fury.

"And with this we will destroy what is left of your reputation and ensure that the president remains in power, under our thumbs," Zidane said. "Arrange the camera."

Frappier moved from the side of the bed to the foot, where he moved the tripod over slightly for a better angle.

The sound of the Beast approaching had become a not-so-subtle roar. Ray's direct approach wouldn't end well for Giselle and me. My eyes tried to catch hers, and I willed her to rally and remember the gun in the hiding place.

"What a way to go," I said.

Zidane laughed, and Giselle's face contorted with surprise. Our eyes finally met as she looked down on me in anger. I nodded up toward the headboard.

"Slap your hands on the headboard, honey." I winked. "Let's go out with a bang."

Anger shifted to surprise, and finally her eyes opened wide with recognition.

Just then the Beast must have touched down in the water ahead of us, which made a loud splash. The propellers must have sliced into the wake, which caused Zidane to glance sharply to his left out the bedroom door.

Then the sound of a high-horsepower speedboat roared as it closed in from the opposite direction.

Zidane ran from the cabin.

53

F RAPPIER WATCHED ZIDANE HURRY OFF and then glanced from us to the video camera. He bent over to study the play button—

"Now!" I said.

Giselle reached over me and banged her fist on the center of the wood headboard. The hidden compartment popped open above my face.

"What are you doing?" Frappier said.

She grabbed the 9mm Sig Sauer, spun around, and pointed it at him.

"Don't move, asshole."

The man's eyes bulged open.

"Grab my pants," I said. "There's a knife on my belt to cut these ropes."

Frappier slowly moved to his right, closer to Giselle.

"I said don't move!"

He lunged for her—

BOOM!

She fired at point blank range. Frappier's head whipped backward before he collapsed in a lifeless heap.

"Quick," I said. "Untie me!"

Rushed footsteps sounded from the galley.

Giselle jumped up and assumed a double-fisted firing position, buck naked. Zidane ran into the doorway and froze at what he saw.

The snaggletoothed sneer was gone, but his mouth dropped open as his eyes narrowed to slits.

"Be calm now, Madame," he said.

"On your knees, Zidane," Giselle said.

He slid his left foot forward. She slightly altered her aim and—

BOOM!

A bullet ripped through the wood door a foot away from his head. He raised his hands, which I could see were shaking.

"On your knees, now!" she said.

This time he complied. My eyes shifted to Giselle as she lifted my shorts up with her right foot and flung them onto the bed. Still bound, there was nothing I could do to free myself.

The Beast's engines idled loudly, and I could tell Ray was as close to the boat as the wingspan would allow. I thought I heard a couple of splashes, but I wasn't certain.

"Keep your hands in the air!" Giselle said.

With the gun in her right hand, she unbuttoned the sheath that held the knife in its scabbard. She bent slightly lower and cut the strap that held my left hand to the bed. With my hand free, I took the knife, reached over, and cut the strap on my right hand.

"Reilly? You in there, brudda?"

"Yes, in the aft starboard stateroom."

Boom-Boom peeked around the corner, a Spectre M4 machine pistol extended ahead of him. When he saw Zidane on his knees with his arms up, he pointed the gun toward him.

"Frisk him for weapons," I said.

Boom-Boom glanced up, saw me naked, and then looked past me to Giselle, still in a firing stance and also naked. His jaw fell open.

"The hell's going on here? Why you naked, Queenie?"

"You say naked?" Diego peered around the corner and I couldn't help but smile. "Look at you people, all shiny and white."

His bright smile caused me to smile back at him. When Boom-Boom finished frisking Zidane, he stood with two handguns and a switchblade.

"Who the hell's this?" Diego said.

"Meet Alphonse Zidane, murderer and blackmailer," I said. "Oh, and he's also the head of President Huibert's security."

"Zidane?" Diego's eyes darkened. He stepped forward and kicked Zidane hard in the side—the man fell over and balled up.

"Son of a bitch killed Maurice."

Brass Knuckles. Dead. Ray told me he'd been killed when the black helicopter attacked Boom-Boom's compound.

The sound of the boat engine grew louder and then cut to low as it came up next to the catamaran.

I cut the ropes holding my ankles, jumped up next to Giselle, reached past her, and took my robe off a hook by the closet and wrapped it around her. I took the gun so she could get her arm into the sleeve. She was far from shy, focused instead on securing Zidane.

A loudspeaker suddenly broke the momentary quiet. "Everyone inside come out with your hands up!"

I handed Giselle back the gun, pulled on my shorts, and walked to the doorway. Diego was panting heavily, his eyes locked on Zidane.

"Don't kill him," I said. "I'm pretty sure this is either the Royal Police from Tortola or the FBI."

"Lucky for this asshole," Diego said.

"I'll be right back." Then I raised my hands and my voice. "It's Buck Reilly! I'm unarmed and coming out!"

Slowly I walked into the salon and saw several men in suits on the back deck, all with handguns or shotguns pointed at me.

"Stop right there, hotshot!" Booth peered out from behind an agent holding a shotgun. "We heard shots fired. What's the situation?"

"One bad guy's dead, the other is in our custody."

"*Our* custody? Who's in there with you?"

"Giselle Huibert and, ah, two good citizens who helped me save her."

Behind Booth I could see that Ray was on Zidane's boat, his arms up, with another federal agent guarding him.

"That's Ray Floyd out there, my partner. He's with us, too." I paused and couldn't resist. "They beat you here, Booth. Saved the day."

I could see him grit his teeth before half-looking behind him. There was another man there, dressed in dark, casual clothes, but I couldn't see him clearly.

"Go check it out," Booth said.

I peered back over my shoulder. "Drop your weapons, everybody."

I heard the sound of a swift kick to a solid object followed by a deep grunt. I didn't need to see it to know what had happened.

"Arms up in there!" an agent said. "You, step forward and sit in a chair."

I stepped into the galley and sat on a stool next to the bottles of rum I'd brought aboard.

The agents disappeared inside. One issued orders for everyone to walk out slowly, while the other clasped handcuffs onto Zidane's wrists.

Diego and Boom-Boom stepped out of the room and joined me at the bar. I'd pulled out five glasses on the counter and was pouring shots of Pilar dark rum.

Booth stepped inside, followed by the casually dressed man—oh shit.

Him I recognized. The VIP complication Booth mentioned earlier on the phone.

"Giselle?" he said. "*Où est-tu?*"

"François?" Giselle's voice rang out from inside the stateroom.

"Don't let him in here!" one of the agents said.

"Shit," I said.

Diego and Boom-Boom looked at me and shook their heads.

I drank a shot of Pilar.

"Giselle! *Sortir!*"

Giselle came out of the room and fell into the arms of her husband. He squeezed her tight as he wept. She was quiet, but her eyes were pressed tightly closed.

Diego refilled my glass.

The remaining FBI agents walked inside, followed by Ray Floyd.

"Damn, Buck," Ray said. "What a scene."

The two agents inside the stateroom pushed Zidane out the door and into the waiting arms of two other agents.

"*Vous miserable traître!*" François spit on Zidane as he passed by.

Ray joined me at the bar. Diego picked up a shot glass and handed one to Boom-Boom and another to Ray. We held them a moment. Giselle let go of François and walked over next to me. She took the last glass off the bar and held it up.

"*À votre santé, et merci mes amis.*"

She downed the rum, and we all followed suit. The dark liquor barely burned at all. I'd brought the bottle from Key West—it was my favorite rum, and this was supposed to have been a celebration. I thought I'd found love, and now I felt it slipping away.

Again.

"Monsieur Reilly," François said. "Thank you for taking care of my wife. Special Agent Booth has assured me that if it had not been for you, these swine would have killed her."

All I could do was nod.

"Please come to Paris, where I will award you with the Legion of Honour."

I cleared my throat. "Yeah, thanks."

"We need to get you to safety, Mr. President," Booth said. He glanced at me. "And Madame First Lady."

"Buck?" Giselle said. "Can I see you in private for a moment?"

François did a double take but said nothing. His brow furrowed as if he realized for the first time that I wore only shorts and Giselle only a robe. Diego whistled under his breath.

I followed her into the stateroom. She closed the door and turned and wrapped her arms around me. She held me so tight I thought she might rupture my kidneys. When I felt her shaking, I leaned back and wiped the tears from her eyes.

"I don't know what to do …" Her voice broke.

"Come with me, Giselle. That's my plane outside. We could be in Key West in—"

She gently placed her hand over my mouth. "Please, stop." She shuddered and hung on to my biceps, staring up into my eyes as tears sprang from hers.

I felt hot streaks down my cheeks that dripped onto my chest. I didn't want to blink. I didn't want to miss seeing her for one second.

She dropped the robe and I took her beauty in one last time.

Once she was dressed, she moved to the camera on the tripod. It was still recording. She hit "end" and removed the camera from the tripod.

"Keep this safe," she said.

I bit my lip. It quivered like a wild caterpillar.

"This is not good-bye, Buck Reilly."

Breathe deeply, Buck. In, out, in, out.

The look in her eyes said it all.

That and the fact that she wouldn't engage mine.

She gathered herself up and I struggled to do the same. She squeezed my hand, opened the door and walked out.

EPILOGUE

IT WAS A COUPLE OF MONTHS BEFORE THE NEWS CREWS left me alone and I was able to resume my abnormally normal life in Key West. No more CNN, France 24, BBC, *Entertainment Tonight*, TMZ, or Ellen DeGeneres hounding the staff of the La Concha or camping out at Key West International Airport. Like everything, what was hot one day faded to old news after time.

Giselle had remained out of the limelight in France after her very public return with François to the Èlysée Palace, where adoring crowds lined the streets and brought flowers by the metric ton to honor her defeating the conspirators who'd nearly killed her. Gossipmongers, who even in progressive France sought to delight in her relationship with the famous/infamous American, had besieged her as well.

After the first month, the official head of public relations for the French president initiated overtures to have me come to Paris to receive the Legion of Honour, as François had promised. No way I was going to do that—I didn't want to reignite the speculation about Giselle and me—and it would've been too hard to see her, so I ignored the calls until they stopped.

Booth had hit the jackpot when he returned to St. Thomas with the French president and first lady, and miraculously, CNN just happened to be there to capture the moment. There's no doubt in my mind that Booth tipped them off, and his subsequent trip to the White House to be personally commended by the president of the United States, again covered by national television networks, was the crowning achievement of his career. But the true media darlings were Boom-Boom and Diego, who were also there to be pardoned for past crimes in recognition of their help in keeping the first lady safe while on the run in the Virgin Islands. I had ignored pleas from the White House to attend, but laughed my way through a half bottle of Pilar blond rum as I watched it all on CNN.

The experience had affected me in ways I still didn't fully understand, and as I drove my 1966 Land Rover Series 2A home from the airport, with the canvas sides rolled up and the salt air blowing my again long hair wildly around, I could still smell Giselle's scent, taste the salt of her skin, hear her accented English as she spoke my name.

I parked the Rover behind the La Concha and entered through the back door.

"Hey, Buck," Frank, the concierge, said. "Got some newlyweds from Long Island who'd like to charter you to Fort Jefferson tomorrow. You up to it yet?"

"Sure, Frank, I'll do it for you." It would be my first charter in two and a half months.

He patted me on the back and winked. "Thanks, Bubba."

The elevator opened onto the sixth floor, and I found the door to my corner suite overlooking Duval Street unlocked. What the hell?

With my senses aroused, I pushed the door open slowly.

Inside I found candles burning—I sure as hell hadn't lit them. The suite was small, so it only took a second to see that there was a lump in my bed underneath the covers.

My heart thudded in my chest as I walked quietly to the bed. As I extended my arm to reach for the covers, the lump giggled.

"Excuse me," I said. "This is the Tennessee Williams suite. Are you in the right room?"

Another giggle, then words muffled by the covers. "I certainly hope so."

That voice—

She slid the covers from over her head and down to her bare chest.

"Giselle! What the hell?"

I spotted a red velvet sash around her neck, with a five-armed Maltese Asterisk medal nestled between her cleavage.

Her laugh reached deep inside my chest and enveloped my heart.

"I'm here on behalf of the president to award you with France's highest civil award, the Legion of Honour."

She reached up and pulled me down on top of her—I was so shocked that my legs crumpled when she pulled me. Our lips connected and we held a long kiss. She scratched her nails up the length of my back as she pulled my Last Resort Charter and Salvage T-shirt over my head.

"How on earth did you get here?" I said.

"By plane, of course." She giggled.

I kissed her again. Her lips were warm and wet.

"But you're still with François. I've seen you on television."

"I'm French, remember?"

Without her seeing, I pinched my arm to make sure I was awake.

It hurt.

Adrenaline surged through my limbs. I couldn't believe she was here.

"How long are you staying?"

"So many questions, Buck." She pulled the covers down. I soaked up the sight of her lovely naked body before she flung the covers over my back and pulled me down on top of her.

"We can talk later, *mon cher.* "

Much later ...

THE END

ACKNOWLEDGEMENTS

Even fiction needs to be accurate when describing locations, settings and content that revolves around historical background. I try to visit every location that is included in the Buck Reilly series, and considering this story took place in the Virgin Islands, I recently made the personal sacrifice to head down and re-check the status of several sites, even though I'd been there many times before. Reality is that post-hurricanes Irma and Maria, two years ago, there is still much that has not been rebuilt, and several places that have been restored were done very differently, and this was before Hurricane Dorian, which thankfully spared the Virgin Islands.. So for those of you who also love to island-hop, don't assume your favorite places are as you last saw them.

Research takes local help when out in the field. Thank you to the following people for their help in researching locations and making connections with key collaborators for scenes in White Knight, several of whom appear as themselves at key moments in the story: Captain Jay Rushing, Captain Alex Dooley, Justin Bartosh in the USVI; Foxy Callwood of Foxy's on Jost Van Dyke; Nick Norman, Kelly Norman, Tony Jonas and David Wegman in Key West. And one of my oldest friends, Edward "Bert' Harrell in Virginia.

You may have noticed my continued interest in the French people and culture. I attribute that to my youth when my family would gather on Sunday nights to watch Jacques Cousteau's Undersea World. Cousteau's ship was a crucible for adventure and undersea exploration, and the French crew captured my imagination and led me to get certified as a Scuba diver at age 13, move to Key West at 18, attend University in France at 23 and be an annual visitor to St. Barths in the French West Indies since the 90s. While much of the story appeared to malign the fictional French president, clearly Buck thought highly of the French First Lady, and things turned out differently than he, and maybe you, thought it would.

It also takes a team to produce a high quality product in any endeavor and writing books is no different. Thank you to Renni Browne, Shannon Roberts, Doug Wagner, and Ross Browne of The Editorial Department, who have edited every Buck Reilly novel; Tim Harkness for creating the book cover, the series logo and marketing materials; Ann-Marie Nieves of Get Red PR for her advice and for being my longtime publicist.

Thank you to the fans of the Buck Reilly series, for your patience, dedication and support. Special thanks to Ron and Linda Weiner, Holly, Bailey, Cortney and future son-in-law Will Prendergast for their love and support as I multi-task my way through life.

ABOUT THE AUTHOR

John H. Cunningham is the author of the best selling, eight book, Buck Reilly adventure series, which includes Red Right Return, Green to Go, Crystal Blue, Second Chance Gold, Maroon Rising, Free Fall to Black, Silver Goodbye and White Knight. Through the years, John has been a bouncer at a Key West nightclub, a diver, pilot, magazine editor, commercial developer, songwriter and global traveler. He has either lived in or visited the many island locations that populate the series, and has experienced or witnessed enough craziness and wild times to keep the Buck Reilly series flowing. John mixes fact with fiction and often includes real people in his novels, like Jimmy Buffett, Chris Blackwell, Matt Hoggatt, Thom Shepherd, Dave McKenney, Keith Sykes, Marius Stakelborough, Bruno Magras and Bankie Banx to augment the reader's experience. Adhering to the old maxim, "write what you know," John's books have an authenticity and immediacy that have earned a loyal following and strong reviews. Buck Reilly is a reflection of us all, including our frailties, strengths, dreams, fears, successes, mistakes and occasional victories. No government agency, former Navy SEALS, unlimited cash, or secret agents are coming to his rescue, because, well they're not coming to mine either. How about you?

John lives in Key West and New York City. His choices for the places and plots that populate the Buck Reilly series include many subjects that he loves: Caribbean settings, amphibious aircraft, colorful characters, and stories that concern themselves with the same tensions and issues that affect all of our lives.

Book links:

RED RIGHT RETURN (Buck Reilly book 1):
http://www.amazon.com/Right-Return-Reilly-Adventure-Series-ebook/dp/B00D8HOSN2/ref=pd_sim_kstore_2?ie=UTF8&refRID=0H9XXB0JPPWTQPP251FB

GREEN TO GO (Buck Reilly book 2):
http://www.amazon.com/Green-Buck-Reilly-Adventure-Series-ebook/dp/B00D6Q0WOE/ref=pd_sim_kstore_1?ie=UTF8&refRID=1AH2GWXXGX0MV0N3RDM8

CRYSTAL BLUE (Buck Reilly book 3):
http://www.amazon.com/Crystal-Blue-Reilly-Adventure-Series-ebook/dp/B00EWSAZ92/ref=pd_sim_kstore_2?ie=UTF8&refRID=14902YRMCYTEGSMTTYHQ

SECOND CHANCE GOLD (Buck Reilly book 4):
http://www.amazon.com/Second-Chance-Reilly-Adventure-Series/dp/0985442271/ref=pd_sim_14_2?ie=UTF8&refRID=0CEEBYEWA7C7E50NGRGH

MAROON RISING (Buck Reilly book 5):
https://www.amazon.com/Maroon-Rising-Buck-Reilly-Adventure-ebook/dp/B016QUC76C

FREE FALL TO BLACK (Buck Reilly book 6):
https://www.amazon.com/Free-Fall-Black-Reilly-Adventure/dp/0998796506

SILVER GOODBYE (Buck Reilly book 7):
https://www.amazon.com/gp/product/B07G6BRQWX/ref=dbs_a_def_rwt_bibl_vppi_i0

Music links:

"THE BALLAD OF BUCK REILLY" (Download the song or all of Workaholic in Recovery from iTunes at): https://itunes.apple.com/us/album/workaholic-in-recovery/id908713680

"RUM PUNCH" by Thom Shepherd, and co-written by John H. Cunningham, is available on iTunes at: https://itunes.apple.com/us/album/rum-punch-single/id1051324975

"LONG VIEW OFF A SHORT PIER" by Dave McKenney and co-written by John H. Cunningham, is available on iTunes at: https://itunes.apple.com/us/album/back-in-time/id1161935367?ign-mpt=uo%3D4#

"Hanging Out at Le Select" by Keith Sykes and co-written by John H. Cunningham, is available on iTunes at: https://music.apple.com/us/album/hanging-out-at-le-select-single/1439181610

SILVER GOODBYE by Donald James and co-written by John H. Cunningham will soon be available on iTunes

"SILVER GOODBYE" by Donald James and co-written by John H. Cunningham, available soon on CD Baby and iTunes

Silver Goodbye
Concept inspired from John H Cunningham's book "Silver Goodbye".
Co-written by Donald James Morrison and John H. Cunningham

Three years old on her mama's hip
Watching her daddy climb aboard that shiny airship
Sea bag in his hand

Sun reflecting off aluminum sides … daddy turned and waved goodbye
It was his final trip

It taxied down the runway took to the sky
She looked at her momma said please don't cry
It's just a silver goodbye

At 16 she fell hard for the high school's favorite football star
When they shared …that first spring break

After graduation they headed south…for an island life on a southern Key
Crazy in love

Momma hugged her said live your life,
Don't stand still and I wont cry
It's just a Silver Goodbye

Chorus
Those silver wings will carry us home
We may be gone but not for long
And though the time must pass by
They're in our hearts no need to cry
It's just a Silver Goodbye

It didn't take long until little ones…filled the beach with happy songs
She sent messages to her mom… saying we love you

Plans were made to visit home…ride the wings and return
From a Silver Goodbye

A letter arrived in the PO box on their little island paradise
Sayin' I'm gone…but not for long
Mommas writing right there on the page said

I got my wings it's my turn to fly
I'll see your daddy … no need to cry.

I know one day we'll see you again. We'll meet you at Heaven's gate …
until then
It's just a silver goodbye

Chorus
Those silver wings will carry us home
We may be gone but not for long
Although the time must pass by
They're in our hearts no need to cry
It's just a Silver Goodbye
It's just a Silver Goodbye
It's just a Silver Goodbye

CPSIA information can be obtained
at www.ICGtesting.com
Printed in the USA
BVHW070920260620
582152BV00002B/83